'I look very like my mum (apart from my glasses) – little, with black eyes and mad curly hair – but Mum's loud and funny and isn't scared of anything. I'm much quieter and I worry about things.'

Jess and Tracy Beaker are the perfect team. Jess thinks Tracy is the best mum ever (even when Tracy shouts at her teachers). Tracy is fun and daring, but she also works hard to give Jess the family home she desperately wanted when growing up in the Dumping Ground. Their flat might be a bit mouldy but it's their happy home.

But when Sean Godfrey – Tracy's rich new boyfriend – comes onto the scene, Jess is worried things are going to change. What if Sean wants to turn Jess's brilliant mum into a new person altogether? Sean's superstar mansion and fancy cars might have been Tracy's childhood dream, but maybe the Beakers' perfect home was right in front of them all along . . .

ABOUT THE AUTHOR

JACQUELINE WILSON wrote her first novel when she was nine years old, and she has been writing ever since. She is now one of Britain's bestselling and most beloved children's authors. She has written over 100 books and is the creator of characters such as Tracy Beaker and Hetty Feather. More than forty million copies of her books have been sold.

As well as winning many awards for her books, including the Children's Book of the Year, Jacqueline is a former Children's Laureate, and in 2008 she was appointed a Dame.

Jacqueline is also a great reader, and has amassed over twenty thousand books, along with her famous collection of silver rings.

Find out more about Jacqueline and her books at www.jacquelinewilson.co.uk

Jacqueline Wilson

Illustrated by Nick Sharratt

MY MUM TRACY BEAKER

DOUBLEDAY

DOUBLEDAY

UK | USA | Canada | Ireland | Australia
India | New Zealand | South Africa

Doubleday is part of the Penguin Random House group of companies
whose addresses can be found at global.penguinrandomhouse.com.

www.penguin.co.uk
www.puffin.co.uk
www.ladybird.co.uk

First published 2018

001

Text copyright © Jacqueline Wilson, 2018
Illustrations copyright © Nick Sharratt, 2018

The moral right of the author and illustrator has been asserted

Text design by Becky Chilcott
Printed and bound in Great Britain by Clays Ltd, Elcograf S.p.A

A CIP catalogue record for this book is available from the British Library

HARDBACK ISBN: 978–0–857–53522–1
INTERNATIONAL PAPERBACK ISBN: 978–0–857–53523–8

All correspondence to:
Doubleday
Penguin Random House Children's
80 Strand, London WC2R 0RL

Penguin Random House is committed to a
sustainable future for our business, our readers
and our planet. This book is made from Forest
Stewardship Council® certified paper.

For Nick Sharratt
Best illustrator ever – and best friend too

HAVE YOU HEARD of my mum Tracy Beaker? You'll know her if you live in Marlborough Tower. The whole of the Duke Estate knows my mum. *Everyone* knows her – in the shops and down the market, in the library and the fried-chicken place and the chippy and at my school.

When we first moved I called our block *Marble* Tower by mistake. That made Mum crack up laughing.

'You make it sound like a palace!' she said, and blew a raspberry. 'I *wish*!'

The towers aren't made of shiny white marble, they're just ordinary brick, and near the ground they're covered with graffiti tags and very rude words. Everyone says the Duke Estate is a rubbish place. Our tower is often ankle-deep in real rubbish, and the boys keep setting fire to the waste bins, which doesn't help. But it's our first proper home together, just the two of us. Before that we lived with Cam, but lots of big girls live there too so it got a bit squashed. Cam's a foster mum. She looks after them all. She looked after us as well, but Mum wanted us to have a proper home, just her and me.

Marlborough Tower is a dump outside but we've made our flat really lovely. Mum painted the living-room walls red so it looks really cosy, and got a purple sofa with red cushions. Mum sits at one end, I sit at the other. Sometimes I put my feet on Mum's lap and she tickles them.

We've got a television and a bookcase, because we both love reading, and on the wall we've got a picture of a mother cuddling her daughter. We found it at a boot fair for only a couple of pounds and we both loved it straight away. It's by an eighteenth-century French

2

painter – a woman, which makes it even more special. The mother and daughter look a bit like us, with our curly dark hair.

We have all sorts of great boot-fair and junk-shop finds. We have mother-and-baby china dogs going for a walk along the windowsills, and a little cluster of china ladies with balloons chatting together on the side table. Sometimes we pretend they have a sing-song and warble 'Feed the Birds' from *Mary Poppins*. There's a pretend parrot in a cage, three plaster ducks flying up the wall, and little bluebirds kissing beak-to-beak on top of the bookcase.

The kitchen is yellow, so it feels sunny even if it's pouring outside. We have Toby jugs all along the windowsill, grinning at us. We got them cheap because most are cracked and a couple have lost their handles. We keep spoons in one, forks in another and knives in a third. During the summer I pick daisies and dandelions to put in our lady Toby jug, and in the winter there are plastic daffodils. On top of the kitchen cupboard we have a circle of tiny teddy bears having a picnic around a huge jar of honey, and a very fat pot-bellied teddy clings to the fridge handle.

Our bathroom is green. I used to spend ages kneeling beside the bath playing mermaids with my old Barbie dolls. I wrapped silver foil around their legs to look like fish tails. I have my own bedroom, though it's not much bigger than a cupboard. It's blue like the sky, and crammed with all my old toys and cuddly teddies. Mum is brilliant at winning them down the amusement arcade. Cam says I'm spoiled. I *know* I am, and it's lovely.

I don't always sleep in my bedroom though. If I'm worried about something I go into Mum's bed. I take Woofer with me. He's my favourite cuddly toy. He's a bit droopy now and doesn't look much like a dog any more, but I still think he's special. We're not allowed *real* dogs on the Duke Estate, worst luck.

When Mum first got fostered by Cam, she painted her bedroom walls black so it looked like a bat cave. Mum's always been a bit weird. I'm so glad that her

 room now is a deep rose colour. She often has rose candles burning so it smells like roses too. Her bed's bigger than mine, and she has a pretty white bedcover made of broderie anglaise – that's material with little holes in the shape of flowers. When I curl up with Mum, I run my finger along the pattern.

So, you see, our flat really *is* like a little palace, though it's a bit damp. Mum's been down the council heaps of times about it, but they never do anything. She has to keep repainting the walls herself to hide the dark patches. The windows always get covered in condensation too. Mum made me Puddle Monitor, so I have to whip round every morning and wipe all the sills with a j-cloth. They go black and gungy if you don't. I have to mop every paw of the china dogs too, which takes a while. But we're on the fourteenth floor, so there are fantastic views. We pretend we're seagulls flying high in the sky. We spread our arms and make that funny squawking noise.

We once saw Tyrone way down below us. He didn't look big and scary at all, he looked very small and silly.

'OK, little seagull, let's poop on him!' Mum said to me.

We didn't *really*, it was just pretend, but it was fun. We like it at Marlborough Tower. Like I said, everyone knows us. Well, they know my mum, and so they know me too. I look very like my mum (apart from my glasses) – little, with black eyes and mad curly hair – but Mum's loud and funny and isn't scared of anything. I'm much quieter and I worry about things.

'You're a girl in a million,' says Mum. 'You're *my* girl.'

That's what a lot of people call me. Tracy Beaker's girl. They don't always remember my name. I'm Jess. Jessica Bluebell Camilla Beaker. Jessica because Mum just liked the name. Bluebell because that was the name of Mum's doll when she was very little. Camilla because that's the name of my foster granny, Cam, and she's lovely. And Beaker because that's my mum's name.

I don't see much of my dad, but he knows my mum too, obviously. People know my mum at all the other places she lived before I was born, and all the places she worked, and all the different homes she was in when she was a little girl. My mum was in care until Cam came along and fostered her. I think there was once an actual television programme about her. Yes, my mum used to be a little bit famous!

My mum's boyfriend actually *is* famous. Well, he is if you're into football. He's called Sean Godfrey – does that ring any bells? You know, he's that big guy with the fancy hairdo and the six-pack and the flash clothes. He used to play for a Premier League team. He was one of the stars. People still make a big fuss of him when he walks down the street. It's 'Hi there, Sean,' and 'How are you doing, mate?' and 'You still look pretty fit!' and 'My lad's football daft – have you got any tips for getting him into a team?'

Mum just rolls her eyes. She makes out she's not impressed by his football and his looks and his money, but she is really. He runs his own gym now, and it's doing really well.

That's how they met. Mum joined the gym because she wanted to learn kick-boxing. She thought it would be fun. And a good way of dealing with her Anger Issues.

My teacher, Miss Oliver, said Mum had Anger Issues. It was when Tyrone and his mates started picking on me at school. At first it was just calling me silly names like Curlynob and Four Eyes and Geeky Beaky, and then they started flicking me with their fingers, which is surprisingly painful, though I tried not to show it.

They couldn't do too much to me in lessons, and I hid from them in the playground. I haven't made many friends at Duke Primary, so I went to the Peace Garden to read. It's my favourite place. It's got a hedge all round it so you feel safe. There are flowers and a small fountain and a bench and a little winding brick path. Best of all, hardly anyone goes there.

But one lunchtime Tyrone came looking for me. He barged right into the Peace Garden, his mates following, and my tummy went tight, but I tried not to show I was scared. I just went on reading.

'Why do you always have your head in a book, Geeky? Hey, I'm talking to you!' said Tyrone, standing right beside me. I kept my head bent, making out I was too engrossed in my book to hear him. Then he snatched the book away, though I kept looking down, my eyes flicking from side to side as if I was reading a story written on my school skirt. That really annoyed him, so he suddenly shoved me right off the bench, onto the brick path. My glasses fell off, and I hit my head and grazed my knees.

I didn't cry. I just lay there.

'It's your own fault. You shouldn't just ignore people,' said Tyrone. 'Don't make out you're hurt!'

I *was* hurt, but I managed not to cry. I throbbed all through afternoon lessons, and by going-home time I had a big bump on my forehead and my knees were still bleeding.

'What on earth's happened to you, Jess?' Mum asked as I limped across the playground. She gave me a great big hug.

'I just fell over, Mum,' I said. I was scared I might burst into tears and I didn't want the other kids to laugh at me.

'Don't give me that!' said Mum, holding me at arm's length. 'Some kid's beaten you up! Who was it, Jess?'

I pressed my lips together. I couldn't tell her in case Tyrone stamped on me for being a tell-tale the *next* time he knocked me over. He was standing with his mates watching me. He had his hands on his hips as if he wasn't the slightest bit worried – but all the same he looked a bit trembly. Like I said, everyone knows my mum. She's very small – Tyrone's already bigger than her – but she can be very, *very* fierce.

'Oi, you!' Mum said, seeing him staring. 'Did you do this to my Jess?'

'Nah!' said Tyrone, shaking his head, and his mates shook their heads too.

'Don't stand there lying your heads off! It's written all over your faces! How dare you pick on a little kid half your size! I'll show you!'

She went charging up to them, fists clenched.

'You're not allowed to hit us! We'll report you!' said Tyrone's best mate, Piotr.

'And *my* mum will come and sort you out. And my brothers!' said Tyrone.

I don't think Mum would have actually thumped them – but she certainly looked as if she might. She didn't stop running, and Tyrone and his mates started running too, charging right out of the playground and down the road.

'I'll get you! I know where you live, you big bullying toerags!' Mum yelled.

Then she came running back and gave me a quick hug. 'Didn't Miss Oliver tell them off?'

'She didn't see,' I said.

'What sort of a teacher *is* she? Useless old bat! Come with me,' said Mum, and she pulled me across the playground, back into the school.

'Oh, Mum, please, don't make a fuss,' I begged. 'Miss Oliver wasn't on playground duty at lunchtime so she wouldn't have seen anything. And anyway I was hidden away in the Peace Garden.'

'*Peace* Garden!' Mum practically had steam coming out of her ears. 'I'll tell Miss Useless Oliver she should be looking after the kids in her care.'

'*Please* don't, Mum,' I implored, but when Mum goes off on one she won't listen to anyone, not even me.

Miss Oliver was in the classroom sticking our pictures on the wall. We'd done a painting in the style of Van Gogh. He was a Dutch painter who used wonderfully bright colours in his swirly paintings. His favourite colour must have been yellow because he painted yellow beds and yellow chairs and lots of yellow flowers too.

I did a picture of Mum and me. I dressed us both in yellow T-shirts and jeans, though we haven't actually got any that colour, but I drew us too small, and there was too much blue sky and green grass above and below us. We looked like yellow ladybirds. You practically needed a magnifying glass to see us. I knew Miss Oliver wouldn't put mine up.

'Hello, Jess. Hello, Ms Beaker,' said Miss Oliver. She peered at me through her little round glasses. 'Oh, Jess, it looks as if you've been in the wars.'

'Yes, in your blooming Peace Garden at *lunchtime*,' Mum exploded. 'She's been sitting in your classroom all afternoon with a huge great lump on her forehead and two bloody knees and you haven't even bothered to stick a plaster on her. What's the matter with you?'

Miss Oliver went red. She has white-blonde hair and very pale skin so it looks odd when she blushes. She hardly ever does. Even when she's cross she stays very calm. 'I'm so sorry, Jess. I didn't see you properly, dear. You should have come and told me.'

'You didn't *see* her? You need new glasses, mate,' said Mum.

I just about died. You don't call a teacher *mate*. And it wasn't Miss Oliver's fault. I sit right at the back of the class, and I was leaning forward to do my painting so she wouldn't have seen my forehead, and my knees were under my desk, blood dribbling down into my socks unseen.

'I've said I'm sorry,' said Miss Oliver, with an edge to her voice. 'I'll fetch the first-aid box.'

'Sorry isn't good enough! It's your duty to look after the children in your so-called care! I was brought up *in* care, and the care workers did their level best to keep a proper eye on us all the time. My mum wasn't around and I didn't have anyone to fight my corner – but *I'm* here for Jess. I won't have my little girl beaten up by young thugs twice her size while you sit here playing with pieces of paper, as calm as custard! You need reporting. I won't have it. I WON'T HAVE IT!!!'

By this time I wanted to crawl under the table.

Miss Oliver sat very still, her hands clasped. 'Please try to keep your voice down, Ms Beaker,' she said. 'I understand your concern, but I don't think we'll get anywhere by shouting at each other. Come here, Jess, and let me look at the bump on your forehead. Do you have a headache?'

I had a *terrible* headache, but it wasn't because of the bump, it was because my mum was yelling so loudly. I shook my head.

'Your knees look very sore too. Shall we clean them up a bit and put on some antiseptic?' Miss Oliver asked.

'*I* can do that when we get home. I'll take responsibility for my daughter now, thank you very much,' said Mum, pulling me back to her side. 'I just want you to control the kids in your care like a *proper* teacher, and punish those boys who thumped my Jess. Especially the big brutish one.'

Miss Oliver quivered at the word *proper*. 'Was it Tyrone, Jess?' she asked quietly.

'It might have been,' I mumbled.

'It wasn't just one boy. I saw them in the playground. I'm sure the big ugly one and all his horrible mates beat up my little girl – it's a miracle her glasses weren't broken,' said Mum. 'Don't you have a no-bullying policy at this dump of a school?'

'We do indeed. So, did Tyrone and Piotr and Jack and Simon and Raj *all* beat you up, Jess?'

'Of course they did! I just *said*!' Mum insisted.

'Jess?' Miss Oliver asked quietly.

I'd bent my head so low my chin was digging into my chest.

'No, it was just Tyrone. And he didn't actually beat me up. He just pushed me off the bench,' I whispered.

'Oh dear. Well, I'll have a serious talk with him in the morning,' said Miss Oliver. She looked at Mum. 'I'm sorry this happened to Jess. I'll do my best to make sure it doesn't happen again.' She gave Mum a dismissive nod, and went back to

sticking another painting on the wall. A blue-and-green picture with two little yellow ladybird blobs in the middle.

'Don't you treat *me* like a little kid!' Mum said. 'It's not good enough. I won't be fobbed off like this! I WON'T HAVE IT!'

'And I won't have you barging into my classroom and shouting at me,' said Miss Oliver. 'You need to deal with your Anger Issues, Ms Beaker.'

'Anger Issues! Don't give me that care-worker rubbish! And I'm *Miss* Beaker, not Ms, and proud of it. It's just me and my daughter, and I'm not letting you tell me what to do, you bossy old bag,' Mum shouted.

I took hold of her hand and pulled. 'Mum, please, let's go home,' I begged. 'Please please please!'

She looked at me and saw that behind my glasses my eyes were blurry with tears. She squeezed my hand tight and let me pull her to the door.

'I won't have it,' Mum repeated, but more quietly now. Her voice was a bit shaky.

Hand in hand we went down the corridor and out through the doors. Mr Smith, the school caretaker, was sweeping up rubbish. He saw Mum's fierce face and the tears rolling down my cheeks.

'Oh dear, have you been a naughty girl, Jess Beaker?' he said, shaking his head and clucking, pretending to be shocked. He was just teasing. He's a gentle, smiley man who's friends with everyone.

I gave him a wobbly smile. Mum ignored him. She clung onto my hand and we walked quickly down the street, not speaking. I kept glancing up at her anxiously. She saw, and tried to give me a smile, but hers was wobbly too.

We were almost running now. My forehead throbbed and my knees stung, but we were both desperate to get home. Then, when we thought we'd made it, we couldn't use either lift. One broke yesterday and the engineers were still struggling to fix it. The other had been working OK that morning, but now someone had deliberately jammed it between floors. So we had to walk up the stairs. Fourteen flights.

It took us a long, long, long time. Especially as we came across Mrs Alfassi sitting on the third-floor steps, gasping. She's always been big, but now she's even bigger because she's going to have a baby. She can't speak much English yet, and we don't know her language, but it didn't matter. Mum heaved her up as carefully as she could, and we took an arm each and helped her up the stairs to the sixth floor.

Then we found old Mrs Reynolds from the ninth floor struggling up the steps with a bulging Lidl carrier in either hand. We carried them for her, and she gave me a mini Bounty bar from her big handbag. I don't actually like coconut but it would have been rude to refuse.

And when we reached the eleventh floor, there was our friend Fadwa trying to carry her little boy *and* his scooter, so Mum took him and I took his scooter – and had a little go on it as we walked along to their flat on the thirteenth. I had to bend right down because it's a very small scooter, but it was good fun, even though it made my knees start bleeding again.

'It's like we're going up the Faraway Tree,' I said, dabbing at them quickly. 'We might meet Moon-Face or Silky the fairy next.'

Mum smiled properly then, and I hoped she'd calmed down – but when we reached our flat she took me to the bathroom and looked at my big bump and my bloody knees, and screwed up her face as if she was going to burst into tears too, even though Mum never cries.

'It's all right, Mum! They don't really hurt that much now. I don't mind,' I said, putting my arms round her.

'You poor little kid,' she said, sniffing. 'Maybe we should take you to A and E to check you haven't got concussion or blood poisoning.'

'I'm fine, Mum. Really,' I insisted.

'Well, I suppose it would be a bit daft to trail all the way downstairs and get the bus to the hospital and wait five hours, and then come back and climb all the way up here all over again,' said Mum. 'I'd better be Nurse Beaker then.'

She sat me on the toilet while she bathed my bumpy head with cold water, and then carefully mopped my knees with soap and hot water to get all the dirt out.

'I'd better wash my mouth out with soap while I'm at it,' she said. 'I went a bit over the top with your Miss Oliver, didn't I?'

'Yes, you did,' I said. 'You were awful! Mum, people don't *really* wash their mouths out with soap, do they?' My tongue curled up in my mouth at the very thought.

'Doesn't it taste disgusting?'

'That's the point. My teacher did it to me once when I was really cheeky. It tasted awful, but I didn't let on to Mrs Vomit Bagley. It frothed all over my lips, so I licked them and said, "Yummy, yummy, yummy," like it was a big treat. It didn't half annoy her.'

'Didn't Mike go and tell the teacher off?' Mike worked at the children's home where Mum lived. He was the care worker she liked best.

'I didn't tell him. He'd have gone nuts if he'd heard what I said to Mrs Vomit Bagley,' said Mum. 'But don't you worry, Jess – you can say even worse things to Miss Oliver, and I'll still come and stick up for you. I just want to be the best mum ever for you.'

'I know,' I said, hugging her. Mum's own mum, my Granny Carly, wasn't around much when she was young. She's not around much now. Last year she even forgot my birthday. Cam's like my *real* granny. She never, ever forgets. 'You *are* the best mum ever.' I keep having to tell Mum this, but I don't mind, because it's the truth.

She pulled a face. 'Sorry I embarrassed you, yelling at Miss Oliver. I was just so mad about that big bruiser. Wait till I get hold of him. Tyler, isn't it?'

'Tyrone.'

'He doesn't live in Marlborough, does he?'

'No, he lives in Devonshire, but you can't have a go at him, Mum. He's got two big brothers, and his mum's much bigger than you and ever so tough,' I warned her.

'I'm not scared of them,' she said.

'*I'm* scared of them. They'd *really* beat you up. Then what would I do?'

'I'd beat them up worse,' said Mum, her chin jutting.

'Oh, Mum.'

'And I'll beat up Miss Oliver too if she doesn't look after you when you're at school,' said Mum, but I hoped she was just teasing now.

I rolled my eyes. 'I wish you wouldn't always have a go at my teachers, Mum. I quite *like* Miss Oliver.'

'She looks like a mean old bat to me,' she said. 'She doesn't exactly make a fuss of you, does she? Weren't you moaning that she never puts any of your paintings up on the wall?'

'She put my painting up today, when you were having a go at her. She stuck it right up on the wall for everyone to see!'

'Oh no! I wish *I'd* seen it! What was it of?'

'You and me,' I said.

'Oh, Jess!' Mum looked really upset. 'If I hadn't been in such a royal strop, then you'd have shown me. Why do I always have to lose my flipping temper, eh?'

'Perhaps you can't help it, Mum. You've got Anger Issues,' I said.

She gave me a look, and I wondered if I'd gone too far. But then she burst out laughing. 'OK. Well, I'm going to have to deal with them, aren't I? I promise I won't lose my temper like that again, OK?'

I stared at her. 'Yeah, right,' I said. Mum can't *help* losing her temper. She's famous for it.

But the next day she enrolled for kick-boxing lessons at Sean Godfrey's gym.

'It'll give me an outlet for my Anger Issues,' she said.

And that's how Sean Godfrey became her boyfriend.

MY MUM'S BEEN going out with Sean Godfrey for the last three months. I keep telling myself that it's not that big a deal. Mum's had lots of boyfriends. One at a time, of course.

'I'd never two-time anyone,' she says. 'I don't play games like that.'

She brings them home to meet me before it gets serious. It's like I'm her mum, and have to give my approval! I haven't actually liked any of them much. To be honest, I mostly can't work out what she sees in them.

It's easy enough to work out what *they* see in Mum. She's great fun – she always makes people laugh. She's not exactly pretty, and she wears dead casual clothes – mostly jeans and T-shirts, but with red glitter high-tops so she looks very sparkly. They're her lucky boots. When one pair wears out she buys another.

Mum's favourite film is *The Wizard of Oz*. Have you seen it? They often show it on television at Christmas. It's the one about Dorothy and her little dog, Toto. It's filmed in black and white at first, and then there's a hurricane and they get blown away to Munchkinland, and it's so colourful there it makes you blink. Mum's great at singing the Munchkin song, and she does a brilliant Wicked Witch of the West cackle. Dorothy wears sparkly red shoes and – spoiler! – at the very end she clicks her heels together and says, 'There's no place like home,' and then she *is* home.

When Mum is bored with her date, she clicks her own red boots together. She always gets bored with her boyfriends. She's very picky. She likes them to look smart and make an effort, and they have to have good manners and be respectful – though she can't stick it if they let her boss them around and try to please her too much. Don't ask me why. You'd think she'd like someone kind and gentle.

'You don't understand, Jess,' she says. 'You need a man with a bit of oomph.'

Mum's boyfriends often have far too much oomph. They try to boss *her* around, and then there are big rows and she breaks it off. Yet right at the beginning she always thinks they're The One – she's mad about them, and secretly hopes that they'll be like a dad to me (even though I've already *got* a dad), and that we'll be able to leave Marlborough Tower and get a lovely house and all live happily ever after like in a fairy tale. But Mum can't find the right handsome prince. Her relationships never last longer than three months. Miss Oliver would say she had Relationship Issues.

Mum had already broken it off with my dad when she found out she was going to have me.

'Was I a mistake then, Mum?' I asked.

'The best mistake I've ever made,' said Mum, giving me a hug. 'The bestest ever.'

She means that too. She doesn't want to get back with my dad, but she tried to stay in contact because of me. But then he started messing us about – promising he'd come and take me out on Sundays and then not turning up. Mum can't bear people who break promises. So she put a stop to that, and I haven't seen him for ages.

I don't really mind. I suppose I love my dad because he *is* my dad, but if he *wasn't*, I don't think I'd like him much at all. He's called Si Martin, and he's very good-looking with curly dark hair (not much chance of me having long, fair Alice-in-Wonderland hair with *my* parents, worst luck). He's a DJ at a nightclub. He used to be the DJ at Storm, the club in town, and Mum went there with friends from work. That's how they met. She thought *he* was The One. When she told me this, she raised her eyebrows and shook her head at herself. That's because heaps of other girls thought he was The One too. So when Mum found out that he was two-timing her, she broke it off.

I suppose he should be *my* One too, seeing as he's my dad. I don't think he was ever that thrilled to see me, if I'm absolutely honest. He was never nasty – he never told me off, even when I turned the wrong knob on his music system and accidentally mucked it up. It's just that he didn't know what to do with me.

If it was sunny he'd take me to the zoo, but if it was rainy we'd have to go back to his flat, and then we were stuck. He'd sit on his sofa cracking his knuckles and giving me nervous little glances. I'd sit on his swivel chair and whirl myself round and round, and wish I could whirl myself right through his window and whizz back home.

I'd try hard to think of things to tell him. I'd rehearse it in my head, but when I actually said it out loud, it sounded so lame I started stammering. Dad would nod and ask questions, but I could tell he wasn't really interested.

He ended up downloading all these tunes and asking me what I thought of them. It wasn't really my sort of music at all, but I tried to work out which ones he liked best – usually the ones when he closed his eyes and shook his head in time to the beat.

'This is great, Dad,' I'd say.

'You've got good taste, little girl,' he'd reply, pleased.

Mum said I should have told him straight that I wasn't into that kind of music. She has no problem telling anyone what she doesn't like. But I wanted Dad to like *me*.

'Still, at least you can tell *me* anything, Jess,' Mum says.

I don't like Sean Godfrey – but I can't tell Mum that because she's nuts about him. She thinks *he's* The One now.

It's not just because he's a celebrity. Mum knew him long before he was famous, when he was just a kid.

'Though he's changed so much I didn't even recognize him. He knew me straight away though,' said Mum.

'You mean he was at the children's home with you?' I asked, interested.

'No, he wasn't one of the Dumping Ground lot. I knew him when Cam first started fostering me. He was my mate for a bit. We used to hang out in this old empty house, me and these two boys.'

'Did Cam let you?'

'She didn't know, did she?' said Mum. 'I was a bit of a handful then. Don't you dare get up to any of the things I did, Jess!'

'But that's not fair!'

'Life isn't fair,' said Mum. 'Anyway, these two boys – one was this weird little guy, Alexander, who was a total geek, ever so brainy, and he was bullied at his school. And then there was this big fat ugly kid, Football.'

'Miss Oliver says we must never call anyone fat or ugly,' I said.

'But he was. And really tough. *He* was a bully.'

'Like Tyrone?'

'Yep. Probably worse.'

'Did he bully you and this Alexander?'

'I'd like to see anyone bully me!' said Mum. 'He was mean to Alexander sometimes, but I'd stick up for him. I wonder what's happened to Alexander now. He probably lives in Silicon Valley, King of the Computer Nerds. Still, I know what's happened to old Football.'

'The bully?'

'Yes, but he's so different now. It's *his* gym. *He's* Sean Godfrey. Football was just his nickname when he was young. I never knew his real name.'

'Is he still f-a-t and u-g-l-y?' I asked, spelling out the words.

'He's still big, but he's not fat any more. He's very toned because he works out. And actually he's not really ugly either. He used to look like a skinhead, but now his hair is carefully styled. He's even got his eyebrows styled! He thinks he's a real Jack the Lad now. If you didn't know him, I suppose you'd think he was pretty fit.'

'But you don't think that, do you, Mum?'

'Well, he looks OK, but he's still a silly kid inside. You should have heard him going on about his football career! He's got these trophies and an old football strip on display in his office. Talk about a show-off!'

'What were you doing in his office?'

'He invited me in for a natter after I'd had my kick-boxing lesson. To catch up on old times. It was just an excuse to let me know that he's a great big success now,' said Mum. She gave a little sniff. 'Fancy, old Football. I couldn't help being impressed – he's turned his whole life round. He's really made something of himself.'

'So have you, Mum!' I said.

'No I haven't,' she said abruptly. 'I'd better change out of these clothes and have a bath.'

She let the taps run for a long time. She was in the bath even longer. I think she was upset at the thought that *she* hasn't made anything of herself, career-wise. She's had lots of careers. I think she's been good at them all, but other people don't always agree.

For a while, when they were short of care workers, she did a stint at the Dumping Ground. Cam told me that she was very good with the children but got a bit too involved. I think it's great that she really cared about them – though she didn't always stick to the rules. She still doesn't. That's what makes her fun.

Anyway, after that she went to college because she hadn't worked hard at school and needed to get some A levels. She wanted to do media studies at university. She funded herself by getting an evening job in a wine bar, but it turned out she was better at working at the wine bar, and in the end she gave up on college, and eventually managed the wine bar herself. She was good at it too. It was called something silly like the Grape Harvest, but no one called it that. Everyone called it Tracy's Bar.

But then she met my dad and started me. She had to give up running the bar for a while, and then didn't go back because she couldn't take me along too. She could have got a childminder, but she wouldn't.

'I'm going to mind my own child, thanks very much,' she said.

So she did any old job as long as I could be strapped into my baby harness, or toddle along beside her, or ride my kiddie scooter, and come with her. First she got a cleaning job, but I was a menace when I learned to crawl – I kept unscrewing the tops of all the lethal cleaning fluids, which terrified Mum.

Then she delivered meals for old people, and they all made a fuss of me, but one old lady tried to pick me up and dropped me, so Mum decided it was time she tried something else. She'd done a bit of gardening at the Dumping Ground so she got a job as a gardener, and we both loved that. I played Jungles in the long grass, and picked the dandelions and daisies, while Mum mowed and dug and planted, but everyone wanted such

neat, boring gardens, and Mum can't seem to manage
neat and boring so they stopped
employing her.

Her best job of all was
being a dog walker. Every
morning we took out three
chihuahuas and a Yorkie, all owned by a mad artist
lady. The chihuahuas were called Eeny, Meeny and
Miny, and the Yorkie was Moe. They looked the
sweetest, silliest dogs ever, but the
chihuahuas were spoiled and yappy,
and Moe could be very grumpy.

We gave Buster the pug a lunchtime
walk, and he was a total sweetheart and
trotted to heel very happily. In
the early afternoon we walked
Rover and Rosie, two beautiful
Labradors. They were gentle and
loving, but you had to watch
them because they'd eat anything, and
drooled whenever we passed a full
litter bin.

In the late afternoon we walked
Nelson and Juliet. Nelson was a
lovely Staffie who was blind in one eye,
and Juliet was a highly strung French bulldog who'd
cost a fortune. You had to watch *them* too, because

they liked each other enormously but they weren't allowed to mate.

One way and another we did an awful lot of walking. I sometimes found it quite hard to keep up because I was still only little, so Mum bought me a red scooter. It was wonderful, but Moe didn't like it, and one day, when I went too near him on my scooter, he bit me on the ankle. It probably looked quite funny – me being bitten by a small hairy dog that looked like a floor mop – but it didn't feel funny at all. He bit right through to the bone, and I had to go to hospital for a tetanus injection.

After that Mum gave up dog walking altogether, even though I promised I wouldn't let myself get bitten again, and for a while we were quite poor. I missed those dogs so much – even mean little Moe. When we were out I sometimes pretended I was walking my own imaginary dogs. I had four: Wolfie, a long-haired German shepherd as big as me, Faithful, a loving cream Labrador, Pom-Pom, a very girly Pomeranian,

and Snapchat, a teacup chihuahua. They even went to school with me and sat by my desk and ran around with me in the playground if I didn't have anyone else to talk to. I suppose I'm way too old for imaginary games, but I sometimes summon up Wolfie and Faithful and Pom-Pom and tiny Snapchat when Tyrone and his mates start bullying me.

Mum's last job but one was as a receptionist in a car salesroom. She went out with one of the guys there, and he taught her how to drive. She got quite interested in cars. Cam's a writer as well as a foster mum, so when she got paid for a series of funny children's books, she helped Mum buy a little second-hand car. It's quite old, and we're not sure it will pass its MOT this year, but we couldn't really have a flash new car even if we could afford one – it wouldn't last five minutes on the Duke Estate.

Cam's series didn't make as much money as we'd hoped, but she dedicated the first book to me, which made me feel very proud. Mum's always liked writing too, so she had a go at a children's book herself. She read me bits when I came home from school. I thought it was ever so funny but very rude. Mum sent it to Cam's editor, Marina, but she thought it was not *that* funny, and much *too* rude. Mum got upset.

'She thinks you've got a fantastic, lively writing style, Tracy,' said Cam. 'You're just a bit too outrageous, that's all. I'm sure she'd think about publishing it if you toned it down a little.'

'I don't *want* to tone it down,' said Mum. 'And what's wrong with being outrageous? I'd have loved this sort of book when I was little.'

'I know you would. But you were a very odd child,' said Cam.

'I had a very odd childhood.'

This gave Mum an idea. She decided she'd write her autobiography.

'Really?' said Cam nervously. 'You can't write whatever you like about real people, Tracy. They'll sue you.'

'Let them try! I'll change their names a bit. You wait, Cam. This is going to be a real bestseller – for adults, not just kids. It's going to be a misery memoir!'

'Oh, Tracy!' said Cam, pulling a face.

'What's a misery memoir?' I asked.

'They're dire books people write about their awful childhoods, all self-pitying and full of shocking details.'

'Exactly!' said Mum triumphantly. 'They sell shed-loads. Jess and I will be set up for life. Mine will be the most tragic misery memoir ever because I had such a terrible childhood.'

'Do you really think so?' said Cam quietly.

'Yes!' said Mum. 'It was *total* misery.'

I nudged her fiercely. 'But you were happy when Cam fostered you, weren't you, Mum?' I hissed.

Mum realized she'd been very tactless. She often is. She can't seem to help it.

'Oh, Cam, I didn't mean I was miserable when *you* fostered me, you banana!' Mum tried to give her a hug.

'Well, I looked after you for most of this totally miserable childhood, didn't I?'

'I meant *before*. When I was in and out of care. I don't know which was worse. Living with my real mum was no picnic, especially when she got that boyfriend who started slapping us around. And then there was that creepy couple who sent me back the minute they realized they were having their own baby. And the Dumping Ground was dreadful – all those kids running riot and having tantrums and going ballistic.'

'That was just you, Tracy,' said Cam.

'I was a little angel compared with some of the others! Remember Justine Littlewood and how she took my friend Louise away from me? They were so mean to me, you've no idea,' said Mum, shaking her head self-pityingly. 'Justine

Spiteful Littlewood is *definitely* going in my book.'

'You could sometimes be a bit mean too,' Cam pointed out. 'Look at the way you treated that dear little boy – the one who had the same birthday as you.'

'Weedy Peter Ingham! Oh yes, him! Well, he was such a drip he asked for it,' said Mum. 'It's all coming back in vivid detail. I'm going to start writing it straight away.'

She worked on it for weeks. She sniffled over the sad bits, then suddenly burst out laughing when she remembered playing a trick on someone to get her own back. She read me passages. Some of them made me cry because Mum had been so unhappy. Some made me snort with laughter. Some astonished me.

'Mum! You couldn't *really* have done that! You're making all this up!' I said.

'It's all absolutely one hundred per cent true,' she said.

'That's what I'm worried about,' said Cam, when Mum showed her passages too. 'You *can't* write all this stuff about real people.'

'Of course I can. People will be thrilled to be in a book. Especially if it's a bestseller.'

But it wasn't a bestseller. It didn't sell any copies at all because it didn't get published. Marina turned it down.

Mum and I went to see her in her office after school. Her authors' books were lined up on shelves all round the walls.

'Look, Mum, there's Cam's!' I said.

I had a copy of each title at home, but it was still exciting to see them all in a row with Cam's name on the spines. I stroked them proudly.

'You can have a look at one if you like,' said Marina.

She's a very elegant, softly spoken lady with dangly earrings and her hair in a topknot. She was wearing a cream sweater and beige trousers, the sort of clothes you'd think would get dirty in five minutes, though these were spotless. She had a photo of two little girls on her desk, blonde mini versions of Marina.

I took my favourite of Cam's stories and sat pretending to read it, while I listened to the conversation anxiously, hoping that Mum wouldn't be too fierce.

She got right to the point.

'Why aren't you going to publish my memoir?' she asked.

'It's a really interesting read and a fascinating story, but somehow your writing style isn't quite right,' said Marina.

37

'But when I wrote my children's book, you said I had a great writing style!' Mum said indignantly.

'Yes, but not for a misery memoir. It needs to be much more sad and serious. Besides, misery memoirs have rather gone out of fashion now.'

'So what's *in* fashion?' Mum demanded.

'Novels about strong women seeking revenge.'

'That's right up my street!'

'But by the time you've written one I think that trend will be over. I'm sorry, Tracy, I know it's frustrating.' Marina leaned forward towards Mum. 'In actual fact, I've written a novel myself – well, a children's book. My two absolutely love it. I've tried to get it published, but no one thinks it's quite right. I know just how disheartening it can be.'

It seemed crazy that a publisher couldn't even get her own books published. They were having a good chat about it when Marina's mobile rang. She looked apologetic as she answered it – and then suddenly gasped.

'Oh no, Ava!' she said. 'I can't believe it! She's just walked out?'

Marina listened, shaking her head, screwing up her face. She ran her hands through her hair and dislodged the topknot so that little wisps escaped.

'I'll come home straight away, darling. Oh no, wait a minute, I've got this book launch party at six and I'm giving a speech! If only Dad wasn't away. Oh Lord, what am I going to do?' she wailed.

'What's up?' asked Mum.

'My au pair's had a row with Ava, my eldest – she can be a bit of a handful – and now she's packed her bags and walked out. My two girls are in the house on their own and they haven't had their tea and my mother lives three hours' drive away and I don't really know the neighbours properly—'

'You know *me*,' said Mum. 'Where do you live? Jess and I can pop round and I'll sort out their tea.'

'But I couldn't possibly ask you to do that,' said Marina.

'Of course you can. Don't worry, I used to work in a children's home. I'm good with kids, aren't I, Jess?' said Mum.

'Brilliant,' I said.

Marina wavered. I don't blame her. She'd only known Mum for half an hour – though she'd known Cam for years and years, ever since Mum was little. She'd heard heaps about my mum. Hmm. Maybe *that* was why she hesitated.

'Maybe I'd better try an agency for emergency nannies,' she murmured.

'But then Ava and her little sister would be on

their own for ages before she came – and she'd be a complete stranger,' said Mum.

'All right,' said Marina, suddenly making up her mind. She turned back to her phone. There had been fierce 'Mum? *Mum? MUM?*' noises coming out of it.

'Shh, darling. No need to panic. I'm sending my friend Tracy round to keep an eye on you and Alice and give you your tea,' said Marina. 'Here – have a little word with her.' She gave her phone to Mum, putting it on speaker so that she could hear too.

'Hi, Ava. Hi, Alice,' said Mum. 'I hope you're OK with this. I'm bringing my daughter, Jess, with me. You can all play together while I make tea.'

My tummy went tight. I always feel a bit anxious meeting new children, especially if I have to play with them. I didn't like the sound of Ava, and Alice was probably just as bad.

'Are you the Tracy who wrote the children's story?' Ava asked. 'The one with all the rude bits? Mum started reading it to us.'

'What did you think of it? I bet you liked it,' said Mum.

'It was funny,' said Ava.

'Yes, isn't it? Your mum's missed a trick not publishing it,' said Mum. 'What do you like for tea?'

'Not boring old pasta or fish or anything with broccoli,' said Ava. 'We don't like *any* of that rubbish healthy stuff.'

'Well, I'll give you a surprise – and I bet you both like it.'

'OK then. You can come.'

'Is that OK with you too, Alice?' Marina asked.

Ava seemingly wouldn't give the phone to her. 'She's nodding,' she said.

So that was how Mum got a brand-new job – and I made a best friend.

ON THE WAY to Marina's house Mum went to a drive-through McDonald's.

'Mum!' I said. 'You're supposed to cook them something.'

'This is quicker – and I bet they'll like it better,' she said.

I wasn't going to argue. *I* like McDonald's too, and so does Mum. We go there for a treat. Most days we eat pasta and fish and lots of broccoli, because Mum is determined that I should grow up healthy.

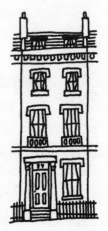

Five minutes later we arrived on Marina's doorstep. It was a very posh old house in a terrace of cream-painted houses.

'Isn't it lovely?' said Mum, clutching our big carrier of food. 'We're going to have a house like this one day, Jess, you just wait and see.'

She bent down and opened the letter box. 'Hi there, girls,' she shouted. 'It's the Tracy Beaker Takeaway Service!' She grinned at me. 'That'll make them come running.'

It did. Ava was just as I'd imagined. She was a bit older than me, and looked just like her mother, thin and elegant, with long fair hair. She wore amazing clothes – a fantastic soft blue sweater and tight jeans, both clearly designer. She had astonishing blue high heels too, but they were much too big for her – she wobbled when she walked. I think they were Marina's.

Alice was younger, and still wearing her school uniform, like me. She was a tiny bit chubby and she'd lost the ribbon on one of her plaits. She was blinking at Mum and me, nibbling her lip. I knew her tummy felt tight too, but she smiled when she saw we'd brought McDonald's.

Ava looked pleased too. 'Though Mummy doesn't actually allow us to eat burgers and fries,' she said.

'OK,' said Mum cheerily. 'You two can just sit and watch. But *we're* eating them, aren't we, Jess?'

I nodded. Alice looked very upset.

'Mum's just joking,' I said quickly. 'We've bought some for you too.'

'We won't bother messing up any plates. Let's just eat out of the boxes. And there's Coke or milkshakes – I wasn't sure which you'd like best,' said Mum. 'I don't expect you're allowed them either, Ava, so you can have plain tap water.'

Ava ate a cheeseburger and fries, and had a Coke *and* a milkshake. She said they would be facetiming with their dad soon, so Mum quickly cleared away – one swipe and into the bin, another swipe and table wiped.

Ava wanted to message her friends, but Mum said we should all sit round the table and play a game to impress their dad.

'That's what parents want their kids to do – play old-fashioned games,' she said. 'We do it all the time, don't we, Jess? And we read and paint and bake.'

'Boring!' said Ava, yawning.

'I like reading,' said Alice softly. 'I don't paint because of the mess, but I like drawing. I've never baked, but I wish I could because I love cakes.'

'We'll play Consequences,' said Mum. 'Ava, find

us four pieces of paper – Alice, four pens or pencils. Spit spot!'

'Who do you think you are, Mary Poppins?' said Ava.

'Will you give us a spoonful of sugar?' Alice asked hopefully.

'No chance,' said Mum, tweaking her nose.

Ava and Alice had never played Consequences before! Alice got a bit worried when we had to write down a man's name, and then turn the paper over and pass it to the next person.

'I don't know which man to put. And I'm not very good at spelling,' she whispered to me.

'It doesn't matter. It's just a game. And I'm not very good at spelling either,' I said. I was fibbing – I nearly always get ten out of ten when we have spelling tests at school – but I wanted to comfort her.

'This is the lamest game ever,' said Ava, but when we came to read out the finished Consequences she fell about laughing. Mum is very good at ridiculous – and frequently rude – suggestions.

We were all laughing when their dad phoned.

'Hey, girls! What's all the giggling? Where's Aggie?'

'She's walked out on us. And Mum has to work

late so she's got this weird friend Tracy to look after us,' said Ava.

'Ava!' said her dad. 'You mustn't call people weird! Is Tracy in the kitchen with you?'

'Here I am,' said Mum, pulling her chair over and waving. 'I'm here with my daughter, Jess. Marina's coming back around eight. Don't worry, your girls are fine.'

'We like Tracy, Dad,' said Alice. 'Guess what she gave us for tea!'

'I gave them a little bit of salmon and broccoli and a baked potato,' Mum said quickly. 'I hope that's OK.'

'Sounds excellent.'

When Ava and Alice had said goodbye and shut the computer, they both looked at Mum.

'You lied to my father!' said Ava.

'Yep,' said Mum. 'I was being kind to him.'

'What?'

'Well, now he can relax and feel you're being fed just the way he likes.'

'But it's still a lie, isn't it?' asked Alice.

'Not a great big whopper. And I was being kind to you girls too, because if I'd faffed around making a proper meal, I wouldn't feel like baking. But I fancy making a cake now. Who wants to help?'

'Me!' said Alice.

'Me!' I said.

Ava hesitated. 'OK. Me too!'

Mum peered into the larder. It was like a little supermarket in there, every shelf neatly packed. They had all kinds of fancy things we hadn't heard of, but Mum found self-raising flour and caster sugar and, after a lot of ferreting about, a packet of icing sugar. I found butter and eggs in the fridge.

'OK, we'll wash our hands,' said Mum.

'Spit spot,' said Alice, giggling.

'And then we'll don our aprons, fellow bakers.'

She wore the father's blue-and-white striped butcher's apron. It came down to her toes. Ava wore Marina's apron, very crisp and white. There weren't any aprons left for Alice and me, but Mum found us tea towels.

'Right. Ready, steady, BAKE!' she said.

'Can we make red velvet cake? No – a lemon polenta! No – a croquembouche!' said Ava.

'A what?' said Mum.

'It's a profiterole tower,' she explained. 'You have them at weddings.'

'Do you now? Well, we're not at a wedding. We're making fairy cakes,' Mum said firmly.

'Fairy cakes!' Ava rolled her eyes, but she seemed happy enough to take her turn at stirring and spooning the mixture into little crinkly cases on a baking tray. Then we all licked out the bowl.

'This is the very best bit!' said Alice.

While the cakes were cooking we made the icing. When they were cooling, Ava went back to messaging her friends and Alice took me upstairs to see her bedroom. I've got the best bedroom of anyone in Marlborough Tower, I know that for a fact, but it's still not quite as nice as Alice's.

Hers is blue like mine, but the ceiling is painted with a pearly white moon and silver stars. I lay on Alice's bed to get the full effect.

'It's just like we're floating in space,'
I said.

'Sometimes I pretend Basil's a
spaceman,' said Alice, holding him up
and making him swoop through the air,
his long ears flapping.

Basil is the name of her blue toy rabbit.
He's very big and soft and cuddly. She has
an entire rabbit warren in her bedroom.
Basil is the biggest. The smallest is Little
Titch, a weeny china rabbit only as big as my
thumbnail. There are all shapes and sizes of
rabbit in between, and different colours too
– red and green and pink as well as white
and brown.

'I often pretend that they've all escaped,
and then they hide all over the house,' said
Alice. 'Or sometimes they've got rabbit flu,
and I lie them on their backs with their paws
in the air, and I'm the vet and I have to give
them medicine and nurse them back to
health. I play all kinds of rabbit games. Ava
says I'm a hopeless baby, playing
with cuddly toys at my age.'

'Doesn't she have
cuddly toys herself?'

'She has bears. Three of them.'

'Does she pretend she's Goldilocks?' I said, joking. I couldn't imagine Ava playing a pretend game in a million years.

'They're those very expensive bears with a yellow tag in their ear. Ava says you're not supposed to play with them, they're more like ornaments. She's got fed up with them anyway and says I can have them, but I don't really want them. They look like they'd bully my rabbits,' said Alice. 'I'll show you.'

She took me to have a peep in Ava's room. We had to be very quiet because Alice isn't allowed to go in there. It was a much deeper blue, with lacy white curtains and lots of framed pictures on the wall – and a special fitted wardrobe.

'She keeps it so neat – look,' said Alice, opening it up.

Most of Ava's clothes hung on hangers – her shirts, her dresses, her jackets, her coats. Her T-shirts were in a neat stack, her jumpers too, and her jeans lay side by side, their legs tucked up tidily. Her shoes were on racks, all clicking their heels together, though they were already home.

'Goodness,' I said. 'It must get annoying at times, having a sister like Ava.'

Alice nodded in agreement.

'If I had a sister, I'd much prefer her to be like you,' I said.

'Perhaps we can be friends,' Alice suggested. 'Friends are better than sisters because you can choose them.'

'Do you have a *best* friend?' I asked.

Alice went a bit pink. 'Not really. At school I'm in a sort of threesome with Katie and Angela, but they like each other best.'

'I'm not even in a threesome,' I said. 'All the other girls had made friends before I started at my school.'

'Then *we* could be best friends,' said Alice. 'If you'd like to . . . You don't have to if you don't want.'

'I *do* want!'

I couldn't quite believe it. I'd been hoping to find a best friend for so long, and now, just like that, I had one.

Mum called up to tell us that the cakes were cool enough to ice, so we ran downstairs. Icing was the best bit. We dripped it on and then spread it like butter. Mum had found a big packet of Smarties for decoration.

'Our granny gave us the Smarties. We're only meant to have one a day,' said Ava.

'One a *day*?' said Mum. 'Oh well, suit yourself.'

It suited Alice and me to decorate our cakes with

copious Smarties. I picked out the blue ones and made a B for Basil cake for Alice. She was very touched.

She made me a face cake, with two brown Smartie eyes and a big red Smartie smile.

Ava iced her cake very carefully indeed, and designed a perfect flower. Alice and I looked at her enviously.

'Whose cake do you think is best, Tracy?' Ava asked.

Mum pondered as she finished adding icing to her own cake. She made a face cake like Alice's, giving it two eyes and a red smile. Then she went to the larder and brought out a packet of currants. She pressed lots of them round the edge, making curly black hair.

'It's you!' said Alice.

'Yes,' said Mum. 'And mine's definitely the best cake.'

'You can't choose *your* cake. That's not fair. You're an adult,' said Ava.

Mum just smiled at her. She never sticks to any of the rules. My mum's Tracy Beaker.

We were still quite full of McDonald's, so we saved our cakes to show Marina when she got home. She was very impressed. We had tea with her and ate cake. Mum and I had proper brown tea, and Marina and Ava had green tea, though it looked brownish too. Alice had milk. She wouldn't eat her Basil rabbit cake.

'Go on, Alice. They taste OK actually,' said Ava, nibbling her flower cake enthusiastically.

'Yes, but I want to keep it. Jess made it for me and it's lovely,' she said.

'It'll go stale, silly.'

'I don't care.'

I'd already had a mouthful of my face cake, but I kept the rest of it. It was only a little nibble. We both ate plain iced cakes instead.

Then Marina looked at her watch. 'Goodness, it's late – and it's a school night too. Bedtime, girls! Say goodnight to Tracy and Jess, and thank Tracy for looking after you so well.'

'Night. Thank you,' said Ava. Then she smiled at us. 'It's been fun,' she added surprisingly.

'It's been the best ever,' said Alice, and she gave me a hug. 'It's not fair, I don't want to go to bed. I want to stay up with Jess. She's my friend.'

'We'll come again,' said Mum. She looked at Marina. 'In fact, we could come permanently, if you like, seeing as your au pair has done a runner.'

Marina had started to tidy the kitchen, wiping down the sticky surfaces. Then she threw the cloth into the waste bin. She saw all the McDonald's cartons inside and frowned.

Mum sighed. So did I. It looked as if she'd blown it.

'Well, we'll have to establish a few ground rules,' said Marina. 'But we could give it a trial for a week or so and see how we all get on.'

So now Mum works for Marina and we all get on splendidly. Mum likes it much more than the car-showroom job, especially as she split up with her car-salesman boyfriend and it was awkward still working for him. And I love it because I get to see my friend Alice every day, and Ava isn't too bad, though I don't like her anywhere near as much.

I didn't mind not having a best friend at school any more, now that I had Alice *out* of school. It was great going to their house. And then it was great going back to our flat, just Mum and me.

Only now Mum has this boring old Sean Godfrey for a boyfriend, and he keeps coming round. He stays ages after I get sent to bed – I often can't get to sleep. I lie awake worrying about him.

Still, they've been seeing each other for just over three months – he's already past his sell-by date. Mum will be getting sick of him any day now.

IT WAS SEAN Godfrey's birthday yesterday, and he asked Mum if she'd celebrate with him that evening. Mum doesn't usually go out on school nights. We all have tea at Marina's (sometimes pasta and fish and the dreaded broccoli, worst luck – it looks as if the McDonald's meal was a one-off). I get to play with Alice, and then, when Marina gets home, Mum and I go home  too. We cosy up at either end of the sofa and have a little chat or watch television, and then I go to bed and Mum reads to me.

I can read, obviously, but it's lovely to share a story. Mum says she's catching up because no one ever read to her when she was young – not until Cam fostered her. Then I go to sleep. Once Mum nodded off mid-sentence as well, and didn't wake up until the middle of the night.

She doesn't go out on school nights because it would mean I'd have to stay with Cam. There would be a huge rush in the morning because Mum would have to drive over early to collect me, and then drive the other way to pick up Ava and Alice, and we'd all be late for school.

But Mum has a thing about birthdays. They're very special to her. When she was at the Dumping Ground she hated having the same birthday as Peter because they had to share the cake. Mum didn't like sharing the cake and the candles and her birthday wish. The wish was the most important part. She told me she always wished her mum would come back – but she didn't.

My Granny Carly is OK with me, but she wasn't a very good mum to my mum. Sometimes she gave Mum heaps, sometimes nothing at all. Mostly she still doesn't turn up when she's supposed to.

Mum always makes *my* birthdays extra special. Last year she took me out for a meal in a posh Italian restaurant, and they made me a special ice-cream cake with sparklers, and everyone sang 'Happy Birthday'. She gave me a book about mermaids and a book about dogs, and a silver bangle, and a big box of colouring pencils, and a bottle of my very own blue nail varnish – though I'm not allowed to wear it at school.

Mum makes a big fuss of Cam on her birthday too. She gives a lovely present to each of Cam's foster girls on *their* birthdays, even if they're only staying for a few weeks. Anyone just has to say to my mum, 'It's my birthday,' and she'll rush around buying cards and flowers and chocolates.

So she felt she had to go out with Sean Godfrey on *his* birthday.

'But Thursday's a school night,' I reminded her.

'Yes, I know. I asked if we could go out on Friday or Saturday instead, but Friday is his special social night at the gym, and on Saturday a whole crowd of his football mates are taking him for a lads night out,' said Mum. 'So it's going out on Thursday, his actual birthday, or not going out at all.'

'How about not going out at all?' I said.

'Oh, come on, Jess, don't give me a hard time,' said Mum. 'What's up with you, eh?'

I shrugged. I still can't stand Sean Godfrey. For a start I don't like the way he looks. He's so *big*. When he takes Mum out, he wears very bright suits in daft colours like pale blue and *orange*. Mum says they're 'bespoke', which means they're very expensive because someone makes them specially for him. I don't think they're very good at their job because his suits always look way too tight – the jacket hardly buttons up and his legs look silly.

He wears very flash jewellery too – a big watch and chunky rings and a gold bracelet with his name engraved on it. It makes him look like a little kid at nursery school with a name badge because he can't talk properly yet. *He* doesn't talk very clearly actually. He mumbles. Mum tells me to speak up when *I* mumble.

Sean Godfrey's always OK with me. He tries to be nice. He tries much harder with me than my dad, but he does it all wrong. He cocks his head and winks and says, 'Hey, kid,' out of the side of his mouth like he's a gangster or something. He fishes out his smartphone – the very latest model, naturally – and asks if I'd like to play around on it, as if it's a big treat. Well, it *is*, but after a few seconds I give it back, pretending I'm not interested.

Then he crumples up some paper and starts playing keepie-uppie – he can do it for ages. He counts, just to show you how good at it he is. He's always fidgeting around. Sometimes he does shadow-boxing, demonstrating how to punch someone. I suppose it might come in useful the next time Tyrone knocks me flying. Still, he's kept out of my way recently.

If Mum puts on some music, Sean Godfrey will play invisible instruments. If it's piano music he'll waggle his fingers. If it's rock music he'll play air guitar, pulling silly faces. He hams it up to make me laugh. I just look at him.

Sometimes he ruffles my hair and says I'm a funny kid. *He's* the one who's funny. Funny peculiar, not funny ha-ha.

I just don't get what Mum sees in him.

'Yeah, he's a bit of a whatsit,' said

Mum. She always says 'whatsit' when she means a rude word. She's very careful not to swear in front of me. 'But deep down he's OK. Quite sweet actually, when you really get to know him. Maybe I wouldn't think that if I'd only just met him, but we go way back.'

Mum and I go way back too, but she insisted she really *had* to go out on Sean Godfrey's birthday, whether I liked it or not. So it was a real hassle on Thursday. Mum picked Ava and Alice up from school and gave us all tea at their place, and then Marina came home early as Mum had to take me to Cam's for the night.

'Why can't Jess have a sleepover with us?' Alice asked.

'Oh yes, *could* I?' I asked.

'That would be fine,' said Marina.

'Yes, but it's my job to look after your girls, not the other way round,' said Mum.

She's very independent. She never asks for favours. Well, she asks Cam, but that's different, she's family. I love Cam second to Mum. She's much, much nicer than Carly. If I was just staying with Cam, it would be a real treat, but I'm not so keen on her foster girls. They're 'hard to place', which means that most people don't want them because they're not little and cute any more.

Nowadays they try not to put kids in children's homes like the Dumping Ground. They think they'll do better in proper family homes. Cam did a great job fostering Mum, who was considered *very* hard to place, so when a teenage girl ends up in care nearby, they ask Cam to look after her. Cam generally says yes, even when her house is completely full up.

She always has two girls in the loft extension. It always feels a bit weird, because that's where Mum and I used to live. We had our own little living room and shared the bedroom, and we even had our own bathroom – though it wasn't big enough for a bath, and if I sat on the toilet while Mum was having a shower I got soaking wet too. We didn't mind a bit, we thought it was funny, but Cam's girls moan and complain.

On the first floor there are two lovely bedrooms, but the girls sometimes fuss about them too because they're a bit shabby. Cam herself often has to sleep downstairs on the pull-out bed in the study where she does her writing, but she never moans or complains.

Some of Cam's girls stay for a long time. Jax and Rosie have been there for ever. Jax is very loud. It's not just her music or her voice – the whole house rocks when she thunders up and down the stairs, and there are always smashing noises in the kitchen when she does the dishes. She broke the special elephant mug that Cam keeps just for me, and didn't even say sorry.

Rosie is the exact opposite – she's as quiet as a mouse. She even cries quietly. At  mealtimes she sits there silently with tears running down her cheeks. She doesn't like eating. Cam has to coax her like a baby.

 There was once a real baby called Micky, who came with his mum, Lorraine. She was very young, so Cam looked after her too, but she left ages ago. And Jean and Sarah and Chantelle. And Lily. She was my favourite. She was lovely. Whenever I was at Cam's she made a big fuss of me because she missed her little sisters and brother. When she went back to her mum I felt sad, though happy for her.

A most horrible girl called Renée came  in her place. She was mean to everyone and made the whole house smell of cigarettes even though there's a strict no smoking rule. She said it wasn't her, even when you could see the smoke coming from behind her back.

Another girl, Marie, kept staying out really, really late – sometimes the police brought her back and she yelled at them, and yelled at Cam too. But she said sorry the next day and begged Cam to keep her. That's the thing. No matter how mad and scary the girls seem, they all behave like little kids wanting to be Cam's favourite.

I'm actually her favourite because I'm family. When Mum dropped me off I had to go into the sitting room with all the others. I felt shy because I didn't know two of the girls, and Rosie was doing mad press-ups in a corner, and Jax was jumping about practising some daft dance routine, making the floorboards creak. The new girls were lounging on the comfiest sofa and boasting about their boyfriends.

I don't get why girls want boyfriends. I don't think much of any of the boys in my class. Especially Tyrone. I don't see why Mum has to have boyfriends either, Sean Godfrey in particular.

For a while Cam was busy with the girls, but then we went off to her bedroom to sort out my camp bed, and we had a lovely time together, just her and me. She asked all about school, and I asked her all about her latest story, and then we cuddled up on her bed

with the old photo album and she showed me photos of Mum when she was little. There's only two of her when she was a baby. In one she's yelling her head off. In the

other she's with Carly. This one's all tattered and smeary, because Mum used to take it to bed with her and hold it to her chest. Then there's one when she's about my age, and scowl-

ing. It's the photo they used in the papers to see if anyone wanted to foster her. No one did.

So Mum stayed at the Dumping Ground. There are a few photos from those days, but they're all group ones. There's Mum's birthday party, but she's scowling at Weedy Peter. There's a whole series of photos of all the Dumping Ground kids at the seaside. Mum's charging around in the thick of things, making a

sandcastle, frying sausages, doing handstands on the beach. I like the photo of her racing against a little boy, and grinning because she's in front. I think the boy is Peter.

There are lots of photos of Mum after she went to live with Cam. I like them all, but my favourite pages are when Mum's grown up, with a big bump making her jumper stick out.

'That's me!' I said.

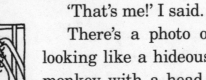

There's a photo of newborn me, looking like a hideous, wrinkly little monkey with a head of frizzy curls, but Mum is sitting up in bed and cuddling me as if I'm the most beautiful baby in the world.

'My girls,' said Cam, stroking the photo of Mum and me together.

'I love Mum so much,' I said. 'Though she can be a bit embarrassing at times.'

'Don't I know it,' said Cam.

'The worst time was when she got mega-stroppy with Miss Oliver,' I said.

'Yes, poor you! And poor Miss Oliver. Tracy's always had a problem with authority, especially teachers.'

'Still, I suppose it's good that she sticks up for me,' I said. 'But it's bad bad bad that she started doing kick-boxing because of it.'

'I'm not sure Tracy doing kick-boxing is a great idea,' said Cam.

'She hasn't kicked anyone yet, as far as I know. She just goes to classes at Sean Godfrey's gym. I wish she'd kick *him*.'

'Ah, the new boyfriend,' said Cam. 'The flash footballer. You know, he was the saddest, scruffiest kid ever, though certainly daft about football. I can't believe he's done so well for himself.'

'He's a terrible show-off and he wears stupid clothes. I don't get why Mum acts so soft with him.'

'I've never heard Tracy called soft before! It sounds as if she's really keen on him then.'

'She *can't* be! And anyway, she's been going out with him for more than three months so she must be getting fed up. Any day now he'll be history, you wait and see,' I said fiercely.

I was wrong wrong wrong. When Mum came to collect me in the morning she looked different. Her eyes were shining and she was pink in the face. We had to whizz over to Marina's to pick up Ava and Alice, but when we'd dropped them off at their school and driven to mine, Mum suddenly blurted out, 'Jess, I've got something to tell you.'

My tummy went tight. I didn't want to hear what she was going to say. 'Must go, Mum. Miss Oliver goes nuts if we're late,' I said hastily, and made to open the car door.

'You've got five minutes, Jess. Listen!'

'I can't, Mum. I need to sort out some homework. Tell me later.'

'It's good news, I promise. *Great* news,' said Mum.

'What?' I said warily.

Mum reached out and held my hand. 'You know Sean and I have been seeing each other for the last few months?'

'Three months and one week.'

'Have you been keeping count then?' Mum asked.

'Sort of.'

'And you like Sean, don't you?'

I stared at her. She was my mum. She was supposed to know me through and through. I'd never actually said, *I can't stick Sean Godfrey*, but surely it was obvious.

'Are you breaking up?' I asked hopefully.

'Who said anything about breaking up?'

'You always do. After three months,' I said.

'Well, I'm not breaking up with Sean. It's the exact opposite. Oh, Jess, we're going to live together, you and me and Sean,' Mum said. 'Can you believe it?'

I didn't want to believe it. I wanted to put my hands over my ears and go *la-la-la* so I couldn't hear another word. I started scrabbling in my school bag, just for something to do.

'Well, say something! Isn't it wonderful? What are you looking for?'

'It's this homework, I *said.*'

'Never mind your silly old homework. What do you think about us being a proper family at last?' Mum asked eagerly.

'We're a family already,' I told her.

'Yes, I know, but it'll be so different with Sean being part of things.'

'I know it will,' I said, nibbling at my lip.

'Stop doing that, you'll make it sore! Oh, Jess, come on, talk to me. Tell me what you really think,' said Mum.

'It'll be too much of a squash,' I said.

'What?'

'Sean Godfrey's too big. He takes up too much room. For a start he'll need most of the sofa so we won't be able to sit together. And there's not room for three at the kitchen table. And whenever he has a shower he'll splash everywhere,' I said.

'Don't be daft, Jess. Don't you get it? He won't be coming to live with us! *We'll* be going to live with *him*. We're going to be living at Sean's, right on the other side of town. It's ever so swish, with huge leather sofas – they're big enough for all of us. And he's got a proper dining room, and his kitchen has a big fancy trestle table for when you have breakfast. And wait till you see *his* shower. It's so powerful it's like being in a rainstorm. And two of the bedrooms have baths too, those roll-top ones with clawed feet. You'll absolutely love it.'

'No I won't,' I said. 'I love it at Marlborough Tower, just you and me.'

'But it's a dump, you know it is, no matter what we do to it. And I can't see how I'll ever earn enough to get our own place – certainly not a fantastic house like Sean's. He's really serious about it, Jess. He's actually asked me to marry him! You always said you wanted to be a bridesmaid. Well, now's your chance!' said Mum.

I couldn't swallow properly. My eyes were prickling. I felt sick.

'I can't stop you marrying Sean Godfrey if you're daft enough, but I'm not not *not* going to be your bridesmaid!' I said, and I jumped out of the car, ran through the gate and raced across the playground, desperate to get away.

5

I WAS RUNNING so hard I could barely see, my eyes blurry as I dodged in and out of the clusters of children straggling into school. I was scared Mum might come chasing after me and make a scene with everyone staring.

I couldn't let her catch me. I ran full-tilt – through the school entrance and down the corridor, though this was strictly forbidden. I rounded the corner – and barged right into someone bending over to tie a lace. It was a very big someone.

He tipped forward onto his nose and shouted something very rude indeed.

'Tyrone!' I gasped.

He scrambled up, his face strawberry pink with fury. 'Jess Beaker!' he said, his eyes popping with astonishment. Then he clenched his fists.

I was for it now! I tried to dodge past him, but then stopped. He had bright red blood spurting out of his nose.

'You're bleeding!' I said.

Tyrone put his hand to his nose – and when he took it away again it was running with blood. 'Help!' he said thickly.

'We'll get Miss Oliver!' I said. 'Quick! It's dribbling all down your shirt! Come *on*!'

I took his arm and hustled him towards our classroom. I banged the door open and Miss Oliver looked up from her desk, startled.

'Good heavens, what's happened?' she said, rushing towards us. 'Let me look at you, Tyrone. I can't believe you've been fighting with poor little Jess again. She's half your size!'

'It was *Jess*! I wasn't doing nothing!' he protested.

'*Anything*.' Miss Oliver corrected his grammar automatically as she sat him in her chair and clamped a wad of tissues to his nose. 'There. Hold it tight and keep still. Are you hurt too, Jess?'

'I don't think so, Miss Oliver,' I said shakily. 'Look, the blood's coming right through the tissues. What if he bleeds to death?'

'No one's allowed to bleed to death in my classroom,' said Miss Oliver. 'Fetch me some more tissues, Jess.'

Just then the bell went for the start of morning school. Our classmates started coming in. They stared at Tyrone in awe. He was looking very pale now, and had started to shiver.

'Oh, Tyrone, I'm so sorry,' I said, clutching his hand. 'Please don't die. I don't want to be a murderer!'

'There's no need to get into such a state, you two. It's just a nosebleed. Tyrone will be as right as rain in five minutes,' said Miss Oliver firmly, but she was looking a bit worried too. 'Jess, run and get the towel hanging by the sink. Tyrone, pinch your nose really hard.'

'It hurts enough as it is, Miss!' he mumbled.

'Miss *Oliver*,' said Miss Oliver. 'Perhaps we'd better take you to Mrs Michaels' office. You come too, Jess.'

I'd never been sent to Mrs Michaels' office before. I had never done anything bad enough.

Mrs Michaels is small and round, and she's got

a young-looking pageboy haircut, but  don't let that fool you. She can be *soooo* scary. When someone set off the fire alarm deliberately, she had the whole school quaking. Even the teachers seem a bit frightened of her. I once saw poor Miss Evans, who can't keep her class quiet, coming out of Mrs Michaels' office *weeping*.

When Miss Oliver steered Tyrone and me into her office, Mrs Michaels sighed. 'Oh dear, that's an almighty nosebleed, Tyrone. Sit down, head forward, paper towels, and try not to drip over my new carpet,' she said briskly. She turned to Miss Oliver. 'How did it happen, Miss Oliver? I do hope Tyrone hasn't been fighting again!'

'Apparently Jess knocked him flying,' said Miss Oliver.

I wanted to fall right through Mrs Michaels' new carpet and disappear.

She looked at me in astonishment. 'I don't believe it!' she said.

'I know.' Miss Oliver lowered her voice. 'Have you met her mother?' she murmured.

I wasn't quite sure what she meant, but I suddenly stopped being frightened and felt fierce. 'Are you having a go at my mum, Miss Oliver?' I asked.

'I wouldn't dream of it,' said Miss Oliver hastily.

'Did you mean to knock Tyrone over, Jess?' Mrs Michaels looked as if she was struggling not to laugh.

'Of course she didn't!' Tyrone snorted. 'We weren't fighting! She just came barging into me by mistake.'

'Don't try to talk, Tyrone. We'll time you. If you're still bleeding after fifteen minutes we'd better call an ambulance,' said Mrs Michaels.

'I'm not going to no hospital!' Tyrone protested.

'I'm not going to *any* hospital,' said Miss Oliver.

I started shivering now. I'd watched the TV hospital dramas. I pictured Tyrone lying on his back in a pool of blood, with great pincers attached to his nose. Suddenly Mrs Michaels' new carpet started going up and down like waves.

'Oh dear, Jess – you're feeling faint, aren't you?' said Mrs Michaels. 'Sit down and put your head between your knees. I don't want two casualties cluttering up my office.'

I sat down in that weirdly embarrassing position. Still, it did stop the carpet behaving like the sea.

When I felt less wobbly, Mrs Michaels took Tyrone and me to a side room with two narrow beds.

'Is this your bedroom, Mrs Michaels?' I asked, wondering if she actually lived at the school.

'Well, it certainly feels as if I'm here twenty-four seven,' she said. 'But I keep this room as a little sick room. You'd both better rest for a while. I'll leave the door open and keep my eye on you.'

It felt strange lying down beside Tyrone, as if we were on a sleepover together.

'Did I actually faint?' I whispered.

'No, but your eyes went all funny,' said Tyrone. 'You didn't half look spooky.'

'Well, you look spooky too, with all that blood,' I said. 'Is it stopping yet?'

'It might be a bit.' Tyrone snuffled experimentally. 'No, it's gushing now.'

'Shut up!' I said, feeling queasy.

'Look, *you* did it to me!'

'I know. I'm ever so sorry.'

'Well, I barged into you before, didn't I? So we're kind of even now.'

'I suppose.' I thought about it. 'So then will it be *your* turn to knock *me* over?'

'Nah. You're all right, Jess Beaker. Don't you worry, I won't have a go at you any more, and I'll make sure no one else does either,' said Tyrone. 'I'm your mate now. I'll look after you.'

I wasn't really sure I *wanted* Tyrone to be my mate, even though I didn't have any particular friends at school, but I felt it would be churlish to say *No thanks* when his blood was turning the towel dark red.

'Do try and stop bleeding, Tyrone,' I begged.

'I'm doing my flipping best.'

'I'll try to magic it to stop.'

Mum did this for me whenever I had a headache or a sore tummy or a snuffly nose. She'd stroke my forehead or my tummy or my nose and say, 'See here, nasty bug, you're to stop upsetting my girl. I'm working my secret powers on you. You'll suffer if you linger, believe you me! Oh, it's getting frightened. It knows I mean business. It's packing its bags right this minute. There, your headache/sore tummy/ snuffly nose is starting to get better, isn't it?'

I know it sounds ridiculous, but it nearly always *did* seem better. Of course it could have been the stroking, or simple coincidence, but it always seemed like it really was magic.

So I gingerly made my hand hover over the soggy towel covering Tyrone's nose and willed the bleeding to stop. I didn't say anything out loud, like Mum does – I didn't want Tyrone to think me a complete nutter – but even so, it worked! It was difficult to tell at first but, when Tyrone lowered the towel, his nose was still a mess but there was no fresh blood – and it stayed that way.

Mrs Michaels had a look and pronounced him better. She seemed very relieved. She put on little plastic gloves and washed his face with a clean towel, and then we both peered at him closely. His nose stayed dry, though it was a bit pink and swollen.

'I suppose you might have broken it,' said Mrs Michaels. 'Maybe your mother had better pop you up to A and E to get you X-rayed.'

'I'm not having no X-ray,' said Tyrone. 'I'm fine now, Miss— Mrs Michaels.'

'Well, if it starts bleeding again you must come to me immediately. Take it easy today. No sport. And as for you, Jess Beaker . . .'

I quivered.

'Watch where you're going!'

I watched, all right. At lunch break I wondered anxiously if Tyrone had got tired of being my mate and would be seeking revenge – but he seemed fine. He was mucking about with his gang in the playground, but every so often he'd look over in my direction and yell, 'You OK, Jess Beaker?'

I nodded and said yes, but I wasn't really feeling

OK. I'd been distracted by the entire Tyrone incident, but now I kept thinking about Mum and Sean Godfrey. I couldn't concentrate at all in class. Miss Oliver asked me a question twice and had to snap her fingers at me before I heard her. When the bell went for home time she told me to stay behind.

'Are you feeling all right, Jess?' she asked. 'Do you feel faint again?'

I shook my head.

'Do you think you hurt yourself when you bumped into Tyrone?'

I shook my head.

'But you've not been yourself today, have you? What's going on in that head of yours, mm?'

I wriggled uncomfortably.

'Tyrone's going to be fine. It was just a nosebleed – nothing to worry about. You're not in any trouble,' Miss Oliver said.

I wasn't worrying about Tyrone any more. I was worrying about Mum.

'Can I go now, Miss Oliver?' I mumbled.

'Yes, of course,' she said. 'You'd better not keep your mother waiting.' Perhaps she didn't fancy Mum barging into her classroom again.

I got my school bag and jacket, but then I spent a good five minutes in the girls' cloakroom pulling faces at myself in the mirror. For the first time ever I didn't want to hurry out to meet Mum. I thought she'd still be mad at me for rushing off earlier.

When I emerged at last, the playground was empty. Mum was standing at the gate, looking out for me. Her face was all screwed up, but when she spotted me she smiled.

'*There* you are, Jess!' she called. 'Are you OK?'

I nodded.

'Tyrone hasn't been picking on you again? I saw him coming out of school and he gave me a funny look.'

'No, he's fine. We're sort of mates now,' I said.

'*Really?*'

Mum went on about it as we drove to Ava and Alice's school. She didn't say anything about me rushing off this morning. She didn't mention my being a bridesmaid. The word Sean never crossed her lips.

When we picked up Ava and Alice, Ava went on and on about getting the star part of the Pied Piper in the end-of-year play.

'I'm going to wear this amazing costume, half red and half yellow, and for the actual performance I'm going to dye half my hair red too, so I'll look really incredible, and I'm going to have extra recorder lessons so I can play my magic pipe.' She burbled on about it for the entire journey. I didn't say anything. Alice was very quiet too.

'Are you in this *Pied Piper* play too, Alice?' Mum asked.

'Yes,' she said.

'So what part have you got?' Mum persisted.

'I'm a rat.'

'Yes, poor old Alice – imagine being a rat!' said Ava. 'And her costume will just be boring old brown with a yucky tail. I'm sooo glad I'm not a rat.'

'I'd have loved to be a rat when I was Alice's age,' said Mum. 'I'd have been a really wicked rat, rushing around biting people – especially sisters who show off.'

She thought that might make Ava shut up, but when we got to her house she demonstrated her Pied Piper dance, recited her first few lines over and over again and made her recorder squawk through the Pied Piper tune.

'Yes, I do think you could do with a few extra lessons,' said Mum. 'How about you rehearsing *your* part, Alice? Do you have to squeak and scurry about?'

'She's a bit rubbish at squeaking,' said

Ava. 'She sounds more like a cat than a rat. And she doesn't know how to scurry. She just plods. Can we bake a cake again, Tracy? We could do the icing half red and half yellow, like my Pied Piper costume.'

Marina had filled a shelf in her larder with all sorts of colourings and decorations because she liked it when we made cakes. So we made a Pied Piper cake – yellow sponge with a red raspberry jam filling, and the icing on the top half yellow and half red, as Ava had suggested. While we were doing the icing, Mum coloured some marzipan dark brown and made cute little rats running around the edge of the cake.

Alice cheered up and ate most of them.

'I still think my rat costume is horrid,' she confided to me when we were lying in her bedroom looking up at the stars on the ceiling.

'It's better than a bridesmaid's costume,' I said.

'What?' She looked at me as if I was mad. 'I'd give anything to be a bridesmaid! Ava and I were supposed to be bridesmaids at my auntie's wedding. It was in the winter so we had crimson velvet dresses, and they were the most beautiful dresses ever.'

'So you've been a bridesmaid then?'

'No, because on the wedding day I woke up with a

funny tummy. I didn't say anything, and I ate a big breakfast to keep me going till the wedding breakfast, which is actually a wedding lunch – isn't that weird? Anyway, Mum had just got us ready at this hotel when I started to feel really bad, and then I was sick all down my bridesmaid's dress. You can't get stains out of red velvet. It smelled too much anyway. So I had to stay in the hotel room with Dad while Mum took Ava to the wedding, and *she* got to be the bridesmaid without me. Everyone said she looked beautiful. She had lots of fancy ice cream and banoffee pie and wedding cake at the reception too.' Alice sighed. Then she remembered what had started her reminiscing. 'So why on earth don't you like bridesmaids' costumes?'

'My mum wants me to wear one at her wedding,' I said, in such a tiny voice that Alice had to strain to hear me.

'Your mum's getting married?' she said, puzzled. 'What, you mean to your dad?'

'No, she doesn't like him much any more. She's marrying this horrible man who owns a gym, Sean Godfrey.'

'My mum goes to a gym,' said Alice. 'She wants a flat tummy. It looks flat enough to me.'

'Alice, I just said my mum's getting married! You might be a bit sympathetic,' I said.

'Don't you like your new dad then?'

'He won't be my dad!' I said furiously.

'All right, don't get so cross!' said Alice. 'I'd have thought you'd like someone to give you piggybacks and presents and take you to the pantomime like my dad does.'

'I don't *want* him to do that stuff,' I said. 'I think he's horrible. And I think my mum's horrible for getting together with him.'

As soon as I said it I felt dizzy. I'd been cross with Mum heaps of times, but I'd never said she was horrible before.

'Jess? Are you all right?'

'I think I might be going to faint,' I said. 'I very nearly fainted at school because Tyrone had a nosebleed.'

'You can't faint if you're already lying down,' said Alice. 'I don't think so anyway. Jess, do you *really* think your mum's horrible?'

'Yes,' I said, because Mum was spoiling everything.

When Marina came home I heard Mum talking to her, obviously telling her about Sean Godfrey. Marina was exclaiming delightedly. Perhaps Mum was asking her to be the matron of honour at her wedding, with Ava and Alice as bridesmaids.

'As if *I* care,' I muttered.

I was dreading going home because I was sure Mum would start going on about Sean Godfrey again, but she didn't even mention him. She talked about Ava and Alice and *The Pied Piper*. She asked me if Miss Oliver was going to put on an end-of-year play. I said she certainly hadn't mentioned it, so Mum said I should tell her it would be a good idea.

'You can't tell teachers stuff like that,' I said.

'I did when I was at school,' said Mum. 'And my teacher put on *A Christmas Carol* and *I* got to be Scrooge, the star part. I was a big success. I want you to star in something, Jess.'

'I don't *want* to be in a play!'

'Don't be daft, you'd be brilliant.'

'No I wouldn't. Why can't you see I'm not a bit like you? I'm like *me*,' I said fiercely.

I stomped off to my room. I didn't want to cosy up on the sofa with Mum. I wanted to be by myself.

I sat up in bed reading, but it was a sad book about a Victorian girl who was desperate to find her real mother. I wasn't in the right mood for it. I tried another of my favourites, about a girl whose dad was so scary she had to run away with her mum, but then her mum started to get ill. I didn't feel like reading that one either. The words kept going blurry anyway.

I lay down in the dark and clutched my toy dog, Woofer. He wasn't very comforting. I whistled for Wolfie and Faithful and Pom-Pom and Snapchat, and they jumped up on the bed beside me, but they wouldn't settle down. They had their ears pricked, listening for Mum.

I heard her getting ready for bed. She paused outside my bedroom door. 'Can I come in, Jess?' she called.

I stayed quiet.

'Are you asleep?'

I pressed my lips together.

Mum waited. I waited too.

'Night night,' she said. 'Love you.'

I still didn't say a word. I'd never, ever gone to sleep without saying goodnight.

I couldn't sleep. Mum couldn't sleep either. I heard her getting up to make herself a cup of tea. I wondered about asking for one too because my throat felt dry and scratchy. Then I heard Mum murmuring and realized she was on the phone, even though it was quite late. I heard her say the word *Sean*.

I imagined her telling him all about me. I burned all over. Well, I certainly didn't want a cup of tea with her now.

After a long while she pattered back to bed. I heard her punching her pillow, then tossing and turning. Then her bedsprings creaked and there were thumps on the floorboards. My door burst open. She came right over to my bed.

'Jess?' she whispered. 'Are you awake?'

She climbed into bed with me and cuddled me close. I tried very hard to stay stiff and still, but I couldn't help snuggling up, and then I started crying.

'Don't, Jess! You'll make me start crying too,' said Mum.

'You never, ever cry!'

'I feel like it now,' she said. 'I'm very unhappy.'

'Well, it's your own fault.'

'I know. It's all gone wrong. I thought you'd be thrilled about Sean and me and living in a proper home and not having to worry about money any more. Cam said I was daft blurting it all out like that and it was no wonder you were in a huff,' Mum wailed.

'Cam?'

'I phoned her about an hour ago because I was so worried,' said Mum. 'I forgot it was so late. I woke her up. She was a bit irritated at first. She said I was thoughtless. Do you think I am, Jess?'

'Yes!' I said, because I was still cross with her.

'Do you really hate Sean?'

'I don't *hate* him, but I don't like him much. And I can't understand why *you* do. You didn't at first. The first time you met him you said he looked like an idiot,' I said.

'I didn't! Well, I suppose I might have done, but I changed my mind. You do that too. You thought Tyrone was a total muppet, and now you say you're mates,' said Mum.

'Yes, but I'm not going to marry him and muck everything up.'

'Look, Jess, nothing's going to be mucked up, I promise. It'll be *better*. We'll be just like a normal family,' said Mum. 'It's what I've always wanted for you.'

'No, it's what you've always wanted for *you*,' I said. 'It's not what *I* want.'

'So what do *you* want?' Mum asked. She sat up and switched on my unicorn lamp. She looked at me seriously, and I blinked back at her in the sudden bright light. 'You surely don't want me to break it off with Sean?'

Yes yes yes yes yes yes yes yes yes yes yes!

But somehow I couldn't say it out loud.

6

SEAN GODFREY CAME to take Mum and me out for Sunday lunch. He was twenty minutes late.

'Well, this is rubbish,' said Mum. 'What's he playing at, eh?'

'Don't ask me,' I said.

Mum went to the window for the twentieth time and peered down down down to the parking bays far below. 'Nope. Still no sign of him. How dare he mess us about like this! And he hasn't even texted!' She checked her phone yet again.

'It's a bit rude, isn't it, Mum?' I tried to look annoyed too, but inside I was fizzing over with happiness. Mum can't stand people being late, and she goes nuts if they completely fail to turn up. Cam says it's because at the Dumping Ground she used to spend most of her weekends waiting at the window for her mum to come.

It looked as if Sean Godfrey had blown it. There would be a big row and Mum would break it off, and then it would all be *his* fault, not mine. Mum would get over him in two minutes tops, and then we'd be back to normal. I wanted to whirl around our flat whooping with joy.

But just then Mum jumped, actually banging her head against the window. '*There* he is! Look, see – the red Porsche SUV! He couldn't be more flash, eh? Look at all the kids running and gawping!'

I came and peered too, my heart sinking. He seemed so *big*, even way down on the ground where everyone looked like doll's-house dolls. He was holding a big bunch of flowers too. How cheesy.

We watched him disappear out of sight as he hurried towards the lifts. Then, almost immediately, he bobbed back into sight again.

'What?' said Mum. 'Has he changed his mind?'

'Maybe!' I said, crossing my fingers.

But he was striding round to the side of Marlborough Tower.

'Uh-oh! I guess the lifts have broken down again,'

said Mum. 'He'll be knackered by the time he makes it all the way up here.'

'Don't be disappointed if he gives up halfway,' I said, not quite giving up hope.

But within minutes there was a knock at our door. There he was, grinning sheepishly behind the enormous bunch of flowers, barely out of breath.

'Bit of a climb, that,' he said. 'Sorry I'm late, babe.'

'Don't call me *babe*,' said Mum huffily.

Sean Godfrey tried to kiss her but she turned her head away. 'For goodness' sake, you're half an hour late!'

'Well, I had to hunt down some flowers for you, didn't I? The proper florist was shut. And look what I got you, kid!' He pulled a box of chocolates out from under his armpit, inside his jacket.

The chocolates were protected by their gold box and he didn't seem sweaty, but I still recoiled in disgust. They were the expensive kind – plain chocolate with weird fancy fillings.

Mum was still glaring, but she gave me a nudge. 'Say thank you for the lovely chocolates, Jess!'

'Thank you for the lovely chocolates, Mr Godfrey,' I mumbled.

'Hey, hey, what's with this Mr Godfrey business? I'm Sean!' he said, looking hurt.

'Yes, well, she's being polite,' said Mum. 'Unlike you. I bet it wasn't the flowers that made you so late! You went out with your mates after the match, didn't you!'

'Don't yell at me, Trace! I've got a bit of a headache,' he said.

'No wonder! How much did you drink last night, eh?'

Sean Godfrey looked at me and winked. 'She's really fierce, your mum, isn't she?'

'No she's not,' I said, which was the biggest fib I've ever told in my life – but as if I'd ever side with Sean Godfrey against Mum.

He pulled a silly face at me – and I pulled one back.

'Stop it, you two,' Mum snapped. 'And you're both total amateurs when it comes to face-pulling anyway.'

She made her point by pulling the most hideous face ever, crossing her eyes and wrinkling up her nose and letting her tongue loll.

'Mum!' I squealed. I've always hated her pulling faces. When I was little I was scared that my old smiley mum would never come back.

I think I was feeling that again now because my *real* mum would never, ever go out with a guy like Sean Godfrey.

'Tracy!' he yelled, put off by the face too. 'Put your face straight. You're frightening the kid. And me. I'll go off you sharpish if I have to look at that ugly mug another second.'

'Wha you mea? Fis *is* my fay,' said Mum, her voice scarily distorted because her tongue was in the wrong place.

'Please *stop* it, Mum,' I whined, though I was starting to hope that if she carried on like that Sean Godfrey might really go off her.

He just started laughing. 'Don't worry, Jess, I'll sort your mum out,' he said. 'We'll tickle her, eh?'

I snorted. Mum isn't the slightest bit ticklish. When we're sprawled on the sofa I tickle her feet and she doesn't even wriggle. But Sean Godfrey started tickling her neck, and she squirmed and scrunched up – and suddenly her face was back to normal and she was shouting at him. But she was laughing too. He was laughing back. They were getting all lovey-dovey.

I went and sat on the old rickety chair in the corner.

'What's up, Jess? Come on, put your coat on. What do you fancy for lunch, eh? Sean's taking us to The

Chestnut,' said Mum. 'Leave *off*, now, Sean. No more tickling.'

'What's The Chestnut? A pub?' I said. 'I'm not allowed in pubs.' Were they going to make me stay outside on one of those wooden benches with a packet of crisps?

'Don't be daft. It's got a proper restaurant – it's a gourmet pub, with a fantastic menu. I looked it up online. It does all kinds of fancy stuff, but there's a special kids' menu, and they do macaroni cheese, your favourite,' said Mum.

'I don't want any lunch actually. I feel a bit sick,' I said.

Mum glared at me. 'Let's go and find your jacket, Jess,' she said, sounding fierce. She took my hand, pulled me into my bedroom and pushed me down on my bed. 'Now listen to me,' she hissed, her face very close to mine. 'Don't act like a spoiled brat. You're being a right pain. Sean will think you're always like this. He's trying ever so hard, Jess. Just stop this playacting and perk up, OK?'

'I really *do* feel sick. I truly *don't* want any lunch,' I insisted.

'Don't spoil it all, Jess, please,' Mum begged.

'I'm not spoiling anything,' I said. 'Look, you and him go out to this Chestnut place. I'll be fine here. I'll just lie down and have a sleep.'

'As if I'd ever leave you on your own!'

'Well, take me to Cam's then. She'll look after me.'

'Jess! You're coming out with us. Put your coat on. End of,' said Mum.

So I had to go. I have to admit I felt a little bit thrilled when I got into Sean Godfrey's fancy car, and all the kids out playing gawped enviously. I wished Tyrone was there, but he lived in Devonshire Tower, and kids from there hardly ever hung out with us Marlborough lot.

Mum obviously loved showing off the car – and Sean Godfrey was causing quite a stir. Some of the older boys even asked for a selfie. And their dads. Even a couple of mums.

He loved it too – making a fuss of the kids, telling the guys about the hat-trick he'd scored at some boring football match, and chatting up the mums. That made Mum a bit restless.

'Are we going for this meal or not?' she asked.

'Sorry, ladies, gotta go. Taking the family out,' he said, jumping into the car.

I'm not his *family*. I hated him saying that. I looked at Mum. She was looking so different. She looked . . . pretty. I couldn't work out if it was because she was wearing more make-up than usual, or because she was wearing a new red dress. She didn't have any money for a new dress. I had a sinking feeling that Sean Godfrey had bought it for her.

Then I realized it wasn't the make-up or the dress. It was her expression. She looked so *happy*. I suddenly felt helpless. She loved me more than anyone – probably ten times more than Sean Godfrey – but I'd never made her look like that.

It didn't make me like Sean Godfrey. It made me dislike him more than ever. Though after that I tried not to spoil her day. I still felt sick. In fact, sitting in the back of Sean Godfrey's car, whizzing along at about a hundred miles an hour (well, it *felt* like it), made me feel dizzy, and I had to sit very still with my eyes closed to stop myself heaving.

'Jess? Are you all right, love?' Mum asked.

'Just a bit sleepy,' I murmured.

'She's not going to throw up, is she?' Sean Godfrey asked anxiously.

'She's fine,' said Mum, but she sounded anxious too.

I started to work out a contingency plan. When I was little I was sick in my dad's car, and it still smelled a bit the next time he came to collect me. Now I saw a copy of *Glossip* on the back seat. I opened it up on my lap, thinking I could always be sick into it. Then I realized that I was staring at a photo of Sean Godfrey on the 'Who's at the Party?' page. Of course, he was wearing a ridiculous suit – silver grey and terribly tight – with a midnight-blue shirt. He was clinking glasses with Sandy Forthright, that actress who used to be in *EastEnders*. I was just a tiny bit impressed that Sean Godfrey went to posh parties and was friends with a famous TV star – but then the sick feeling came back worse than ever, and I was in danger of spattering them both.

The car turned sharp right into the pub car park. The second we stopped I got out and stood with my hand over my mouth.

'Oh, you poor love,' said Mum. 'Here, lean on me. Breathe deeply, in and out, come on. You really *do* feel poorly, don't you? Look at her, Sean, she's white as a sheet.'

'Perhaps she's just hungry,' said Sean Godfrey.

Mum snorted irritably, and I felt just a little better. Breathing deeply helped. The sick feeling lessened, and then floated right away. I felt OK again. I suddenly felt ravenously hungry. It was very annoying – I hated Sean Godfrey being right. Still, I was now quite keen to go into the pub.

It wasn't a bit like the Duke's Arms down the road from us. Mum didn't let me go there, but I'd peered inside. It was very dark, which was just as well because the chairs were shabby and the carpet stained. There was a television screen taking up one whole wall, and the guys watched all the big matches. It was always very noisy. Whenever there was no football they played pop music. Their menu was brief and to the point: fish and chips and mushy peas; pie, beans and chips; sausage and mash and onion gravy.

The Chestnut was very light and airy, the walls painted different shades of white and grey, with a contrasting olive-green carpet. The tables were a very pale wood, each with a glass vase of real flowers. They didn't have any television at all, and they just played very soft piano music.

There was a proper menu in a leather case, plus a chalk board of today's specials. *All* the meals sounded special. They had any number of roasts on offer because it was Sunday, and a list of thoroughly described alternatives. They told us about the fish of the day and waxed lyrical about its sauce, and all their chips were triple cooked. There were pies filled with birds – just like that old nursery rhyme 'Sing a Song of Sixpence', only the birds in the pie were pheasant and partridge, not blackbirds. There were sausages too, but there were descriptions of the type of pig they came from, which put you off because you don't want to think about the animals when you're eating them.

I was grateful for the children's menu, with its macaroni cheese, although it turned out to be a bit  weird. The pasta was twice the normal size, and the cheese sauce didn't taste like the packet sort. I wasn't sure if I liked it or not, but I ate it anyway. Mum fancied fish so Sean Godfrey insisted she try the Dover sole, which was extraordinarily expensive. I thought she had finished, but then she turned it over and found there was another half underneath. Mum ate and ate and ate, and said it was delicious. Sean Godfrey had a twenty-one-day

aged steak. I never knew steak came in ages.

We had puddings too. I just asked for a vanilla ice cream because I felt quite full up. It came in three scoops, with violets on top. I didn't know you could eat *flowers*. I wasn't sure about the ice cream either. It had little black dots in it, which put me off. Sean Godfrey saw me peering at them and said they were little vanilla pods. I nodded as if I'd known that all along.

Mum chose chocolate mousse, which came in three flavours – dark, milk and white, with cream and a little doll's-size shortbread finger. Sean Godfrey had something called Eton Mess, and it looked a bit of a mess too, because the meringue part was all broken, but he said it was meant to look like that.

'How did you get to know all this fancy stuff?' Mum asked when he was choosing wine for her.

'You pick it up, don't you?' said Sean Godfrey. 'I was only nineteen when I started playing professionally, and my idea of a good meal was a few pints of beer and a curry down the Indian – but the other lads in the team soon took me in hand.'

'So that's what you're doing with me, is it – taking me in hand?' Mum asked.

'It would be a foolish bloke who tried to take a girl like you in hand, Tracy Beaker,' he said. He was right there. I suppose he has the advantage of knowing Mum from when she was a girl.

When she spilled a little bit of cream down the front of her red dress, she rushed to the cloakroom to wipe it off.

Sean Godfrey shook his head at me. 'Do you know something, Jess?' he asked.

'What?' I said warily.

'I can't believe I'm sitting here with Tracy Beaker,' he said. 'And her daughter.'

'Well, you're not,' I said. 'Mum's in the ladies'.'

'You know what I mean. When I was a tough little toerag I had this mad crush on your mum. Mind you, *she* was tough then. I was a big lad, and a bit of a bully, but she wasn't scared of me. In fact, *I* was secretly scared of *her*,' he said, chuckling.

'A lot of people are,' I said.

'Your mum says *you've* palled up with a big tough lad like I was.'

I was outraged. I hated to think that Mum had been talking to Sean Godfrey about me, telling him all my secrets.

'I don't know who you mean,' I said.

'Tyrone,' he said triumphantly.

Tyrone wasn't the slightest bit like Sean Godfrey. He wasn't slick and rich and cocky. He wasn't even particularly good at football. Sean Godfrey was talking rubbish. And if Mum had blabbed about Tyrone to him, what else had she been saying? Had she told him that I still took a cuddly toy to bed? Had she shared our special jokes? Had she told him that I sometimes had nightmares and had to climb into bed with her?

I had a sudden horrible thought. I swallowed so hard my teeth clanked on my ice-cream spoon. I wouldn't be able to climb into bed with Mum any more – not if there was a great big lump stuck under the duvet with her.

'What's up, kid?' he asked. 'Is the ice cream making your teeth hurt?'

'A bit,' I said, because it was simplest.

'You scared of the dentist? When I was a kid I never went. Half my teeth went rotten and I didn't like to smile. But I've got this fabulous dentist now. See my gnashers?' He flashed his bright white teeth proudly. He looked like the wolf in *Little Red Riding Hood*.

Oh, Sean Godfrey, how big your teeth are!
All the better to EAT YOU UP!

It was a huge relief when Mum came back with a damp spot on the front of her dress.

'Did you fix it, babe?' Sean Godfrey asked.

'*Don't* call me babe! No, it just won't budge, and it's such a lovely dress too,' said Mum.

'Never mind, I'll buy you another one. Red again, because it really suits you.'

'It's OK, I'll just take this one to the dry cleaner's.'

'You're determined to be independent, aren't you? Come on, Tracy, I'm desperate to buy you a whole wardrobe of dresses. And Jess too. What's your favourite colour, Jess?'

'Slime green,' I said quickly.

Sean Godfrey looked surprised, but nodded as if I really meant it. On top of everything else he was a bit thick. Whatever did Mum *see* in him?

When he'd paid the astonishingly large lunch bill, he gave the waitress a huge great tip too. She went all wobbly like jelly, and thrust her notepad at him to autograph. *And* he let her have a selfie. Then more waitresses clamoured for one – and the blushing waiter too.

Mum rolled her eyes. I did too. Sean Godfrey didn't even play football any more. It wasn't like he was a real celebrity – even though his photo was in *Glossip*.

Afterwards he drove us to his house. It was like a real celebrity mansion, set in a private road, with an electronic gate, and then a long driveway, and there it was, very big and brash, with lots of steps leading up to the front door, and a glass extension with a turquoise swimming pool glinting inside.

'Isn't it fantastic, Jess?' Mum murmured to me. 'There are seven bedrooms!'

'Have you been in them all?' I asked fiercely.

'No! Don't be cheeky now. Wait till you see the kitchen! You could fit our entire flat in it, twice over. And the conservatory is just like Kew Gardens!'

Mum insisted on showing me round. We even had a peep at his private study. I wasn't really impressed. It was all so bright and showy it made my eyes ache. And it didn't seem like a real home because it was so incredibly neat. My dad's place is a mess of old newspapers and coffee cups and beer cans, and he leaves his clothes everywhere, even his smelly old trainers. Sean Godfrey's house is immaculate. Mum showed me his walk-in wardrobe. All his shirts were on special hangers, and his jumpers were carefully folded and stacked, and his shoes were arranged in a long row as if they were about to start line dancing.

'Incredible, isn't it?' said Mum. 'He's got someone who cleans, but Sean does all the tidying.'

Sean Godfrey heard but he didn't seem to mind. 'I like everything to be in its place,' he said. 'When I was a kid, our house was a mess and my mum couldn't be bothered to clean. It used to drive me nuts. It's great to have my own place where I can keep it looking nice. I even dust and vacuum my study, even though Rosalie comes every day. It just gives me a kick to know that it's all mine.'

I thought Mum would scoff, but she went all soft again. 'Oh, Sean! You've come a long way since we played house together, with our cardboard-box furniture,' she said, and she gave his arm a squeeze.

I went to the window and stared at the pool. I didn't want to see Mum and Sean Godfrey kissing. The turquoise water sparkled invitingly in the sunlight. All around it were slatted wooden loungers, padded with brilliant white towels.

We went swimming once a week with the school. I hated the journey because I didn't always get a partner and had to walk with Miss Oliver looking a right Billy-No-Mates. The pool we went to was very old. You could still see the name DUKE STREET PUBLIC

SWIMMING BATHS painted on the brickwork, though it was called the Duke Leisure Centre now.

The changing rooms were old too, and they weren't very clean. It wasn't nice taking off your shoes and socks because you might find yourself standing on clumps of wet hair or a used plaster.

I didn't mind the swimming part though. I could already swim because Mum had taken me when I was quite little – I even liked putting my head under the water. I sometimes swam a few strokes below the surface, pretending I was a mermaid, but Miss Oliver blew her whistle because she didn't want anyone copying me and drowning.

I was allowed to swim a length, which was lovely, but you always had to watch out for someone else barging into you, and whenever you lifted your head out of the water there was this loud echoing yell from all the other children. I imagined swimming in Sean Godfrey's serene, silent pool.

'Do you fancy a swim, Jess?' asked Mum, standing beside me.

I shrugged. 'I haven't brought my swimming costume,' I said. I wasn't going to swim in front of Sean Godfrey in my knickers!

'I've brought it with me in my shoulder bag. And mine,' said Mum. 'Sean will lend us towels, won't you?'

'Is he going in too?' I whispered.

He had sharp ears. 'Nah, I'm not that fussed about swimming. I'll go in the Jacuzzi and let you girls have the pool to yourselves,' he said.

'He's not actually that great at swimming,' Mum said when we were changing in one of the seven bedrooms. 'We could both beat him, easy-peasy.'

'So what does he want a pool for? Just to show off?' I said, stepping into my costume.

'There's nothing wrong with that, is there?' Mum was putting on a white bikini.

'That's new!' I said.

'It's only Primark,' she said.

'So you want to show off too.'

'Stop being so lippy.' Mum looked at herself in the mirror. 'Actually, I haven't *got* much to show off. You should see some of the girls down at Sean's gym! They've got fantastic figures, and they're all the same shade of honey brown, with beautiful long blonde hair. It makes you sick. I can't imagine what Sean sees in me.'

'You're much better than any girl at his gym. You're Tracy Beaker, Mum!' I said.

'Oh, Jess. You crack me up sometimes,' she said, giving me a hug. 'Come on then, let's go and swim.'

The pool was glorious. The water was soft and silky and didn't smell of chlorine. Sean Godfrey sat in the Jacuzzi and watched us for a while, which was a bit off-putting, but then he got out and went to have a shower, so we had the whole pool area to ourselves. We swam, we floated, we dived down to the bottom, we bobbed up spouting water like dolphins, we played at being mermaids.

Then Sean Godfrey came back wearing a white dressing gown and flip-flops. He was carrying a tray of fancy drinks with straws and little paper umbrellas! 'Cocktails, ladies,' he said, pretending to be a waiter.

We dried ourselves with great fluffy towels, and then lounged on the chairs, sipping our drinks. Mine was pomegranate juice with a dash of lime and cherries on a stick. It tasted very grown up and delicious. Mum's was pink and fizzy, and she let me have a sip. It made my nose tickle. I didn't like her drink anywhere near as much as mine.

We posed like celebrities, and Mum took heaps of photos of us to put on Instagram.

Then we showered and got dressed again, and Sean Godfrey asked if we'd like to watch a movie. I thought he'd just put a DVD on the television, but we went downstairs into a room that looked like an actual cinema! There was an enormous screen that took up one whole wall, and a lovely great squashy sofa. We had heaps and heaps of films to choose from. I couldn't make up my mind.

'OK, *I'll* choose,' said Mum. 'We'll watch my favourite, *The Wizard of Oz*.'

I groaned. Mum *always* chooses that film. I *quite* like it, but we've already watched it heaps of times.

Sean Godfrey groaned too. 'I ordered all the Disney princess films specially for Jess,' he said.

'We'll watch them another time. Let's see *The Wizard of Oz*. Please!' said Mum.

'You're still a kid at heart, aren't you?' said Sean Godfrey, and she got her way.

We lay back on the sofa in the dark. Mum reached out and held my hand when the twister part started. I wondered if she was holding Sean Godfrey's hand too. I couldn't really  see. He was quite funny when Dorothy's house landed in Munchkinland. He sang along in this silly little voice until Mum made him shut up.

She watches *The Wizard of Oz* as if it's really happening all around her. Right at the end Glinda,

the pretty pink witch, tells Dorothy how
to get back to Kansas. She just has to
click her heels and say, 'There's no place
like home.'

Mum murmured the words along with her, her
hand clutching mine. I wondered which home she was
thinking of. Was it ours? Or was it Sean Godfrey's?

SO IT'S SETTLED. We're going to move in with Sean Godfrey. They're going to get married. And my mum won't be Tracy Beaker any more.

'Yes I will!' said Mum. 'I'm keeping my own name after I'm married. I'll always be Tracy Beaker and you'll always be Jess Beaker, right?'

It's *not* right, even if we do keep our own names. It'll be wrong wrong wrong. Cam agrees with me, and she's the one who knows Mum best after me. When Mum told her about getting married, Cam said all the right things: *Oh my goodness, how lovely! It's great to see you looking so happy! That's just wonderful news! Blah blah blah.* Then, in a different tone altogether, she added, 'Are you *sure*?'

Mum said she was certain. Cam gave her a hug. Then she gave me a big hug too. She whispered in my ear, 'How about you, Jess? How do you feel?'

'It feels . . . funny,' I whispered back.

Cam didn't say any more, but the following Saturday we had a day out together, just her and me. She got her friends Jane and Liz to come and keep an eye on the girls. We took the bus to Battersea and went to the zoo there, which is one of my all-time favourite places. I like the lemurs best, with their big eyes and stripy tails. I love the way they lie on their backs and sunbathe. I'd give anything to have a lemur for a pet. I like the squirrel monkeys too, with their dear little faces and soft yellow fur. I wish I could cuddle one. You're not allowed to touch them, but you can go to the petting zoo and stroke the rabbits. You can stroke the goats too if you want, but I don't really fancy it. They have yellow eyes and they smell a bit too goaty.

Cam likes the pigs best. I think they used to be mini pigs but they've grown into great big giant pigs. They like to have their backs scratched. I don't blame them – I like to have my back scratched too.

We washed our hands very thoroughly indeed on our way out of the petting zoo – you have to if you've touched any of the animals.

Then we walked through the park and sat on a bench in the sun, and Cam produced a picnic out of her backpack. We each had a cheese-and-tomato sandwich and a little banana-and-cream-cheese roll, and then an apricot slice and an apple, with elderflower cordial to drink.

'You make very good picnics, Cam,' I said. 'Did you make them for Mum when she was little?'

'She was more of a McDonald's girl. I used to take her there for a treat,' said Cam.

'Did she get lots of treats?'

'Her mum sometimes bought her a whole load of stuff.'

'My Granny Carly buys me stuff too, but it's always the wrong sort,' I said. 'When I told her I wanted a dog, she gave me this huge mechanical toy dog that moves its head and lies down and makes woofing noises. But then it went wrong and flopped over to one side, and the woof noise sounded more like a growl. I didn't like it any more, and Mum had to put it in a cupboard, but I still knew it was there in the dark, waiting to get me.'

'Oh yes, I remember that dog. I thought it looked rather scary,' said Cam. 'Still, I suppose it was a thoughtful present.'

'But she often forgets my birthday altogether. She remembers me at Christmas – she buys me clothes, mostly frilly party dresses that are too small. I'm hardly ever asked to parties anyway. There was one with a man who brought animals to show us, but when it was my turn to hold the rabbit, it wee'd all down my party dress and spoiled it.'

'Oh dear!' said Cam. 'I suppose she's trying to dress you up a bit because she likes to look girly too, even at her age.'

'She says I look as if Mum kits me out at a jumble sale,' I said.

'Charming,' said Cam. 'I think your clothes look great, Jess.'

'I *did* get my jacket from a jumble actually.'

'Bargain,' said Cam. 'Anyway, you'll be able to get heaps of new clothes if you're living with Sean Godfrey.'

'I don't want any clothes from him,' I said.

'You still don't think much of him?' Cam asked.

'That's right.'

'For any particular reason?'

I thought hard.

'Does he ever get cross with you?'

I shook my head.

'Does he ignore you when he's with you and your mum?'

I shook my head again.

'Does he make *too* much of a fuss of you?'

Another shake of the head.

'Does he act the fool?'

Shake.

'You know Little Noddy? Well, you've turned into Little Shaky,' said Cam.

I laughed and felt a bit better. 'He's OK, I suppose, though I think he looks stupid. His suits! And he's got this flash red car. And a great big mansion. I don't want to live there, even though he's got a swimming pool. I don't *have* to live there, do I, Cam?'

'Well, I think your mum's got her heart set on it. And she's got her heart set on him too.'

'Do *you* like him?' I asked.

'Well. I don't really know him that well. He was a bit of a lout when he was a kid, but I don't think that was necessarily his fault. He's very smooth and Jack the Lad now. He does seem very, very fond of your mum, and I suppose that's all that matters,' said Cam. 'And she seems very, very fond of him.'

'Mm,' I said.

'Is *that* why you don't like him?' Cam asked.

'Maybe,' I said, looking down at my knees.

'Come here,' said Cam, and she put her arm round me and pulled me close. 'You'll always come first with your mum. She loves you with all the love in the world.'

'Then why aren't I enough? Why does she want Sean Godfrey too?' I mumbled against her shirt.

'She wants to be a family.'

'But we *are* one,' I wailed.

'I know, but she wants a bloke too.'

'*Why?* You don't want a bloke, do you, Cam?'

'No,' said Cam, laughing. 'I've never really fancied blokes.'

'Don't you fancy anyone?' I asked.

'Oh, give it a rest, Jess. Liz and Jane keep quizzing me, wanting me to hook up with someone. But I'm fine just the way I am,' said Cam.

'Me too,' I said. 'Cam, if I really can't bear living with Sean Godfrey, could I come and live with you and all your girls?'

'Yes, of course you can. Though I'm not sure what your mum would say!'

'She wants me to be her bridesmaid, but I don't want to wear a frilly dress and look daft,' I said.

'She wants me to walk her down the aisle, and I'll look daft no matter what I wear,' said Cam. 'I'm the one who gives the bride away.'

'Well, that's easy-peasy. *Don't* give Mum away. Keep her just for us,' I said firmly.

Cam laughed and ruffled my hair. I squirmed.

'Yeah, your mum's always hated me doing that too!' she said. 'But you've both got such lovely bouncy, wild, curly hair I can't help it. Poodle hair.'

I rolled my eyes. 'Woof woof,' I said.

'Hey, I've just thought of something!' Cam said excitedly. 'If you and your mum go and live with Sean Godfrey you'll be able to have a dog at last!'

'Really? Like, an actual poodle?'

'Whatever breed you like. Or you might prefer a mixture. I know where we'll go! Let's check out Battersea Dogs and Cats Home! They have heaps of rescue dogs looking for a home.'

'Oh, let's!'

We went through the park. I kept pulling on Cam's hand to make her go faster. By the time we got there we were both out of breath. Then we walked round all the kennels, going very slowly now, so I could talk to every dog. There were great big huskies and weeny little chihuahuas and all sizes of dog in between. Some were so friendly they came rushing up to the bars and tried to lick us. Others were anxious and barked a lot. A few seemed sad and lay on their beds looking mournful. I wanted each and every one, especially the sad sort.

'Do you think I could have two?' I asked Cam. 'Or maybe even three? Sean Godfrey's got lots of spare rooms. They could have a room each!'

'I think you'd better start off with one,' she said.

'But I can't choose. Hey, Cam, when you first went to Mum's children's home, did *you* find it hard to choose which child you wanted?'

'I wasn't looking for anyone. I was just there to write an article.'

'But you chose Mum anyway,' I said.

'No, *she* chose *me*!' said Cam.

'And did you take her home straight away?'

'I had to have a very careful think about it. And so did all her care workers. You can't just make a snap decision over something as important as that,' said Cam.

After we'd been round twice – *and* enjoyed a detour to the cattery – I knew exactly which dog I wanted. He wasn't very big, he wasn't very small, he was exactly the right size. He was a beautiful black terrier and his fur was almost as curly as my hair. He didn't

rush over to lick me, but he didn't
bark at me either. He lay on his bed
with a cuddly toy and a rubber
bone, looking very sweet but just a
little bit sad.

Outside his kennel was a sign with his name on.
Alfie.

'Alfie!' I called softly, so as not to frighten him.
'Hey, Alfie!'

He looked up at me with his big brown eyes. It
was just as if he'd recognized me. He jumped up and
came trotting over.

'Oh, Cam, look! He likes me! Oh, please please
please can I have Alfie?'

It wasn't as simple as that. It was just like Cam
fostering Mum. For a start the Battersea people
wanted to meet Mum and talk it over with her too.
And Sean Godfrey, because it was his house.

'But it's not going to be his dog!' I whispered to Cam.

'No, Alfie will be *your* dog,' she said, but she was
looking anxious. 'Oh dear, we should have talked it
over with them first. I should know better.'

'So we can't take Alfie right away, even though he
wants to come with me?' I asked.

'Not just yet,' said Cam.

'But what if someone else comes along and gets
him first?' I wailed.

The Battersea lady said they would reserve Alfie for me, so long as Mum and Sean Godfrey and I came back soon.

The moment Mum came to pick me up from Cam's that evening I said, 'Are you going to see Sean Godfrey tomorrow?'

'Why are we using surnames, Jessica Bluebell Camilla Beaker?' Mum asked.

'He *is* coming round though, isn't he? It's Sunday. Doesn't he want to take us to that Chestnut place again?'

'Well, I was thinking we might have a Sunday together, just you and me,' said Mum.

'Oh!' I gave such a cry of despair that she gazed at me in astonishment.

'You *want* us to see Sean?'

'We have to take him to Battersea tomorrow!' I insisted.

'It's my fault, Tracy,' said Cam, looking shame-faced. 'I took Jess to the Dogs and Cats Home.'

'What? Oh, I see! Well, that's actually quite a good idea. Great idea, in fact. When we move in with Sean we *could* get a dog. We could have a cat too. Sean's got so much space. Maybe you could have a pony, Jess!' said Mum. 'Or a donkey. I love donkeys.

And what are those shaggy things with goofy faces? Alpacas! Maybe we could have a couple of them as well!'

'I don't want any alpacas or a donkey or a pony or a cat. I just want my dog, Alfie!' I said.

'Alfie does seem a lovely little chap,' said Cam.

'But we have to go and get him tomorrow or someone else will choose him,' I said urgently.

'Well, we're not moving in with Sean right away. We've got to plan it all out. But as soon as we're settled I promise we'll go to Battersea and get this Alfie – or we'll find another dog just as special, or even better,' said Mum.

'Mum!' I was shocked. 'How could *you* of all people say that! Remember when Cam went to visit the Dumping Ground and you wanted her to foster you? What would you have done if she said she had to plan it all out first? What if someone horrible came along and fostered you in the meantime? Then Cam would have fostered someone else – Justine Littlewood, for instance!'

Mum had told me heaps about Justine Littlewood – another girl at the children's home. She was her worst enemy ever. She took Mum's best friend away and they ganged up on Mum. She always sounded like the meanest girl in the world.

Mum looked at me. 'How come you've got so good at arguing?'

'It's because I take after you,' I said.

'OK, OK. We'll go and see Alfie tomorrow.'

I couldn't sleep properly for thinking about him. I was planning it all out too. My very own dog! I'd love him so much. I'd take him for a long walk every day – *two* walks – and I'd play ball with him and teach him tricks. Maybe he'd be really clever and we could work up a little act together, but if he was too shy I wouldn't force him to show off in front of anyone. I'd give him treats, but not *too* many because I didn't want him to get fat. We'd have big cuddles every day, and I'd let him sleep on the end of my bed so he would never feel lonely.

Alice would think me so lucky! She and Ava had wanted a dog for ages too, but Marina wasn't keen on the idea. I'd let them both play with Alfie – so long as Ava wasn't too bossy.

Cam's girls would be dead jealous as well. I'd take Alfie with me whenever we went to visit. Alfie would play with the girls – so long as they weren't too rough. He'd make a big fuss of Cam herself because we'd never have got together if she hadn't taken me to Battersea Dogs and Cats Home.

I was scared Mum might have changed her mind during the night. I slid into her bed ever so early. She put her arms round me, and then almost immediately went back to sleep.

'No, Mum, wake up! Promise I can still go and fetch Alfie today? Promise promise promise?'

Mum opened one eye and squinted at her alarm clock. 'It's practically the middle of the night! Go back to sleep!'

'Not till you promise we can get Alfie,' I bargained.

'All right, I promise, if you let me go back to sleep for a bit,' Mum said.

'Hang on a minute! Let me record you saying it on your phone.' I reached out and scrabbled around in her bag.

I got it out and saw that there was already a message from Sean Godfrey. I couldn't help looking at it. I wish I hadn't. It was sickeningly lovey-dovey.

'Leave my phone alone!' Mum mumbled. 'I *promised* you could fetch Alfie.'

'Today?'

'If you keep on, I'm going to throw you out the window,' said Mum. 'When have you ever known me to break a promise?'

I thought about it. I couldn't think of a single time.

'You've *never* broken a promise!' I said. 'You're the best mum ever.'

But she'd already gone back to sleep.

I WASN'T A bit tired myself, even though I'd been wide awake most of the night. For a while I lay beside Mum, planning more things I was going to do with Alfie. Then I got a bit peckish and went into the kitchen to scoop a handful of cornflakes out of the packet. That gave me a great idea. I'd make us breakfast in bed.

I hadn't made Mum breakfast in bed since the time I forgot about the toast and the smoke made the fire alarm go off. Luckily, when she'd got over the shock, she just thought it was funny. The time before that I tripped carrying the tray and the orange juice went all over Mum's cream rug. She didn't find that funny at all because the stain wouldn't come out. And when I was *really* little and not allowed to boil a kettle, I'd dunked a teabag in stone-cold water, hoping that Mum would drink it anyway. And she did, though it must have tasted revolting.

This time I was going to make her a breakfast fit for a queen. I got out our best tray with the two cats on it.

'Watch out!' I said. 'Better run fast when you see my dog Alfie coming. I haven't trained him yet.'

We had little blue cats on our nicest mugs too.

'I'm going to have to buy some dog mugs,' I told them as I carefully poured boiling water onto the teabags and added milk without a single splash.

I spread the golden toast with butter and honey, and poured a portion of cornflakes in two bowls, not adding milk till the last moment so they wouldn't go soggy.

We had orange juice in the fridge, but I decided that might be too much of a risk. I made the tray look pretty by snipping a rose from Sean Godfrey's bunch and putting it in an egg cup. Then I carried the tray into Mum's bedroom, step by cautious step.

'Breakfast is served, Your Majesty!' I said.

You're expecting me to trip at the last minute and

spill everything all over the bed, aren't you? But I didn't! I hung onto the tray until Mum had sat up, and then I put it carefully on her lap.

'Wow, Jess! You're a little star,' she said.

'Sean Godfrey is coming, isn't he? You did message him last night?'

'*Sean!* And you know I did.'

'And what if he's late like last Sunday?'

'He won't be. And stop fussing – Battersea Dogs and Cats Home doesn't even open until ten thirty today, I checked,' said Mum. 'Come on, jump into bed with me and share this lovely breakfast.'

So we ate it together and then had a cuddle. I had a sudden thought and slid down under the covers.

'Jess? What are you doing? Playing at being a bunny in a burrow? Remember, that was one of your favourite games when you were really little,' said Mum. She tried to pull me up. 'What is it?'

'We'll never be able to have cuddles like this when we live with Sean Godfrey,' I said.

'Of course we can have our cuddles. Most days Sean gets up at some unearthly time like half five so he can go and train

127

with a few other obsessives. We'll have a couple of hours' snoozy time cuddled up together, you and me. Though maybe your Alfie will need to go out for a wee at the crack of dawn!' said Mum. 'He's going to be totally your responsibility, OK?'

'Absolutely,' I said. 'Exactly how early do dogs need to get up then?'

We spent the next half-hour looking up how to care for a rescue dog on Mum's phone.

'Hm. I'm not sure about all this weeing and what-have-you. Sean's so houseproud. He won't want his carpets messed up,' said Mum.

'I'm sure Alfie's trained. He's not a little puppy. And if he's not, it'll only take a couple of days to teach him to ask to go out,' I said.

'It took you much longer than a couple of days,' said Mum. 'And even if he *is* trained, he'll be feeling stressed, and that can have a disastrous effect on the bladder. You know Weedy Peter – the boy at the children's home with the same birthday as me – when he first arrived there he was always wetting his bed.'

'Did you ever wet the bed, Mum?' I asked.

'No I did not, cheeky! Come on, you'd better have first bath. Hey, we can have a bathroom each at Sean's – imagine!' Mum stretched luxuriously. 'I can't believe we're actually going to be rich! You'll be able to have a beautiful bedroom like Alice's, and lovely clothes, and you can have all the lessons they have, like ballet and piano, and maybe we'll send you to their posh private school too. Wouldn't that be great, Jess? No more tough kids like Tyrone ganging up on you!'

I tried to picture it. I'm usually very good at imagining, but somehow I couldn't manage it. Perhaps I'd already used up all my imaginative powers for the day thinking about Alfie. We still had hours to wait before we could set off for Battersea, but I was so impatient I could hardly sit still. After I'd got dressed I paced round and round the flat, driving Mum mad.

'Hey, nip down to the newsagent's,' said Mum, frowning at her fingernails. 'I *think* Amir sells nail-varnish remover. My nails are all chipped. Sean's very fussy about stuff like that.'

She gave me a note to put safely in my pocket, and I went down down down all the stairs. The lift was actually working, but at every twist of the stairs I wanted to jump two steps for luck. At the very end I did three steps, and very nearly wobbled over onto my knees, but I managed to save myself and then spread my arms triumphantly like a gymnast.

'What you doing, pretending to be Batman?' Tyrone was lounging against the wall, smoking a cigarette. He was doing it very self-consciously, making a great to-do of holding it between two fingers and narrowing his eyes in supposed bliss as he inhaled. Then he coughed violently, which spoiled the effect.

'What are *you* doing, pretending you're a smoker?' I said. I looked at him closely. His short hair was sticking out sideways where he'd slept on it. He was wearing a grubby T-shirt and trackie bottoms, as if he'd just got out of bed. Maybe he *had* just got up, because he had no socks on and his trainers were unlaced. He wasn't wearing a jumper either, even though it was a fresh morning.

'Do you want a puff?' said Tyrone, offering it to me.

'No thanks!' I said.

'You can have your own fag if you like,' he said, reaching into his pocket.

'I don't like cigarettes,' I told him, shaking my head.

'Where you going then?'

'Amir's.'

'Getting chocolate and crisps and stuff?' Tyrone asked hopefully. 'Give me something, eh? I'm happy to share my fags with you.'

'I don't want to share them! I'm getting my mum some nail-varnish remover. Do you fancy a swig of that?' I said.

'Oh ha ha, very funny.' Tyrone walked beside me, holding his cigarette out ostentatiously. 'What did your mum give you – a fiver? You could buy a KitKat and a packet of crisps out of that. Cheese and onion – they're the best. Go on, get us some. I haven't had no breakfast.'

'What are you doing wasting money on cigarettes then?' I said primly.

'I didn't buy them, I nicked them off my mum's boyfriend.' Tyrone paused. 'I can't stick him.'

I blinked at him. 'I can't stick my mum's boyfriend either,' I said.

'What? Don't talk rubbish – your mum's going out with Sean Godfrey! I've seen him picking her up in his red Porsche SUV. I'd give anything for my mum to go out with Sean Godfrey. Not that he'd pick *her*. Your mum's quite a looker in a funny sort of way. Mine's rubbish,' said Tyrone.

I was shocked to hear him speak about his own mother like that. I struggled to say something polite about her in return, but I couldn't think of anything.

'We've just had a row,' said Tyrone. 'Because I cheeked her boyfriend. So he gave me a clip round the ear and I said some more stuff, and Mum chucked me out the flat.'

'She chucked you out?' I echoed.

'See if I care. Especially as I've got his fags,' said Tyrone, swaggering.

I tried to imagine Sean Godfrey slapping me and Mum throwing me out of the flat. I was a bit ashamed for feeling so sorry for myself. It was far worse being Tyrone.

We walked to the shops in the middle of the estate. Amir was sitting on the floor sorting out the Sunday papers. He grunted at us. He doesn't like children very much.

'Come in separate,' he barked.

He's got this new rule that children have to go in one at a time, so he can keep an eye on them. He says that otherwise one will distract him while the other nicks something. He's probably right.

'You stay outside,' I told Tyrone.

He was bending down, clutching his stomach.

'What's up?' I asked.

'Hunger pains!' he groaned. He was only messing about, but I bought him a KitKat and cheese-and-onion crisps all the same. It meant I could only buy the small size of nail-varnish remover but I hoped Mum wouldn't mind.

'Oh, you star!' said Tyrone when I handed them to him outside the shop. He wolfed down the crisps in less than a minute and then snapped the KitKat in half to give me my share.

'No, it's OK, I've had proper breakfast.' I thought about it. 'You could come to ours and have some too –

cornflakes and toast and that . . .'

'Is Sean Godfrey there?' Tyrone asked eagerly.

'No, but he's coming soon. We're going to Battersea Dogs and Cats Home to get my dog, Alfie,' I said proudly.

'You're getting a dog? You lucky thing! But they won't let you keep it. I got this dog – well, I found him in the street, and he didn't belong to no one, so I looked after him. At first he was frightened, but I was dead gentle and then he really loved me, but some pig shopped me and the council told us we had to get rid of him. *He* went to Battersea. If you see a tan Staffie there, he's my dog, and tell him it's not my fault, eh?' said Tyrone, starting on his KitKat.

'What did you call him?' I asked.

'I just called him Staffie. If you say it, he'll look up at you – he knew his name,' said Tyrone. 'Can I really come for breakfast? Won't your mum be mad?'

'Of course not,' I said, though I wasn't at all sure. When Tyrone knocked me over, Mum had been mega-mad with him. He's still the enemy in her books, and once my mum thinks you're the enemy she goes on hating you no matter what.

She looked astonished when she saw Tyrone with me.

'What are you doing here? Are you picking on Jess again?' she said, hands on her hips.

133

'Mum! You know Tyrone is my mate now,' I said. 'Can he come in for some breakfast? He says he's starving,' I said.

'He's got a KitKat rammed in his mouth!' said Mum.

'Yes, but he hasn't had *proper* breakfast.' I lowered my voice. 'His mum chucked him out because they had a row.'

'I'm not surprised. If he was mine I'd chuck him out too!' But all the while Mum was saying this she was getting out the cornflakes again and putting the kettle on to boil. 'Sit down here, kid. And stop wasting your money on junk food.'

'Jess bought it for me,' said Tyrone, swallowing the last of his bar and getting started on a big bowl of cornflakes.

'She did *what*? With my change? That'll come out of your pocket money, Jess Beaker!' said Mum, starting on her nails.

'That stuff gets up my nose!' Tyrone complained.

'Tough!' said Mum. 'And don't eat those cornflakes dry like that! Pour some milk on!'

'We don't bother with milk at home,' said Tyrone, grabbing a handful of cornflakes.

'Looks like you don't bother with spoons either. Polish up your manners, kid.'

'Is Sean Godfrey really your boyfriend?' Tyrone asked, with his mouth full.

'Yep,' said Mum.

'And Jess really *is* getting a dog?'

'Yep,' Mum said again.

'But we're not allowed to have dogs on the Duke Estate,' said Tyrone. 'I told Jess. I don't want her getting upset when she has to give her dog away like I did.'

Mum didn't look quite so fierce then. 'Yes, but we're not staying here. We're moving,' she said.

'Where?' Tyrone asked, looking alarmed.

'We're going to live with Sean,' Mum said proudly.

Tyrone actually stopped eating. He  stared. 'You lucky beggars,' he said softly.

'You could come to tea when we're there if you want,' I said, surprising myself. I hadn't even asked Alice to tea yet, and she was my best friend in all the world.

'I can't really, can I?' said Tyrone, looking at Mum.

'We'll have to see,' she said, starting to paint her nails silver.

'See if Sean Godfrey will let me come, as it's his house?'

'Yeah, well, it will be mine too,' said Mum. 'And Jess's.'

'And Alfie's,' I said. '*He'll* want you to come because you like dogs.'

Sean Godfrey seemed to like Tyrone too. This

time he came five minutes early! He raised his
eyebrows when he saw Tyrone tucking into his second
bowl of cornflakes.

'You didn't tell me you had a son too, Trace,' he said.

'Oh, very funny,' said Mum.

'So who are you, then, lad? Jess's boyfriend?'

'No!' I said indignantly.

Tyrone went pink and choked on his
cornflakes. 'Pleased to meet you, Mr
Godfrey!' he said, leaping up and
holding out his hand. In his haste he
nudged the milk jug, and it went flying.

'Oh, for Pete's sake!' Mum snapped, rushing for a
dishcloth while Tyrone dabbed ineffectually at the
puddle with the hem of his T-shirt.

'Let me do it,' said Mum, elbowing him out of the
way. 'It's gone all over the floor! I'll have to mop it all
up or it'll smell.'

'Don't bother about it, Tracy. You'll be out of this
dump soon enough,' said Sean Godfrey.

'It's not a dump!' I said, stiffening. How dare he
call it that when we'd made it look like a little palace.

'No, it's not!' said Mum. She stood up straight, her
hands clenched around the dishcloth so that a little
milk trickled onto the floor.

Sean Godfrey looked baffled. 'I've heard you call
it a dump yourself!' he protested.

136

He just didn't get it. Mum could call it anything she wanted, but it was still *ours*, and she'd tried so hard to make a lovely home for us. She looked as if she was about to lose her temper big-time.

'Sorry, ladies!' said Sean Godfrey quickly. He shook his head at Tyrone. 'See the trouble you've got me into?'

He was joking, but Tyrone took him seriously, and bent his head in shame. It was so weird seeing him act like a dumb little kid when he usually seemed so big and menacing.

'Cheer up, lad. Only kidding. Here, have you got a phone? Do you want a selfie?'

Tyrone nodded. 'Please!'

While Tyrone was setting up his phone, Sean Godfrey went over to Mum.

'Sorry, darling. I didn't mean to hurt your feelings – or the kid's. You know me, I just don't think,' he said softly.

'No, you don't,' she said, still sounding angry – but when he gave her a kiss on the cheek she took a deep breath, finished mopping, rinsed out the dishcloth, and then went to get her jacket. It was the first time I'd seen her stop herself flying into a temper. Miss Oliver would have been astonished.

I didn't know how I felt about it. I hated Sean Godfrey thinking that our lovely home was a dump, when it was absolutely nothing of the kind. We kept it so clean and neat, and the colours were lovely, and every chair and cushion and picture was carefully chosen, every ornament a memento of a happy day browsing in junk shops or ambling around boot fairs. Our flat might be very small and cramped compared with Sean Godfrey's mansion, but I liked it much better.

Still, we couldn't have dogs here, and I desperately wanted Alfie. I suppose Mum desperately wanted Sean Godfrey, crazy as that might seem. We had to put up with him saying stupid things.

He was actually being quite tactful with Tyrone. He asked him if he was into football, and they had a boring natter about matches and teams and scores. When we went downstairs, the four of us, Sean Godfrey spotted this bashed-about football in the gutter and kicked it to Tyrone. He kicked it back, and they started playing footie. It was still quite early, so not a lot of people were up, but the kids larking about and the old ladies setting off for church and the guy coming back from Amir's shop with a carton of milk and a Sunday paper all gawped in awe.

Sean Godfrey showed off with a lot of fancy footwork, which made the kids clap, but then he stopped to show Tyrone how to do it. Tyrone was surprisingly good at catching on, and did a passable flick himself.

'Well done, lad! You've got talent!' said Sean Godfrey, patting him on the back.

Tyrone's pinkness became positively neon.

He followed us to the flash red car and ran his hand lightly and lovingly over the gleaming paintwork. 'Fantastic wheels,' he murmured.

'Want to come for a spin?' Sean Godfrey asked.

'What, to Battersea? Then I could see my Staffie!' Tyrone cried.

But suddenly his mum came lumbering up. She still had her bedroom slippers on, and last night's mascara was smudged around her eyes.

'Oi, you!' she shouted. 'I've been looking for you all over, you little tyke! Wait till I get you back home!'

'But, Mum, this is Sean Godfrey, and he's giving me a ride in his car. Sean Godfrey, Mum – you know, the footballer!' Tyrone gabbled.

'I don't care if he's David blooming Beckham, you're not going off in any strange bloke's car.'

'But it's with Jess too, and her mum Tracy Beaker,' said Tyrone.

'Yeah, well, Tracy Beaker!' said his mum as she collared him and started dragging him away. She said something very rude about my mum.

Thank goodness Mum was getting into the car and didn't hear. She certainly wouldn't have been able to control her temper this time.

'Poor old Tyrone,' said Sean Godfrey as we got into the car.

'Is he really good at football?' I asked.

'Well, he's not bad,' he said. 'He can come and join my junior squad if he likes. We do a general fitness workout and then football training. I'm strict with the kids – no point letting them mess about wasting everybody's time – but they seem to have fun.'

'That mother of his would never fork out for anything like that,' said Mum.

'Well, seeing as he's Jess's pal, I'll let him in for nothing.'

'Oh, darling, that's so sweet of you! Isn't it, Jess?'

'You could come too, Jess. It's for girls as well as boys,' said Sean Godfrey.

'No thank you,' I mumbled. 'It's not really my thing.'

I hated most games. I couldn't catch a ball or throw it accurately. I wasn't great at running either. On Sports Day I came last in the egg-and-spoon race! I wish there was a sport called Reading a Book, where competitors had to choose the best book in the library, find the cosiest corner, and read. There could be different categories: the sprint, where you just had to read a page; the five thousand metres, where you read a chapter; the ten thousand metres, where you read two; and the marathon, where you read the whole book. I bet I'd win every race.

Most of the children in my class didn't like reading at all. Miss Oliver once told us about a scheme where children read to dogs to give them confidence. I wondered if she'd let me take Alfie to school!

My tummy felt tight as I wondered whether Alfie was still curled up in his dog bed, waiting for me. Perhaps some other family had come along and they'd decided he'd be better off with them. I got more and more tense the nearer we got to Battersea.

Sean Godfrey was looking at me in his driving mirror. 'Are you feeling sick again, Jess?' he asked, alarmed. 'Try to hold it in, kid! Not on the upholstery!'

'She won't be sick – she's just feeling anxious, that's all,' said Mum. 'We're nearly there, Jess.'

When I got out of the car I felt a bit wobbly, but I

couldn't just stand still and take a few deep breaths. I set off at such a pace I might have found myself winning a race after all. I was so out of breath when we got to the Dogs Home that I could hardly speak.

'We've . . . come to see . . . Alfie!' I gasped to a girl in a blue Battersea T-shirt.

We hurried past all the other dogs. I saw one brown Staffordshire bull terrier, so I paused to say 'Hello, Staffie' to him, but he didn't even glance my way. Then we got to Alfie's kennel . . . and it was empty!

'He's gone!' I cried.

'No he's not – he *can't* be. Look, it says *Reserved* on his kennel. Perhaps he's tucked himself away in a corner somewhere,' said Mum.

'He's not anywhere – look! Someone else has got him! Oh, I loved him so much!' I was struggling not to cry.

'Cheer up, Jess – there's heaps of dogs to choose from,' said Sean Godfrey. 'What about this fluffy little mutt over here? Or there's a German shepherd – they're great guard dogs. We don't actually need to get a dog from here at all – we can go to a breeder and get a proper pedigree dog – any kind you like.'

'We want a rescue dog,' said Mum.

'We want *Alfie*!' I said, and the tears started dribbling down my cheeks.

'Cam said they'd reserved him for you! It *says* so on his kennel! So what are they playing at?' Mum demanded. 'They're not going to get away with this. If they've given Alfie to someone else, then they'll jolly well have to get him back. He's ours, isn't he, Jess?'

'Yes, Mum,' I snivelled.

'No need to get in such a state, Trace! You can't go throwing your weight around in here,' said Sean Godfrey.

'Watch me!' said Mum, and she squared her small shoulders and marched back along the corridor. Sean Godfrey and I had to hurry to keep up with her.

He winked at me. 'Your mum can be very forceful at times, can't she?' he said.

I didn't like him talking about Mum like that. For once I was glad she was in a strop. Maybe she really *would* get Alfie back for me.

She barged her way through to the front of the queue at the reception desk. 'I'm sorry but this is an emergency,' she explained when people objected. 'My daughter was promised a specific dog, Alfie. He was reserved for my Jess, but he's not in his kennel – he's obviously been given to someone else, which is simply unforgivable. Look at my little girl – it's broken her heart. You're going to have to track down Alfie, because Jess saw him first!'

The Battersea lady smiled at Mum reassuringly.

'It's OK! Of course we wouldn't give Alfie to anyone else. He's probably just gone for his walk with a member of staff. All the dogs are taken out for a run. Look, I can see some coming back. Maybe your Alfie is one of them.'

And he *was*! Another Battersea lady had him on a long blue lead. His head was up and he was staring straight at me as if he really recognized me!

'Alfie!' I called, squatting down and holding my arms out wide.

He came running towards me, and then started licking my face, mopping up my tears for me.

'Oh, Jess!' said Mum.

'There now, I told you there was no need to get upset, babe,' said Sean Godfrey. 'Aren't you going to apologize to the girl at the desk?'

'Don't call me babe. And don't tell me what to do,' Mum hissed. Then she turned to the queue and the Battersea lady, and said, 'I'm so, so sorry. I shouldn't have barged in and I shouldn't have yelled at you like that, but I was just so upset. My daughter's been wanting a dog for years, and now at last it's possible and she's just fallen in love with Alfie. You know what it's like.'

They *did* seem to know what it was like, because

everyone was smiling now. We had to go to another room with another lady and fill in more forms, and Mum and Sean Godfrey had to show some identification.

'Though of course we already know who *you* are, Mr Godfrey,' said the third Battersea lady.

And all this time she was holding Alfie's lead, but he was licking my face and bouncing about and scrabbling at my legs, wanting my whole attention.

'He's telling you he wants to be your dog,' said the lady.

'Well, *I* want to be his girl,' I said. 'He's the best dog in the whole world.'

'Do you know his history?' Mum asked. 'Why was he brought here? He looks like he has a nice nature, but does he ever get wound up or aggressive?'

'Like someone I know,' Sean Godfrey muttered, chuckling.

Mum threw him a look. 'I've got to be careful. I don't want Jess getting bitten,' she said.

'I don't mind if Alfie has Anger Issues,' I said quickly. 'I'll be very understanding.'

'Alfie's got a lovely temperament,' the Battersea lady assured us. 'We always get to know our dogs and make sure they go to the right homes. We wouldn't let an aggressive dog go to a home with children. No, his former owner simply couldn't look after him any more so she brought him here for re-homing.'

'How could anyone not want to look after Alfie!' I exclaimed, hugging him.

'It happens, Jess,' said Mum. Maybe she was thinking about Granny Carly not looking after her.

'Sorry, Mum,' I said softly.

'It's OK, sweetheart. Right! Say goodbye to all your Battersea friends, Alfie. You're coming with us,' she said.

I took Alfie's lead and walked out with him. 'Hey, best dog in all the world,' I said. 'You're really mine now!'

Alfie gave an excited bark as if he understood every word. He pulled on his lead, urging me onwards.

'Heel, boy,' I said. He took no notice and went bounding ahead, zigzagging this way and that, winding his lead right around me. Then he stopped to do a wee, which made me giggle.

'That's it, Alfie. Wee-wees outside. Not indoors!' said Sean Godfrey.

'Don't worry, I'm sure he's properly trained,' Mum said quickly.

Alfie seemed uncertain about getting into the car, so I had to lift him in and then keep him cuddled up on my lap. When the car got going he started trembling, so I whispered to him soothingly.

'It's all right, Alfie. You're safe with me. We're taking you to your new home!' Then I stopped. 'Where *are* we taking him?'

'We're taking him to *our* new home,' said Mum. 'Change of plan! We're moving in with Sean straight away.'

WE HAD TO go back home for our things, of course. Mum packed quickly while I took Alfie for a walk all round the Duke Estate.

We attracted crowds of children wherever we went.

'Look, Jess Beaker's got a dog!'

'What's your dog's name, Jess?'

'He's so sweet! Can I pat him?'

'But we're not allowed dogs. You *know* that! He'll have to be put down!'

'Yes, if you don't you'll get evicted.'

I just smiled at them all. Alfie smiled too, and wanted to give everyone a lick.

It felt so great, everyone wishing they were me. But I didn't have time to hang out with all the

Marlborough Tower kids. I went over to Devonshire, which was where all the toughest families lived. The big boys were the worst. The Shireboys had knives, and once a kid from Marlborough was crazy enough to disrespect them and ended up in A & E. Even the little boys were scary and threw stones, and the babies in their buggies looked like they'd spit at you.

'You'd better guard me, Alfie,' I said.

I hoped Alfie understood 'guard' better than 'heel'.

Two boys from Tyrone's gang called, 'What you doing here, Beaker Bum? Clear off back to your own tower or we'll give you what for.'

'You shut up or I'll set my dog on you,' I said.

They didn't shut up. They said worse things.

'Get them, Alfie,' I said, slackening his lead.

Alfie went rushing up to them – and started licking their hands and wagging his tail. He was a total failure as a guard dog, but he was so cute the boys stopped yelling at me and squatted down to pet him instead.

'Is he really yours, Jess Beaker?'

'You're not allowed dogs if you live here!'

'Yes, but I'm moving, see. Me and my mum are going to live over at Sean Godfrey's house,' I said.

They gawped at me. 'You're having us on!' they said in unison.

'No I'm not. His car's parked down at Marlborough and my mum's packing our stuff right this minute. I've come to show Alfie to Tyrone. Is he about?'

They shook their heads.

'Think he's indoors,' said one. 'He's on the ninth floor.'

'There was a bit of a domestic going on earlier,' said another. 'Shouting and slapping and that.'

It had taken all my courage to come over to Devonshire Tower. I didn't dare climb the stairs to the ninth floor and knock on Tyrone's door. His mum looked terrifying, and her boyfriend was probably worse.

But luckily I wasn't put to the test. One of the boys suddenly pointed. 'There he is – over by the playground.'

He was on one of the swing tyres, his back to us. They shouted his name but he didn't turn round. He was hunched over, his head down.

'Doesn't look like he wants company.'

'I'll go and see,' I said. 'Come on, Alfie. I want you to meet my mate Tyrone.'

We walked over to the play area. It was obvious there was something wrong with Tyrone. I could hear sniffling noises. I hoped he wasn't crying. I coughed loudly so he'd know someone was coming.

Alfie hadn't understood about enemies,

but he was brilliant when it came to my friends. He went rushing up to Tyrone and tried to lick his ankles.

Tyrone wriggled and half laughed, half cried. Alfie jumped straight up on his lap and licked his face. Tyrone winced. No wonder. He had a bloodshot eye, and the skin all round it was puffed up alarmingly.

'Oh, Tyrone, your eye!' I said.

'It's nothing,' he mumbled.

'Did your *mum* thump you?'

'Yeah, she did, but it was her boy-friend that punched me in the face for upsetting her. I hate him. I hate her too,' said Tyrone. 'Is this your Alfie then? Wow! You lucky thing, Jess.'

'I looked for Staffie at Battersea. I saw a brown one, but I don't think he was yours,' I said sadly.

'Probably not. I had him ages ago.'

'Tell you what – you can have a little share of Alfie, if you like. We're not going to be living here any more, but I'll get Sean Godfrey to drive me over sometimes, and then you can take Alfie for walks with me if you want,' I said.

'That would be great. With Sean Godfrey too?' Tyrone asked hopefully.

'Yes, if you like. He says you're very talented at football,' I said.

'Yeah, but he didn't really mean it.'

'Yes he did, he told us. And he wants you to join his special squad. For nothing.'

'Oh wow. Really?'

I nodded. I sat on the next tyre and we both swung very slowly and gently so that Alfie wouldn't get seasick. He kept jumping off Tyrone's lap and jumping onto mine, and then back again.

'You're like a jumping bean, Alfie,' I said.

'He's a great little dog.' Tyrone stroked him. 'You're so lucky, Jess,' he said again.

I swallowed. 'I know.'

I kept telling myself just how lucky I was all the way to Sean's house. I walked Alfie all round the huge grounds and showed him a tree far away in a corner.

'This is a good place for wee-wees,' I said. 'Poos too, if you can manage it. But you must never, ever go to the toilet in the house, OK?'

Alfie didn't seem to be listening. He bounded over to the glass extension and peered at the pool. He barked hopefully.

'No, this isn't a pool for dogs. It's for humans. And I don't even know if you can swim or not. Maybe when Sean Godfrey's not around I'll let you try a little doggy paddle. I wonder if they do water wings for dogs,' I said. 'Come on, I'll show you round the house now. But you've got to behave indoors, OK, Alfie? Promise?'

I wiped all four of his paws with a tissue first, which was just as well. Alfie was very keen on the cream rugs. He thought they were specially put there for him to roll on. He liked the cream sofas even more, assuming they were dog loungers. He especially liked the beds upstairs, and threw himself on each one, play-fighting the duvet.

I said, 'No, Alfie,' again and again and again, but he just grinned at me, saying, 'Yes, Jess,' again and again and again.

I showed him the kitchen because I knew it wouldn't have any rugs or sofas or beds. Sean Godfrey was sitting at his huge kitchen table, drinking a beer.

'Hi there, Jess,' he said. 'Like a drink? A juice or something fizzy?'

'No thank you,' I said politely. 'But could Alfie possibly have a bowl of water?'

'Sure,' said Sean Godfrey, and poured half a bottle of Evian water into a china soup bowl.

'See how lucky you are, Alfie,' I whispered. 'Other dogs get ordinary tap water in any old chipped bowl.'

Alfie was very appreciative, and slurped and slurped. I had to wait for him to finish. I didn't know what else to say to Sean Godfrey and he didn't seem to know what to say to me now, though he nodded his head in a friendly fashion whenever he caught my eye.

My dad never knew what to say to me either. I kept rehearsing things I might say to Sean Godfrey inside my head, but they were all too direct. *Do you really love my mum? Will you always look after her? Do you like the idea of us living here? Do you wish I wasn't part of the bargain? Are you pretending to like me the way I'm pretending to like you?*

'Your mum's still upstairs getting your room sorted,' said Sean Godfrey at last, taking another swig of beer. 'We can get it painted all pretty and pink and girly if you like.'

'No thank you,' I said politely, though inside I was thinking, *Yuck!*

'Well, you choose a colour then. And you can have some new cushions and rugs and maybe a little dressing table. And toys too,' he went on.

'Can't I keep my old things?' I asked.

'Well, you can if you want, but I thought you'd like new stuff,' said Sean Godfrey. 'To go with your new bedroom.'

I started to get worried and went to find Mum, Alfie gambolling along beside me.

He wasn't used to stairs, and stood stock-still, puzzled, until I showed him that you went up step by step. He soon got the hang of it, and liked it so much he wanted to tear up and down dementedly, barking with excitement.

'Shh, Alfie! Stop that barking! It's just *stairs*. Come on, we're looking for Mum,' I said.

She was on her hands and knees in one of the bedrooms, delving into the big laundry bag containing my clothes.

'These bags!' she said. 'They were part of my childhood. Whenever I went to a new home I had to shove all my stuff in. It made me feel like *I* was dirty washing. We're going to get ourselves a set of matching suitcases, Jess!'

I squatted down beside her and rummaged through the bag too. 'Where are all my *things*, Mum? All my cuddly toys?'

'What, the ones I won at the amusement arcade? I didn't think you'd want them any more. They're all a bit grubby now, and you never play with them,' said Mum, smoothing out T-shirts and jeans.

'I *do* want them! *Mum!*'

'Look, I've saved old Woofer for you,' she said, throwing him to me.

'I should think so!' I said, catching him.

Alfie leaped up excitedly, thinking it was a game. 'Look, Alfie wants to make friends with him!' I said, holding Woofer out to him.

It was a mistake. Alfie didn't understand. He seized Woofer in his mouth and ran round and round the room with him triumphantly.

'No! Alfie, bring him back!' I called.

'As if!' said Mum.

Alfie came running towards me.

'There, look! *Good* boy, Alfie,' I said, holding out my hand for Woofer.

Alfie still didn't understand. He seemed to think that Woofer was a tuggy toy. He clamped his jaws tight and pulled hard, as if this was a wonderful game. When I eventually distracted him by throwing a pair of my socks, I gazed at Woofer in dismay. He looked extremely shocked, his head lolling, one leg hanging loose, and the stitches on his tummy coming undone.

'Oh dear! Don't worry, I'll see if I can sew him back together again,' said Mum.

I swallowed hard. I was so used to pretending Woofer was real that it was hard remembering he didn't actually have any feelings.

'Alfie didn't mean it,' I whispered into his floppy ear. 'He was just playing with you. Don't worry, I won't let him do it again – he can't help being a bit rough.'

Alfie was now deep in the laundry bag, pulling out more socks, knickers and pyjamas, scrabbling through them joyfully.

'You'd better take him out of here,' said Mum. 'He's driving me crazy.'

Alfie managed to get a pair of knickers caught on the end of his nose and looked so funny that we both burst out laughing.

'Come here, you monkey,' I said,

grabbing him. I sat on the bed with Alfie on my lap, though he struggled to get down.

'Watch he doesn't get his paws on that white duvet!' said Mum.

I looked at it. 'Can't I have my blue duvet?' I asked.

'Well, it's ever so faded now, and it's got that hot chocolate stain. It wouldn't really go with the rest of the room, would it?' said Mum, looking around at the pale grey walls and the biscuit-coloured rug.

'Sean Godfrey said I could have the room any colour I wanted,' I said.

'*Sean,* not Sean Godfrey. Well, yes, you can, but maybe you'd like a different colour scheme. You've had blue for ages,' said Mum.

'I *like* blue,' I said.

'OK, OK. I was just *suggesting.*'

'Sean Godfrey suggested pink. Frilly and girly. I don't have to have pink, do I?' I asked.

'No, you can have anything you like.'

'Then I'll have blue. Again. We like blue, don't we, Alfie?' I said, and I gently made him nod his head.

'You can have blue then. Blue walls, blue curtains, blue bedding, blue clothes – you can wear bright blue face paint and dye your hair navy, OK?' said Mum. 'But don't think I'm always going to give in to you, Jessica *Bluebell* Camilla Beaker. Look, I know this is all a bit of an upheaval and probably feels rather overwhelming. I feel a bit weird too, actually,' she said, looking around the room. 'It's like I'm in a dream. This is all I've ever wanted for us, Jess. I can't quite believe it's all happened for real.'

Alfie started whimpering a little, desperate to get down from the bed. So I let him go, and he immediately ran over to the door, lifted his back leg and did a wee all down the white paint.

'Oh my Lord!' said Mum, using my knickers to try to mop it up.

'It's not his fault, Mum. He was trying to tell me he needed to go – I just didn't realize in time. He drank a whole bowl of water downstairs,' I gabbled. I peered at the door. Some of Alfie's wee had sprinkled the carpet in a very worrying way. 'What will Sean say?' I asked.

'I don't imagine he'd be thrilled – but he won't know because I'll scrub it clean somehow. But you'd better make sure you take Alfie out into the garden regularly. Don't tell Sean just now – I don't want him thinking we're a liability when we've only been here five minutes,' said Mum. 'And I want you to be careful too, Jess.'

'*I'm* not going to wet the carpet!' I said indignantly.

'I should hope not! No, I mean you're to keep your things tidy and not make a mess. No games like Twister! And no potato prints!'

'Mum! I don't do babyish stuff like that any more,' I said.

Twister had been one of my favourite games. I pretended this terrible wind was blowing, and made it toss the cushions and curtains about and send all the books tumbling off the shelf, and then Mum and I had to hide under the table clutching each other. When we were hungry I'd stagger out to the kitchen, almost on my hands and knees, snatch  up a packet of biscuits, then crawl back, and we'd munch companionably, even though the wind was howling around us.

I'd also loved making potato prints. We'd learned how to do them in Infants – cutting a pattern in half a potato, dipping it in a saucer of paint and then stamping a design on a sheet of drawing paper. I did  this at home, but we soon ran out of paper, so I printed on the kitchen wall. I did a very neat frieze above the skirting board, and Mum said she thought it looked great, though even then I knew she was only pretending.

'So I can never play a game or do any art now we live here?' I said.

'Yes, of course you can, just don't go too wild. And clear up after yourself. Sean's very particular,' said Mum.

I pulled a face.

'Don't look like that! He had it very tough when he was young. He never had any clean clothes and his house was a dump. He just likes to keep things nice now. I can understand that, can't you?'

I didn't really *want* to understand. Mum was forever making excuses for Sean Godfrey. And, because it was *his* house, *he* got to say what we did. That evening we had to watch a James Bond film in his cinema room. Lots of kids might have thought this a treat, but I don't like them. I don't think Mum's that keen either, but she made out she was loving every minute. I know for a fact that she was holding hands with Sean Godfrey in the dark.

He cooked us a meal too – great big steaks and very thin chips. The chips were fine but I don't really like meat, especially when it's a vast lump that's still bloody  in the middle. I only had a few nibbles of mine.

'Come on, Jess, eat up. That's prime fillet,' said Sean Godfrey.

'I don't like meat very much, thank you,' I said.

'It's good for you. You could do with eating a bit

more – you're very pale and skinny,' he said.

I *like* being pale and skinny. Who wants to be big and beefy, with a red face like Sean Godfrey? I thought Mum would stick up for me, but *she* told me to eat up too.

I *cut up* my meat but I didn't actually *eat* it. I slipped little bits to Alfie under the table. I think Mum knew what I was doing, though she kept quiet. Sean Godfrey didn't have a clue until Alfie gave an eager woof for another piece.

'You're not giving that prime steak to the dog, are you, Jess?' he asked.

'No,' I said. 'Well. Just a little bit.'

'Do you have any idea how much it cost?'

'I'm sorry. But Alfie needs to be fed too.'

'Yes, and he'll *get* fed. I've bought tins of dog food for him. Tell you what, I'll give Alfie the steak for his tea, and serve *you* a plate of dog food. Is that what you'd prefer?'

'It's all right, Jess,' Mum said quickly. 'Sean's only teasing. Aren't you, Sean?'

'Yes, of course,' he said, pulling a funny face.

I wasn't sure.

'Perhaps eat another three mouthfuls and then you can leave the rest,' said Mum. 'She doesn't have a very big appetite, Sean.'

'Fine,' he said. 'I don't want to *force* the kid to eat.

It's just I thought it would be a treat. When I was a kid I hardly ever got a burger, let alone steak. Most nights we had to make do with a portion of chips from the chippy.'

'When I lived at the Dumping Ground, going to McDonald's was the biggest treat in the world,' said Mum. 'I couldn't believe my luck when Cam took me there!'

She chatted away determinedly to give me a chance to calm down. I put one fingernail-size piece of steak in my mouth and started chewing. I chewed and chewed and chewed, but it wouldn't go down. Alfie's damp nose pressed against my knee. I could feel him trembling with anticipation. He couldn't understand why I'd suddenly stopped feeding him. He gave a little woof to remind me that he was there and he was hungry. I gave him an apologetic pat. It wasn't a good move. Alfie thought I had meat in my hand. He didn't like being teased any more than I did. He barked indignantly.

'You're not feeding him again, are you?' Sean Godfrey demanded.

'No, I'm not – though he's getting upset,' I said. 'It's so unfair, us having our tea while he's not allowed any.'

'Oh, for goodness' sake! Look, I'll take him in the kitchen and give him some dog food in a bowl right this minute. Will that satisfy you?'

He pulled Alfie out from under the table, got hold of his collar and hauled him towards the kitchen.

'Don't! He doesn't like being pulled like that,' I said.

'He's a dog, Jess. He's got to know his place,' said Sean Godfrey, taking Alfie away.

I knew my place in this household too. I was under Sean Godfrey's thumb, and I hated it. Alfie hated it too. He was given a bowl of dog food, but he clearly didn't think it a fair exchange. He hated being shut in the kitchen, away from me, and started howling, scrabbling at the door with his paws.

I put my knife and fork together on my plate, unable to eat any more.

'Now you're just being deliberately awkward, Jess,' said Sean Godfrey. 'Eat up!'

'Don't tell Jess what to do, Sean,' said Mum. 'She's not used to being spoken to like that.'

'Yes, well, it's obvious you've spoiled her rotten,' he said.

Mum went white. She put her own knife and fork together. 'Are you saying I'm not a good mum?' she said.

I held my breath. So did Sean Godfrey. Even Alfie stopped howling for a second.

'I'm not saying anything of the kind. You're a wonderful mum, Trace, you know you are. I didn't mean to upset you, darling. I just hate to see food wasted, that's all. I'm a bit hyped up. I shouldn't have nagged you like that, Jess. I'm sorry.'

Maybe he was. I think he was just scared that Mum might lose her temper altogether and walk out when we'd only just got here. But his little speech worked. Mum took a deep breath, and then reached out and patted his hand.

'I'm sorry too, Sean,' she murmured. 'It must feel a bit odd having us here, Jess and me and the dog, all cluttering up your home. No wonder you're a bit tense.'

He took hold of Mum's hand and held it tightly. 'You're a gem,' he said huskily.

I was allowed to leave the rest of my meat. I found I couldn't even eat much of the chocolate mousse. It was an enormous relief when the meal was over.

Mum and Sean sat over their cups of coffee while I went into the kitchen to comfort Alfie. He leaped up eagerly, so happy to see me. I gave him a big hug and made a huge fuss of him. But I was conscious of a horrible smell. I looked at the floor. There was something terrible on the quarry tiles.

'Oh, Alfie!' I whispered.

Perhaps *that* was why he'd been howling – he was desperately trying to tell me he needed to go out. It wasn't his fault. But Sean Godfrey would go bananas.

I didn't know what to do. If I called Mum, then Sean Godfrey would want to know what was going on. I had to deal with it myself.

There were kitchen towels, thank goodness. And then I wiped the floor over with a j-cloth, and bundled that into another kitchen towel. I found some disinfectant spray and had a go with that for good measure. Then I washed my hands thoroughly, opened the window wide and took Alfie out for a walk in the garden. I held all the kitchen towels at arm's length till I could chuck them into Sean Godfrey's waste bin.

It was an enormous relief to get rid of them. I took a proper breath for the first time in five minutes, and then started running. Alfie bobbed along ahead of me, constantly looking round to check that I was still there.

'We hate Sean Godfrey, don't we?' I said to him.

Alfie agreed.

But Mum liked him. When she came to kiss me goodnight in the new room that was my bedroom, she

166

cuddled me close and said, 'It's all working out OK, isn't it, Jess?'

'I suppose so,' I said. 'But I hate not having half my things. And where are all our ornaments – our china dogs and the Toby jugs and the birds and the little teddies?'

'Sean doesn't really like clutter, Jess.'

'But *we* like it!'

'Well, we'll sneak a few more bits in here and there. Perhaps he won't notice,' said Mum. 'Don't let's stress about it now. We're going to be so happy here, you and me.'

'And Alfie,' I said.

He was curled up in the brand-new dog bed that Sean Godfrey had bought him from Battersea Dogs Home – but as soon as Mum had gone he started whimpering.

I felt a bit like whimpering too.

'Come up here, Alfie,' I said, patting the bed.

He didn't need to be asked twice. He came bounding over and leaped up beside me on the white duvet. I held him close, breathing in his lovely warm doggy smell. When he heard Sean Godfrey laughing downstairs he started growling.

'I wish he'd shut up, don't you, Alfie? We don't like him. We don't like this house. It's all strange and different. Even *Mum's* different. Do you think she's right? Will we really be happy here?' I asked him.

Alfie didn't seem sure. And neither was I.

10

I T WAS A terrible rush to get ready in the morning. I pulled on my jeans and a sweater to take Alfie for a quick wee in the garden, but when I went up to change for school, it took me ages to find my skirt and blouse, and my PE kit was nowhere to be found. Mum must have forgotten to pack it yesterday. I was going to be in trouble. Miss Oliver was always very fierce if anyone forgot their PE kit.

I hurried downstairs for breakfast, Alfie beside me, and then stopped short at the kitchen door. There was a complete stranger standing by the stove, scrambling eggs and grilling bacon – a small lady with long dark hair, wearing jeans. She was young and she was pretty. She couldn't be *another* girlfriend, could she?

'Hello!' she said, smiling. 'I'm Rosalie. Do you like eggs? And bacon? Mr Sean always likes a proper breakfast when he gets back from the gym. There's plenty here.'

I hesitated. The eggs and bacon *did* smell good. I hadn't had much to eat last night. But I always had cornflakes for breakfast.

'Perhaps your dog would like bacon too?' Rosalie asked.

'Yes please!' I said, won over.

'What is his name?' she asked, patting him.

'He's Alfie. And I'm Jess.'

'So you're Mr Sean's lady's little girl?'

'Yes. Well. My mum's Tracy Beaker. She's going to marry Sean Godfrey,' I said.

'Ah, I love a wedding,' said Rosalie. 'Has your mum chosen her wedding dress?'

'I don't think so,' I said, hating the idea of Mum in a long white gown.

'I am very good at baking. I will make your mum a marvellous wedding cake – three tiers, royal icing, little marzipan figures of her and Mr Sean. If she'd like it . . .'

Mum herself came dashing into the room, her hair wilder than ever, her T-shirt on inside out. She looked at the kitchen clock and gasped. 'We're soooo late, Jess,' she said, and then she stopped short, staring at Rosalie.

'Don't worry, Miss Tracy, I'm just about to serve your bacon and eggs,' said Rosalie.

'And who are you?' Mum asked, astonished.

'I'm Rosalie, Mr Sean's housekeeper.' She pretended to look upset, pulling a sad face. 'Didn't he tell you about me?'

'Oh, right, you're his housekeeper!' said Mum, sounding relieved. Perhaps she'd thought Rosalie was another girlfriend too. 'Well, thanks very much, Rosalie, but Jess and I will have to dash.'

Sean Godfrey came into the room, yawning and stretching – he had clearly only just got up too. He was wearing a maroon tracksuit with a gold SG printed on the front. His gold ring was engraved with his initials as well as the identity bracelet. It's a wonder he didn't have a tattooed S on one cheek and a G on the other.

'No gym, Mr Sean?' asked Rosalie.

'A guy needs a lie-in once in a while.' He looked at Mum. 'Where are you off to, Trace? You haven't even had breakfast yet.'

'I've got to pick up Ava and Alice, and it'll take at least half an hour to get there,' Mum gabbled. 'Come on, Jess. Is Alfie on his lead?'

'Who on earth are Ava and Alice?' said Sean. 'Hi, Rosalie! Pile that plate high, darling – and give some to Tracy and Jess too.'

'Certainly, Mr Sean,' said Rosalie.

'I haven't got time for breakfast,' Mum said. 'I take Ava and Alice to school every morning. I told you all about them, Sean.'

'Ava and Alice!' he said in a silly mocking voice. 'Sit down and eat. Then give their mother a call and say you can't come. You don't have to ferry other people's kids around any more. You're not a flipping childminder. You're a Sean-minder now!' He laughed at his own joke.

Mum wasn't smiling. 'I'm not letting Marina down. She's my friend. Jess, come *on.*'

Rosalie shook her head sympathetically and crammed a huge bacon sandwich into my hand.

'Share with your mum. And dog!' she murmured.

Mum dashed out of the front door and then stood still. Sean's big red car was there on the driveway, but *our* car was back in its parking space at Marlborough Tower.

Mum said a very rude word.

Sean Godfrey had followed us, a cup of coffee in

one hand – and a set of keys in the other. 'Here, babe,' he said, tossing the keys to Mum.

'Oh, wow!' she said. 'You mean it? But how will you get to the gym?'

'I'll run there. Do me good – I missed my workout this morning. But drive carefully, for Pete's sake.'

Mum said, 'Promise!' and gave him a quick kiss.

I sat in the back of the car with Alfie on my lap.

'Wheeee!' said Mum, revving up. 'This is the life! Don't you dare get bacon grease on the upholstery, Jess. And don't let Alfie slobber everywhere.'

'He's not the slightest bit slobbery,' I said, offended, sharing my breakfast with him.

'I don't think bacon's good for him,' said Mum. 'We've got to get him into a sensible eating routine. You should feed him that dog food Sean bought.'

'Alfie doesn't like it,' I said firmly. 'Mum, we can still see Ava and Alice every day, can't we?'

'Well, I'm not going to leave Marina in the lurch –

but I don't see how I can keep on working for her now we live so far away. And Sean will create if we have our tea with them every evening.'

'So what?' I said. 'You're not going to let him boss us around, are you? You're Tracy Beaker! *You're* the one who does the bossing.'

'Yes, and that's probably why all my relationships so far have been rubbish,' said Mum. 'I'm going to make this work, Jess. I know that Sean's a bit . . .'

'Irritating?' I said. 'Fierce? Full of himself?'

'Shut it, Miss Lippy. OK, he can be all those things, but he's a sweet guy really, and very, very generous,' said Mum. 'How many other blokes would let me drive their flash car? It's great, isn't it?'

'It's OK,' I said, though I had to admit it was fun driving along with everyone staring at us enviously.

'Men aren't exactly queuing up to go out with me,' Mum continued. 'I was starting to feel like I did at the Dumping Ground, desperate for someone to come along and want me.'

'But Cam came along,' I pointed out.

'Yes, she did, and I was dead lucky, though I didn't always acknowledge it at the time. And now Sean's come along and I'm dead lucky all over again.'

'*He's* lucky to have *you*,' I said.

'Come on, Jess. There's thousands of women out there who'd like to elbow me out the way. Sean's rich, he's good-looking, he's famous – what more could I want?'

'*We* don't want him, do we?' I whispered in Alfie's ear, and he licked my face in agreement.

But I must admit it was wonderful driving up to Marina's house in his Porsche SUV and seeing their faces. Marina was looking tense because we were so late and she was desperate to get to work – but when she saw us she burst out laughing, and made herself even later bombarding Mum with questions.

Ava was very impressed with the car too, but I don't think Alice even noticed we hadn't arrived in our old banger. She only had eyes for Alfie.

I felt my heart swell with pride as I let the girls pat him.

'That's the way, Alice. See, he loves having his back stroked. Gently, Ava! He doesn't really like you touching his head,' I said.

'How do you know if you've only just got him?' said Ava. 'He *does* like it! Look, he's licking me.'

'That's because he's so friendly – but don't pull his ears about like that!'

Alfie protested, growling softly.

'See!' I said triumphantly.

'Will he bite?' Ava started edging away.

'Only if I say so,' I said, though Alfie was such a good-natured dog I couldn't imagine him biting anyone, even a burglar.

Ava believed me, and treated Alfie and me with the greatest respect all the way to their school. Alice kept up a constant chorus: 'Oh, he's so lovely! I wish wish wish I had my own dog. You're so lucky, Jess!'

'Will Sean Godfrey let you drive his car every morning, Tracy?' Ava asked.

'If I want to,' said Mum.

'I wish we had a car like this instead of a boring old Volvo. You're so lucky!'

It was marvellous being thought so lucky. The car caused quite a commotion when we drew up outside their school. It made all the Range Rovers look as boring as golf buggies. Everyone stared, and then the girls shrieked and pointed and came running. Ava swaggered across the playground as if it was her own car. Alice had to be prised away from Alfie, and kept running back to give him one more pat.

'Well!' said Mum when we were on our way to my school at last. 'Looks like *we're* the posh-nobs now, kiddo!'

By the time we got to Duke Primary we were very late indeed. Everyone had gone inside and lessons had started.

'Oh bother, I wanted everyone to see us roll up in the car,' said Mum. 'Oh well, they can have a good peer when I come to collect you this afternoon. What's up, Jess?'

'Miss Oliver hates people being late,' I said anxiously.

'Do you want me to come in with you and explain?' Mum asked.

'No, that might make things worse,' I said quickly, giving Alfie a kiss. 'You be a good boy for Mum, OK? Mum, you will remember to take him outside sometimes so he doesn't have any accidents? And if he *does*, promise you won't get too cross with him?'

'I never got cross with you when you were a toddler and did wees on the carpet, now did I?'

'Mum! You are so embarrassing sometimes,' I said.

I ran across the playground. Mrs Fisher, the school secretary, shook her head at me, and wrote my name down in the Late Book. I ran down the corridor and then entered my classroom timidly.

Miss Oliver was showing everyone how to do sums using a twenty-four-hour clock. 'And what time do you call this, Jessica Beaker?' she said.

'Nine twenty,' I mumbled.

'Why are you so spectacularly late when you only live five minutes away?' she asked sternly.

I took a deep breath. 'Well, actually, we don't live on the Duke Estate any more, we live on a private estate miles away, so it takes us a long time to get here even though Mum was driving the Porsche,' I gabbled.

There was a little gasp from the class.

Miss Oliver shook her head at me. 'Really, Jess. I know you're good at telling stories in your literacy lessons, but I'd prefer you not to invent such a preposterous one as an excuse for getting up late. Do you think I was born yesterday?'

'But it's true, Miss Oliver,' I said. 'You ask my mum!'

'I'd sooner not, thank you. Now sit down – and at playtime you can stay in the classroom to catch up with the sums you've missed,' she said crisply.

I saw that it was pointless protesting any further and sat down meekly – but Tyrone was waggling his arm in the air.

'It *is* true, Miss! Jess wasn't telling fibs. She really *does* live with all the posh-nobs now. Her mum Tracy Beaker has hooked up with Sean Godfrey – you know, the footballer. He's going to give me lessons down his gym. And maybe he'll let me drive his Porsche too,' he said.

Miss Oliver blinked at both of us.

'I saw Jess and her mum go off in Sean Godfrey's car,' said Piotr.

'Jess's mum is Sean Godfrey's girlfriend now, but *my* mum says she doesn't get what he sees in her,' said Aleysha, who sits behind me.

There was a sudden hubbub in class as everyone joined in.

Miss Oliver clapped her hands. 'Quiet, everyone! For goodness' sake, you're like a load of turkeys going *gobble-gobble-gobble*. We're not here to gossip about the Beaker family. Let us get on with our maths,' she said sternly.

When the bell rang for playtime, I wasn't sure whether I still had to stay in or not. I sat at my desk, fiddling with my maths book.

Miss Oliver came over and briefly peered at my sums. 'It looks as if you've got them all right, so you don't have to stay in after all, Jess,' she said.

'Thank you, Miss Oliver,' I said, jumping up.

She looked as if she still wanted to say something, so I waited.

'I'm sorry I didn't believe you at first,' she said quietly. 'And I shouldn't have said it was preposterous.'

It's not often teachers say they're sorry. That's what I like about Miss Oliver. She's strict but she tries to be fair. She was actually looking quite upset.

'It *is* a bit preposterous though, isn't it?' I said comfortingly. '*I* wouldn't have believed it either, Miss Oliver.'

'How do you feel about it, Jess?' she asked.

'Well . . . it still feels a bit weird. But the best thing ever is that I've got a dog now. We got him from Battersea yesterday. He's called Alfie, and he's the most lovely dog ever, and I'm going to teach him tricks, and maybe we'll get really good and end up on *Britain's Got Talent*.'

'Maybe you will,' said Miss Oliver, though I could tell she didn't believe me again. 'I'm glad you've got a Battersea dog. I've often thought I'd love a rescue greyhound. Maybe when I retire. We can keep each other company.'

We got so engrossed in chatting about dogs that there were only two minutes of playtime left when I finally ran outside.

Tyrone was waiting for me. 'Poor you! She's so mean making you stay in doing boring old sums,' he said.

'No, she was OK actually. We had a good talk,' I said. 'Tyrone, thanks for sticking up for me.'

'Well, that's what mates do, isn't it? What's Sean Godfrey's house like, eh? Is it a great big mansion? What about his garden? Is it big enough for him to have his own football pitch?'

'It's quite a big house, and the garden's big too, but not like a football pitch! There's an indoor swimming pool though,' I said.

'Can I come round and see? This afternoon?' Tyrone asked eagerly.

'I'd better ask first, and we have to take my friends Ava and Alice to their house, but I'm sure Sean Godfrey will let you come some time – he likes you,' I said.

'Can I come round too?' asked Piotr, who was hovering.

'Me too. Oh, please, Jess,' said Aleysha. 'I'll be your best friend if you let me come.'

Everyone wanted to be my new best friend. It was heady stuff. I was in great demand at lunchtime too. I swaggered around the playground telling everyone all about Sean Godfrey's house. I started to make up stuff. His swimming pool increased in length and had its own

wave machine and a spiral slide. This
went down so well I considered adding
a freshwater pool with a pair of pet
dolphins, but thought it might be
stretching things too far.

Instead I installed an ornamental fountain in the
main hall, splashing up and down in time to a recording
of Handel's Water Music (Miss Oliver was teaching the
school orchestra to play it on their recorders). I told

them all about Rosalie, our
housekeeper, but gave her
lots of company, so in the end
Sean Godfrey had enough
servants to keep Downton
Abbey spick and span.

We had a couple of specialist chefs –
one to make amazing showstopper cakes
and the other to concoct extraordinary
ice creams in every flavour you could
think of. I invented a rainbow knicker-
bocker glory – a scoop each of strawberry,
tangerine, lemon, gooseberry,
blueberry and blackcurrant ice cream in
a tall glass, with whipped cream and
cherries on top. Everyone stood around
licking their lips enviously.

I was stuck when the boys started

asking me about Sean Godfrey's sporting stuff, wondering which cups and trophies and football kit he had on display, as I'd only had a quick peep into his study, so I told them it was all in a special underground museum that was kept locked.

'But he'll let *me* see it,' said Tyrone confidently. 'He says I've got talent. And he's going to let me drive his Porsche SUV.'

'Don't be daft, you're not old enough. It's against the law,' said Piotr, not as loyal as usual.

'Yes, I know *that*, but it's in his private grounds – it's not against the law then. He's going to let me drive his *other* cars too, even his white vintage Rolls-Royce,' said Tyrone.

I looked at him with new respect. He was almost as good at making things up as me. A huge crowd gathered round, listening, even the Year Sixes. They weren't so easily impressed by my stories, even with Tyrone backing me up.

'You're such a liar, Jess Beaker,' said Clare Turner. Everyone knew Clare because she had amazing hair and wore make-up to school and looked at least fourteen. 'As if Sean Godfrey would ever go out with your mum! I happen to know he's got an actress girlfriend, Sandy Forthright. She's on the telly.'

'That's complete rubbish,' I said. 'My mum's Sean Godfrey's girlfriend. We *live* with him. Sean Godfrey and my mum are going to get married and I'm going to be their bridesmaid.'

'Dream on, loser. Sean Godfrey might be having a little fling with your mum, but Sandy Forthright is his proper girlfriend. There was a whole article about them in *Glossip*. Me and my mum read it. There were all these photos of his house and his swimming pool, and he hasn't got a spiral slide or a fountain in his hall. You're making it all up,' she said triumphantly.

I felt my cheeks flushing red. Was she right about Sandy Forthright? I'd seen her in the magazine I found in the back of Sean Godfrey's car. Was she really still his girlfriend?

I took a deep breath. 'Sandy Forthright's yesterday's news,' I said, as scornfully as I could. 'My mum's *engaged* to Sean Godfrey. And he's only just installed the slide and the fountain. For us – my mum and me. So stick that up your jumper, Clare Turner.'

I marched off, with most of the kids following behind. Mum would have been proud of me. I'd managed to convince them.

At home time I had my moment of triumph when Mum was waiting for me in the red Porsche, parked right outside the school gates. (Which was strictly forbidden, but how else could Mum show the car off to everyone?) All the children ran to get a closer look, and the parents at the gate were agog.

'Hop in, kiddo,' said Mum.

'Mum, can Tyrone hop in too, just for a minute, so he can say hello to Alfie?'

Mum sighed. 'If he's very, very quick.'

I beckoned to Tyrone, and he got in the back with me, and Alfie licked us both and leaped from my lap to his and back again.

'He really likes me!' Tyrone said.

'Of course he does.'

'I wonder if he ever met Staffie.'

'Maybe,' I said.

'I *wish* I'd been able to keep him,' said Tyrone, sniffing.

'Look, like I said before – you can share Alfie, if you like. I mean, he's *mine*, and he lives with me at Sean Godfrey's, but you can take him for walks with me sometimes, and maybe we can go to the park with him, and you can help teach him tricks.'

'You're a star, Jess!' Tyrone breathed. He gave Alfie a big hug – and then he gave me a quick hug too and shot out of the car.

'My, my!' said Mum as we drove off. 'Is Tyrone your boy-friend now?'

'Don't tease! I'm too young to have a boyfriend!'

I felt that Mum was too *old* to have a boyfriend, but I didn't dare say so. The copy of *Glossip* was still tucked in the magazine slot. I edged it out, hoping Mum couldn't see me in the driving mirror, and leafed through it as quietly as I could. I couldn't find a big feature about Sean Godfrey and Sandy Forthright – just the little photo at the back, in the party-going section. He didn't have his arm round her – they were just chatting casually.

I didn't know what to do. Should I tell Mum? All the time we were at Ava and Alice's I kept trying to make up my mind. Marina came home extra early so that she could have a good gossip with Mum.

'I can't believe it, Tracy! I googled Sean Godfrey, obviously. I didn't realize he was so famous!'

'Yeah, he is, isn't he?' said Mum, enjoying it.

'Well, I hope I get to meet him some time,' said Marina. 'So I suppose this means I'll have to find someone else to look after the girls.'

'Oh no!' said Alice, horrified.

'We don't want anyone else, we want Tracy!' said Ava.

'And Jess,' said Alice. 'Me and Jess are best friends, aren't we?'

'Yes!' I said.

'And Alfie's half mine too!'

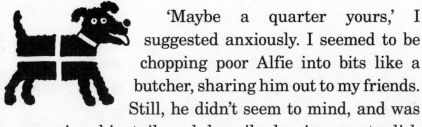

'Maybe a quarter yours,' I suggested anxiously. I seemed to be chopping poor Alfie into bits like a butcher, sharing him out to my friends. Still, he didn't seem to mind, and was wagging his tail and happily leaping up to lick everyone's knees.

'Down, Alfie!' said Mum. 'And calm down, girls. I'm sorry, Marina, I hate letting you down, and this has been the best job ever, but it's just not practical any more. I'll keep coming till you find someone else for the girls, but then I'm going to have to bow out.'

'*Mum!*' I said, anguished.

'But I hope it won't stop us all being friends,' she added quickly.

'Of course it won't!' said Marina. 'You and Jess must still come round.'

'And Alfie,' said Alice.

'And you must come to us,' said Mum. 'One Saturday?'

'*This* Saturday?' said Ava and Alice.

'Please say yes, Mum – and could Tyrone possibly come too?' I begged. I knew this wasn't such a good idea because I was pretty sure that Tyrone and Ava and Alice wouldn't get on, but I knew just how much he wanted to come.

'Well, I'll check with Sean first, but I'm pretty

sure he'll say yes,' Mum said. 'Maybe not *this* Saturday, but certainly some time very soon.'

'That would be great, Tracy. I can't wait to meet him – and I bet he's got a fabulous house!' said Marina. 'Oh my God, you're an actual WAG!'

'What's a WAG?' I asked when we were back in the car. We didn't have to wait to give Ava and Alice their tea because Marina was there to do it.

'It's a silly name for footballers' wives and girlfriends,' said Mum. 'Only Sean isn't a footballer any more, so they can't call me that.'

'Did he have wives and girlfriends when he was playing football?' I asked, fingering the glossy pages of *Glossip*.

'Not wives! But I think he had heaps of girlfriends.'

'Did he ever go out with an actress?'

'Is this Miss Oliver's homework for tonight – write a potted biography of your mum's boyfriend?'

'I just want to know.' I took a deep breath. 'Clare Turner at school says Sean Godfrey's got a girlfriend called Sandy Forthright.'

'Oh yeah, he told me he used to go out with her. She used to be in *Emmerdale* – or was it *EastEnders*? One of those,' said Mum. 'But they split up ages ago.'

'Are you sure? Because there's a photo of them at some party in this *Glossip* magazine,' I said, waving it about.

Alfie thought it was a game and seized hold of it.

'Alfie, don't *eat* it! Stop it – you're ripping it!' I told him.

'Hey, hey, stop mucking about while I'm driving,' said Mum. 'I don't care if Alfie rips it – it's a rubbish magazine. They publish all sorts of gossip and scandal. If there's a photo of Sean and Sandy Forthright, then it was obviously taken months and months ago.'

She sounded so certain and dismissive that I relaxed. When we got back to the house, Mum had a cup of tea and a chocolate cookie with Rosalie, and I had a glass of milk and a chocolate cookie too, and Alfie had a bowl of water and a special dog biscuit because you must never give a dog chocolate. I'm going to be the most responsible dog owner ever.

Mum suggested we have a little swim before Sean Godfrey came back from the gym.

'That would be great!' I said.

She looked at Rosalie, who was chopping up vegetables for supper. 'You come and have a dip too, Rosalie,' she said.

'I can't!' she said.

'Don't worry, Rosalie, we'll teach you,' I said. 'Breaststroke's easy-peasy.'

She laughed. 'I can swim, darling! At home in the

Philippines I lived on an island and all us kids went swimming every day.'

'Do you get homesick?' I asked.

'Yes, I do. I miss my family. And the sunshine. But I can make much more money here.'

'I suppose we've got much more money now, haven't we, Mum?' I said. 'But I'm homesick already. I liked Marlborough Tower – where we used to live,' I explained to Rosalie.

'Marlborough Tower didn't have a swimming pool,' said Mum. 'Come on, let's get changed into our cossies. You too, Rosalie!'

'But I have to do the supper. I'm here to work for Mr Sean, not go swimming,' she protested.

'Well, I'm going to be Mrs Sean sometime soon, so you'll be working for me too, and *I* say come in the pool with Jess and me!' said Mum. 'I'll lend you a costume.'

Rosalie grinned. 'I'm glad you're going to be Mrs Sean,' she said. 'OK, I will!'

She was a brilliant swimmer, much better than us. We had a race, and she won easily. She could swim a whole length underwater too, which looked awesome. I took a deep breath and had a go, but as soon as I disappeared beneath the surface Alfie started barking, and then jumped into the pool to rescue me, making a terrific splash.

Alfie couldn't swim very well, not even doggy paddle, so *I* had to rescue *him*, and then sit on the side of the pool giving him a reassuring cuddle. I was very touched that he was so brave – even though all the towels on the loungers were now soaked.

After they'd got dressed, Mum helped Rosalie with the rest of the vegetables, and supper was nearly ready by the time Sean Godfrey arrived. He was pleased to see Mum and me home already, and thrilled when Mum told him she'd given her notice to Marina.

Mum served the supper so that Rosalie could go home early. Then we all watched another film down in the cinema room, while Alfie fell asleep on my lap. I took him for a last wee in the garden, and then we went to bed.

Mum and Sean Godfrey had seemed all lovey-dovey, but a bit later I woke up because I could hear them arguing. They were in their bedroom at the other end of the landing, so I couldn't make out exactly what they were saying, even though Mum was shouting. I *thought* she said the name Sandy Forthright.

I patted my bed, and Alfie jumped up eagerly and lay beside me. I held him close. What were we going to do? If Sean Godfrey was still seeing this Sandy Forthright, then Mum would go mental. She'd walk out.

This was what I'd wanted. I still didn't like Sean Godfrey. I didn't even like his house, though Rosalie was lovely and the swimming pool was great fun. I'd still much much much prefer to go home to Marlborough Tower. But I had Alfie now. I already felt as if I'd had him all my life. I loved him so much, only second to Mum. If she had this big row with Sean Godfrey and we had to go back to Marlborough Tower, then what would happen to Alfie?

11

I DIDN'T SLEEP very well. I kept a firm grip on Alfie all night long. When Mum shook me awake I peered at her anxiously, but she didn't look distraught. Her eyes weren't red. She sounded surprisingly cheerful.

'Wake up, sleepyhead. And you, Alfie Beaker! I'm going to make sure you both get a proper breakfast this morning. I'll take Alfie for a wee while you jump in the bath, Jess, OK?' she said.

'Are *you* OK, Mum?' I asked, kicking off my duvet.

'Of course! Why shouldn't I be?'

When I went downstairs Rosalie was already in the kitchen making waffles!

'This is the most heavenly breakfast ever!' I said,

decorating mine with raspberries and blueberries and maple syrup and cream.

'You tuck in, Little Miss Skinny,' said Rosalie. 'There's another here if you can eat it.'

'Isn't that for Sean Godfrey?' I asked.

'Jess!' said Mum, her mouth full. 'How many times do I have to tell you? Just call him Sean! And he's not having breakfast now, he's gone for a long run.'

I imagined him running and running and running, further and further and further away. Perhaps Sandy Forthright was puffing along beside him. They were running so far they could never, ever get back. Mum and Alfie and I could stay in the house and drive the red Porsche and swim in the pool and have Rosalie for a friend!

I wasn't daft. I knew perfectly well that it could never happen, but it was lovely daydreaming while I munched my waffle.

Sean Godfrey had left the car keys on the kitchen table.

'Are you driving the Porsche again, Mum?' I asked.

'Yep! And Sean says there's no point my going and collecting our car as it's such an old banger. He's going to get me a flash new car of my own,' she said.

'Seriously?' Mum was as good as me at making things up.

She grinned. 'Seriously!'

When we got in the car, Mum reached into the back for the crumpled copy of *Glossip*, screwed it into a tight ball, then tossed it into the recycling bin by the gate. 'In the trash. Where it belongs,' she said.

I took a deep breath. 'Mum, *is* Sean God— Sean still seeing Sandy Forthright?'

'No! Of course not. He's engaged to *me*. What sort of ring shall I choose, Jess? A diamond? Or how about a ruby? Or a sapphire or an emerald?'

'Whatever. So how come they were photographed together at this party?' I said.

'Oh, that was just unlucky,' said Mum, in a deliberate couldn't-care-less voice. 'They happened to be at the same party promoting something or other, and when Sandy saw the cameras flashing she went marching up to him. She used to go out with him and probably wants him back, but she can't have him. He's mine now.'

'Were you having a row about it last night?' I asked.

'We don't have rows,' Mum said firmly.

'*Mum!* I heard you!'

'Well, it wasn't a real row – we were just getting things straight. I'm not standing for any nonsense. Sean might have played around a bit in the past, but now he's ready to settle down with you and me.'

'And Alfie,' I said. 'He'll never have to go back to Battersea, will he? Promise, Mum.'

'I promise. He's ours now, no matter what,' she said.

'Even if he's sick in your new car and spoils the upholstery?'

'Even if – though *you'll* be the one mopping it up.'

'Even if he accidentally swallows your diamond or ruby or sapphire or emerald engagement ring?'

'Even if – though you'll have to check when it comes out his other end and pick it out of his poo.'

'I'll make very sure he doesn't swallow it then,' I said. We were nearly at Ava and Alice's house. 'Mum, *can* Alice come to tea on Saturday?'

'Soon. But not *this* Saturday,' she said.

'Then can Tyrone come instead?'

'He can come too, but not *this* Saturday either. Someone else is coming. The most important person of all. Cam,' said Mum.

'Cam would like Alice. She might even like Tyrone,' I said.

'Yes, I know. But I want this first visit to be

special, just for Cam. One, because she's my mum and I love her. And two, if she hadn't fostered me, I'd never have met Sean all those years ago when we were kids.'

I understood. 'And three, if Cam hadn't taken me to Battersea I wouldn't have Alfie,' I said.

'Mm,' said Mum.

So we phoned Cam and invited her, and she asked her friends Jane and Liz to keep an eye on the girls on Saturday. Sean Godfrey seemed happy about Cam's special visit. Since the Sandy Forthright row he'd seemed very eager to please Mum.

He bought her a car too. You'll never, ever guess the car Mum picked! She could have chosen any make at all. Sean Godfrey wanted her to have another red Porsche to be the twin of his, but she'd have had to wait several months for all the special fittings – and Mum's never been any good at waiting for anything.

'You know what I'd really like instead?' she said. 'I know it sounds a bit mad – but I'd like a pink Cadillac convertible.'

'*What?*' said Sean Godfrey.

'When I was a little kid it was my dream car. I pretended my mum was a Hollywood actress, and that one day she'd come and fetch me in her pink Cadillac,' said Mum. 'Oh, imagine if I had my very own pink Cadillac now! Oh, Sean, please could I have one?'

'But that's crazy, babe. Why would you want some

ancient vintage car that'll probably be forever conking out when you could have something new and powerful and stylish?' he said, baffled.

'Oh, Sean, please please please! It was my childhood dream!' Mum begged.

'I just don't get you, Trace. You'd think you would want to forget about your crazy childhood,' he said – but he took her to a vintage-car dealer, and when Mum came to collect me from school she was driving a shiny bright pink open-top Cadillac, just like the ones in old American movies!

'Hop in, babycakes!' she said in a dreadful American accent, grinning all over her face. 'Isn't it wonderful?'

'It's very *pink*,' I said.

'Yep,' said Mum happily. 'It's just the way I imagined.'

Maybe it made her start imagining too much. She got in touch with Granny Carly.

On Saturday morning Mum took us all by surprise.

Sean Godfrey was showing off, doing press-ups on the kitchen floor, and Rosalie was making me another pancake, and Mum was having a second cup of coffee and checking her phone when she suddenly said, 'Looks like we're having *two* visitors for tea today?'

I stared at her. 'But it's a special day for Cam. You *said*.'

'I know. But the other day I phoned Granny Carly, just to tell her our new address, and she could hardly believe it. She'd seen all my posts on Instagram, but she didn't realize they were pics of *my* house. We had a long chat, and she said she'd love to come to tea one Saturday. I thought she meant any old Saturday, so I said yes. But she's just emailed again to say she'll be here at three o'clock,' Mum said sheepishly.

'Can't you say no?' I asked.

'Sixty-eight . . . Don't you like your granny, Jess?' Sean asked, mid-press.

'Not much,' I said truthfully. 'And you don't like her either, Mum – you know you don't.'

'Yes, but . . . she *is* my mum.'

'You've said a million times that Cam has always been more of a mum to you than Granny Carly. And you can't put Cam off now, not when she's made arrangements. That would be so mean!'

'Seventy-two . . . Why on earth can't both these mums come?' said Sean Godfrey, starting to pant a little.

'Because they don't really get on,' said Mum. 'Sean, would you stop bobbing up and down like that, it's getting on my nerves.'

'Seventy-four . . . Just let me get to a hundred,' he said.

'Granny Carly probably won't turn up anyway,' I said. 'She hardly ever came when she was supposed to visit you at the Dumping Ground.'

Mum had told me this again and again, but now she looked stricken. 'Of course she'll turn up,' she said fiercely.

'Seventy-nine . . .Tell you what, I'll ask *my* mum round to tea as well. Then they can all have a go at each other,' said Sean Godfrey. He started laughing at the idea, and collapsed on the floor. 'Now look what you girls have made me do!'

'Out the way, Mr Sean,' said Rosalie, stepping over him to serve me my second pancake.

'Have you got a mum, Rosalie?' I asked.

'Of course I have, back in the Philippines. I have many dear relatives. It's why I work so hard for this big fierce man – they all need a share of my wages,' she said.

'Ah, you love me really, Rosalie,' said Sean Godfrey, sitting up. 'Are you going to make your special chocolate cake for Tracy's mum?'

'I'll make the cake,' said Mum. 'And OK, we'll have both of them together, Cam and Carly, even though they've got nothing in common. Apart from me.'

'But Rosalie's famous for her chocolate cake,' said Sean Godfrey.

Big mistake. Mum was more determined than ever to make one herself. Mum's good at making cakes.

She's always made me very special birthday cakes. Last year's one was like our living room – all red, with a purple marzipan sofa and red marzipan cushions. She fashioned two little marzipan people with amazing hair made 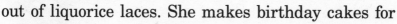 out of liquorice laces. She makes birthday cakes for

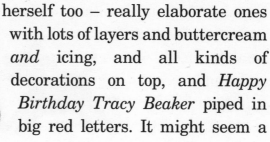 herself too – really elaborate ones with lots of layers and buttercream *and* icing, and all kinds of decorations on top, and *Happy Birthday Tracy Beaker* piped in big red letters. It might seem a

bit weird – it's mostly only Mum and me and Cam eating it, and it goes stale long before we get to the end – but Mum has this thing about birthday cakes because she had to share hers with Weedy Peter. She always wished for her mum to come and see her – and now her mum *was* coming, and *I* wished she wasn't.

Mum took over the kitchen, and wouldn't even let me help her bake, though usually I share the stirring, and she always lets me scrape round the bowl with a spoon. I could see it was annoying for Rosalie, being exiled from her own kitchen, but she just shrugged and went to polish the parquet floors. She let me wrap dusters round my feet so that I could put an extra shine on them while I skated backwards and forwards. Alfie tried to copy me, and Rosalie and I ended up shrieking with laughter.

Mum came to see what was going on. I thought she'd be thrilled to see the floors looking so splendid for our visitors, but instead she got cross.

'You've turned the whole house into a death trap! My mum wears really high heels – she'll skid and break her neck!' she said, huffing and puffing.

Alfie got a bit

frightened and did a little wee. He couldn't help himself, but that made Mum even crosser.

'For goodness' sake, Jess, take that dog out and walk him round the grounds. It's time you started training him properly. You shouldn't keep laughing at him when he does something silly, it will only encourage him. I thought you promised to be a really responsible dog owner! You're useless!'

I took Alfie outside and we moped around. I felt Mum was being extra mean. So did Alfie.

Sean Godfrey came out onto the patio and started skipping with a rope. I sniggered at the idea of a grown man skipping, but he was irritatingly brilliant at it. He turned the rope so quickly I couldn't even see it, and yet he didn't trip once, his feet nimbly dancing up and down.

He saw me watching. 'Do you want a go, Jess?' he asked.

'No thanks,' I said.

We heard a shout from the kitchen, and then a very rude swear word.

'Uh-oh!' said Sean Godfrey. 'Your mum's in a right strop this morning!'

He just wanted to cosy up to me and moan about

Mum, but I wasn't going to join in, even though I was still smarting at being called useless.

'She's just a bit het up because my Granny Carly's coming. She can't help it,' I said. 'I'd better go in and see what's up with her now,' I said. 'Come on, Alfie.'

Rosalie was at the kitchen door, peeping in. 'Doesn't look good,' she whispered to me.

I gave her Alfie's lead and slipped into the kitchen. Mum's cake was on the floor in pieces. Mum was sitting beside it, her head on her knees. She looked like she might be crying – though of course she never cries.

I sat down beside her and put my arm round her. She cuddled up close, and then blew her nose on a kitchen towel.

'Did the cake slip off the baking tray?' I asked.

'It did. How did you know?' Mum said, sniffing and wiping.

'I heard you say a very, very rude word.'

'Well, if I ever hear *you* saying that, I'll be furious.'

I started gathering up the cake pieces. It was lucky that Rosalie kept the floor so clean.

'Can't we stick the bits together with buttercream?' I asked.

'Nope. It's completely smashed,' said Mum. 'It's only good for trifle now.'

'I *love* trifle,' I said.

'And I love *you*, Jess,' said Mum, giving me a hug. 'Sorry I was ratty. I always seem to get in a state when my mum comes.'

'I know.'

'Oh, Jess, what am I going to do? I don't think I can bear starting all over again on another blooming cake.'

'Why don't you make a trifle then – a big strawberry one with lots of cream – and ask Rosalie if she'll make her chocolate cake?' I said.

'Good plan,' said Mum.

She said sorry to Rosalie too.

'That's OK, Miss Tracy,' said Rosalie. 'When my mum came over here on a visit, I got in such a state I forgot about my cake altogether and it was burned black by the time I remembered. And I only have the one mum, and you've got two!'

Mum and Rosalie worked companionably together in the kitchen, while I took Alfie back into the garden and started teaching him to walk to heel. Alfie's not very good at anatomy. He kept forgetting where my heel was. I had loads of treats in my pocket to reward him with if he ever got it right, but he didn't. So eventually we played Hunt the Treat instead. He could do that trick easy-peasy.

We just had a sandwich for lunch as we were going to have an elaborate tea. Mum and Rosalie and I had tuna and sweetcorn on brown bread. Sean Godfrey had a steak sandwich in a baguette.

Then the waiting began. Mum and I couldn't settle to anything. Mum changed her outfit twice. She put on her best red frock and heels, but then thought she didn't look relaxed and casual enough, so she changed into jeans and a T-shirt – and then decided she looked too scruffy. She ended up in her velvet jeans and a prettier top and *then* started fussing about her hair and make-up.

Cam came first, dead on time – dear lovely familiar Cam, in *her* jeans and T-shirt with no make-up at all – and I hugged her, and Mum stopped acting weird and hugged her too. Sean Godfrey kissed her on the cheek and she kissed him back.

'I remember you from when I was a kid, Cam,' he said. 'You haven't changed a bit.'

'I remember you too, Sean. You've changed a lot!'

'I've done all right for myself, haven't I?' He nodded his head at his house, his garden, his pool, his car. 'I hope you approve.'

'Just so long as you look after my Tracy and Jess,' said Cam. 'Here, I've brought some house-warming presents.'

She fished them out of her big bag: a little bunch of daffodils from her garden, a tin of home-made blueberry muffins, a doggy chew for Alfie – and a parcel.

'Don't get too excited,' she said when she gave it to Mum. 'I found it at a boot fair. It's something you wanted when you were little, Tracy.'

Mum tore open the package. She's hopeless with presents – she has to get them undone straight away, *rip rip.* She found herself holding an old-fashioned alarm clock – a kid's one, with Mickey Mouse telling the time with his big gloved hands. I was a bit baffled, but Mum's face screwed up and her eyes went watery.

'Oh, Cam,' she said, and gave her a big hug.

'It's . . . very nice,' said Sean Godfrey, trying to be polite.

'It's exactly like Justine Littlewood's!' said Mum. 'I was so dead envious of her Mickey Mouse alarm clock. Oh, Cam, you're brilliant!'

We took Cam for a tour of the house. She was trying to be polite, but you could tell it wasn't really her style at all. It was all far too big and bare, the few furnishings shiny-new, the sofas so slippery you practically slid off them. It still didn't have any of our stuff in it. Sean Godfrey couldn't see the point of our Toby jugs and our china dogs and our plaster ducks and the rest of our precious things. He didn't even want us to put up our picture of the mother and daughter like us. He said it was too old-fashioned. I've got it in my wardrobe now, and sometimes I squeeze inside and talk to them.

Cam's house is crammed with ornaments and pictures, and she has bright cushions and throws covering up her ancient saggy furniture, and bookshelves round all the walls. Sean Godfrey doesn't

have a single book, just a few magazines. He only has one painting – it's on his living-room wall, along with his framed photos and cuttings, a life-size portrait of himself in his football strip. It's very un-nerving being in a room with two of him.

Cam wasn't that keen on the garden either, murmuring that his neat ornamental flower beds and great green lawns made it look like a park. Sean Godfrey took this as a compliment. She liked the pool though, and said she wished she'd brought her swimming costume.

'Borrow mine,' said Mum, which made Cam laugh because she's quite plumpish now and Mum's a skinny-minny like me.

Cam *loved* Rosalie. She'd been very iffy when Mum told her that Sean Godfrey had his own housekeeper. 'So he can boss her around and tell her what to do?' she'd said.

She found it funny that actually Rosalie often bossed Sean Godfrey around, and told *him* what to do. Rosalie was very complimentary about Cam's muffins. When Cam saw Rosalie's chocolate cake on a plate in the kitchen, she was very complimentary back.

'Are we having tea now?' Cam asked hopefully. 'I skipped lunch deliberately, and I'm starving!'

'Soon,' said Mum. 'We might be having another guest.'

'Jess's new pal Tyrone?' she asked.

'No,' said Mum. 'We will ask him sometime though. If Jess insists.'

'Is it Marina and her two girls? Jess is friends with the younger one, isn't she?'

'They're definitely invited – maybe next weekend.'

'So who is it? I know! Justine Littlewood!' said Cam.

She was Mum's deadliest enemy at the children's home.

'Oh, very funny,' said Mum. 'Hey, I hope she's seen my photos on Instagram! At the Dumping Ground we all used to talk about what we'd do and where we'd live when we were grown up. I wanted to be a writer and Justine wanted to be a model and Louise wanted to be an actress, and we all wanted to live in a great big house with a swimming pool and drive a flash car – and here I am, living the life! I bet Justine's pea-green with envy.'

'So who's the mystery guest?' Cam asked.

'Well. It's Carly,' Mum mumbled. 'I didn't actually invite her to come, not today, but she just assumed that she could barge in whenever. But you know what she's like. I'm pretty sure she won't turn up. And who cares anyway? *You're* here, Cam, and you're the only mum I want.'

Cam reached out and gave Mum's hand a little squeeze.

'So shall I put the kettle on?' Rosalie asked.

'Yes, let's have tea right this minute,' said Mum.

Sean Godfrey wanted us to have tea in the sitting room, with Rosalie serving us from a trolley!

Mum rolled her eyes at this idea. 'Let's have tea in the kitchen, for goodness' sake,' she said.

So we all sat down at the kitchen table, Rosalie too, and I was just trying to decide whether to have a muffin or strawberry trifle or chocolate cake first when the doorbell rang.

'Mum!' said Mum, and she leaped up and ran into the hall.

MY TUMMY WENT so tight that I didn't want muffin or trifle or cake any more. I sat very still. Alfie crept under the table and licked my knees, which was very comforting.

We heard talking and laughing at the front door, and then Mum and Granny Carly came into the kitchen. Carly was holding an enormous bunch of roses and lilies in cellophane, a carrier bag and a big cardboard box. I hardly recognized her. She didn't look the slightest bit grannyish. She'd had her hair straightened and it was blonder than ever. She'd had her eyebrows done too. She looked as if she'd just come back from holiday, with a low-cut white dress to set off her tan, and high heels that made her much taller than Mum.

'Look, Mum's bought us flowers,' said Mum.

'You can't beat roses and lilies,' said Carly, glancing at the daffodils on the table.

Sean Godfrey stood up and took the flowers, blinking in astonishment as Carly flashed her teeth at him.

'So you're the lucky man, eh? Wow, Tracy, he's quite a hunk, isn't he? You've done all right for yourself there, darling!' she said. 'Give your future mother-in-law a kiss then, Sean.'

'I'm glad we're going to be family,' he said, and kissed her. She kissed him back and left a red smudge on either cheek.

Cam stayed sitting where she was and gave Carly a little wave.

'Oh, it's you,' said Carly.

Mum introduced her to Rosalie, but Carly barely nodded at her. She was honing in on me.

'My little Jess!' she cried. 'Come and give me a hug, sweetheart!'

I had to suffer the hug, and the kissing treatment too. Alfie wasn't at all sure about this, and bounded up to us, growling. They were only little *what's-going-on?*

growls, but Carly reacted as
if she was being attacked by
a werewolf.

'Get back!' she cried,
swatting at him with both
hands.

Alfie thought she was playing
and jumped up excitedly, which
made her shriek.

'Get him off me, Sean!' she cried.

'Alfie's not Sean Godfrey's dog,
he's mine, Granny! He's just being friendly,' I insisted.

'He's getting his muddy paws all over my white
dress!' she said. 'Down! Down, I say!'

I'd been trying to teach Alfie to lie down half the
morning without success, but now, awed by Carly's
commanding tone, he lay down flat on his tummy, his
tongue lolling.

'Oh, Alfie, you clever boy,' I said.

Carly brushed at non-existent marks on her dress.
'Whose mad idea was it to get Jess a dog?' she
demanded, frowning at Sean Godfrey.

'Don't look at me,' he said. 'I wasn't too keen on the
idea myself, but we thought it would be nice for
the kid.'

'It was my idea,' said Cam calmly.

'Oh, well,' said Carly, sniffing. 'So why didn't you

get her something cute? A little chihuahua or a French bulldog, not this scruffy mutt.'

'He's beautiful, Granny! He's a special rescue dog from Battersea,' I said indignantly.

'Oh, well, I might have known,' she said. 'Anyway, Jess, put the dog in the corner and see what I've got for you.' She handed me the carrier bag with a flourish.

My heart sank. It was clothes.

'Go on, have a proper look.'

It was a bright pink top with the word *Princess* spelled out in sequins. And there was a skirt that stuck out like a ballet dress, very short and flouncy. I looked at them in utter dismay. I am *so* not a pink, sparkly, flouncy sort of girl.

'Aren't they darling? Go and try them on at once, Jess – you'll look such a picture! Why on earth you wear those dreary old T-shirts and jeans all the time I'll never know,' said Carly, glancing at Cam pointedly.

'She'll try them on later, Mum. We're in the middle of tea right now,' said Mum. 'Sit yourself down. Try a slice of Rosalie's chocolate cake – it's fantastic.'

'Oh, I was forgetting! *I've* brought you cake. I ordered it specially,' said Carly. She opened up the cardboard box. Inside was a huge iced cake that said *Congratulations Tracy and Sean* in silver lettering,

 with little red hearts and pink cherubs all the way round the sides.

'Oh, Mum, that's fantastic!' said my mum.

'Wow, Carly – amazing cake!' said Sean Godfrey.

'Beautiful,' said Rosalie politely, but she didn't sound as if she meant it.

'Lovely,' said Cam, and it was clear that she meant the exact opposite.

I don't think Mum even noticed because she was cutting the first slice of cake excitedly.

'You put your hand over mine so you're cutting it as well, Sean,' she said. 'It's your cake too.' She gave Cam and me a little nod to show us that she was happy to share nowadays. Then she closed her eyes. I think she was wishing, even though all her wishes had already come true.

I had a slice of the cake. It was actually a bit of a disappointment. The icing was so hard you had to bite into it like toast, and there wasn't even any butter-cream inside, just jam dividing the sponge layers. I knew Carly would make a fuss if I left any, so I ate and ate and ate, and at last it was all gone apart from a few crumbs. Alfie wanted to help me demolish it, but I thought iced cake wouldn't be good for his teeth. I wasn't sure if it was good for my teeth either.

The trifle and the chocolate cake and the muffins were still untouched. I hoped Sean Godfrey would help himself – he seemed capable of eating at least half a cow – but he shook his head.

'Sorry, I daren't,' he said, patting his washboard stomach. 'You can't own a gym and prance about with a flabby belly. I put on weight so easily too. Remember what a tub I used to be, Trace?'

She laughed fondly. I already had a pain in my tummy, and that look she was giving him made it worse.

'You've got room for some trifle though, haven't you, Sean?' she said. 'I made it specially.'

'Just a spoonful then, darling.' He opened his mouth as if he wanted her to feed him like a baby. He looked totally *disgusting*.

Mum gave him a smallish portion in a bowl, but he stuck to his guns and literally had just one spoonful.

She looked disappointed. 'Isn't it any good?' she asked.

Sean Godfrey said it was utterly delicious – so why couldn't he have eaten a bit more to please her?

'Would you like some, Mum?' she asked Carly.

'I'm totally full up with cake, sweetheart,' she said.

'I'll have some please, Tracy,' said Cam.

'Me too, Mum!' I said.

'I'd love some, Miss Tracy,' said Rosalie.

Mum's trifle really *was* delicious. It wasn't too difficult to get it down. And then Rosalie offered her chocolate cake to everyone, and she looked so hopeful that I simply had to say yes. She gave me a big slice.

It was the best chocolate cake I'd ever tasted, very rich and creamy. It was light too, but it seemed to get heavier and heavier as it went down into my stomach. I couldn't even give it to Alfie because I knew chocolate could make dogs very ill.

I was starting to feel very ill indeed, but there was still a plate of Cam's muffins on the table – and she'd made my favourite blueberry ones. I knew Cam wouldn't make a fuss if I didn't have one. She'd understand. But I felt so sorry for her – she always had to be the grown-up person – that I helped myself to one.

'Why don't you save it for later, Jess?' she said quietly. 'You must be totally full up now.'

'I've got to have one of my favourite muffins,' I said determinedly.

I took a big bite, and then another. They were great muffins, soft and sweet and truly scrumptious. They really *were* my favourites but I was finding it hard to swallow. I thought of the muffin going down my gullet to sit on top of the chocolate cake on top of the trifle on top of the big iced cake – until my entire stomach was a massive stew of sugar. I suddenly heaved.

'Quick!' said Cam.

I charged out of the kitchen to the loo at the end of the passage. I didn't quite get there in time.

Mum came and mopped me up. After I'd been sick I still felt shivery and tearful, so she took me up to the bedroom for a lie-down. But it wasn't *my* bedroom at home with all my things, and the bed wasn't *my* little bed – and Mum didn't even seem like *my* mum any more, though she gave me a cuddle and told me not to worry.

But Alfie was still my dog, and he came and lay next to me, as still as still, just very gently licking my arm. He knew I felt dreadful and did his best to comfort me. I couldn't go to sleep, and when I tried reading, the words waved up and down and made me feel giddy, so I just lay there, Woofer by my cheek and Alfie by my side.

After a while Mum

looked in to make sure I wasn't going to be
sick again. 'I wish I could stay with you,
sweetheart, but it's getting a bit sticky
downstairs. Mum keeps on getting at
Cam, and Sean keeps yawning because
he's so bored. I need to keep an eye on them!' she said,
giving me a kiss.

Then Rosalie came, and I said I was very sorry,
because she'd had to clear up the mess in the hall.

'Don't you worry, sweetheart,' she said. 'I'm used
to it. My Jane has a delicate stomach. I've often had
to clean up after her.'

'Who's Jane?' I asked.

'My little girl.'

'I didn't know you had a daughter!'

'I have a son too – my Nick. I don't like to mention
them because I might cry. I miss them so. I'm so proud
of my children. I wish you could meet them, Jess.'

'Why can't I?' I asked.

'They're back home in the Philippines. My mother
looks after them. That's what we have to do.

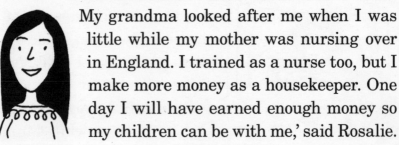

My grandma looked after me when I was
little while my mother was nursing over
in England. I trained as a nurse too, but I
make more money as a housekeeper. One
day I will have earned enough money so
my children can be with me,' said Rosalie.

'Oh goodness, it must be awful for you. *And* them,' I said.

'But I get to go home for three weeks every summer. Mr Sean pays for my plane ticket. He is such a kind man,' she said.

I didn't think it was *that* kind – Sean Godfrey obviously had lots and lots of money.

He put his head round my bedroom door too. 'You all right now, kid?' he asked.

I nodded.

'Have you got that dog on the bed?' he asked.

I nodded again, because it was obvious.

'Well, I suppose we'll let you just this once, as you've been poorly.'

What did he mean 'we'? It wasn't up to him what I did or didn't do. He wasn't my dad. Thank goodness.

He was laughing now and shaking his head. 'There I was, thinking you were a picky eater, and yet you scoffed so much at tea you made yourself sick!' he said, as if it was a great joke.

I didn't say anything. He ran out of things to say too, and headed back downstairs.

'We still don't like him one bit, do we, Alfie?' I whispered, and he agreed.

We didn't have any more visitors until Carly came up to say goodbye.

'There, you never even got to try on your lovely new outfit,' she said.

'Sorry, Granny,' I mumbled.

'Oh well. Wear it *next* time I come, so I can see if it fits. It'll match that ridiculous car of your mother's. Why on earth did she choose such an old crock? She'll be a laughing stock. Dear oh dear, I don't like to see that animal on the bed with you! It'll get the covers all dirty – and you'll probably get fleas!' she said.

'Alfie hasn't got a single flea!' I said indignantly.

'Don't use that tone with me, Jess!' She looked around the room. 'My, your mummy's done well for herself at last, hasn't she? Sean Godfrey! Even *I've* heard of him, and I don't know anything about football. He's quite a catch!' she said. 'Don't pull that silly face, Jess!'

I didn't even know I was.

'You're very lucky. There's not a lot of guys happy to saddle themselves with someone else's kids, but he seems to be making a real fuss of you,' said Carly. 'You mind you do your best to behave yourself. And stop being such a greedy-guts! You're too old to make yourself sick like that!'

I didn't feel very lucky because of Sean Godfrey. I felt very lucky that I wasn't a little girl from the

Philippines, because then Carly might be looking after me instead of Mum.

Cam came up a little later. She lay down on the bed beside me and gave me a gentle hug. Alfie licked us both.

'You poor thing,' she whispered. 'I feel awful. You didn't have to eat my boring old muffin on top of everything else. No wonder you were sick.'

'I love your muffins,' I said. 'I was just trying to make everyone happy.'

'I know,' said Cam. 'It's difficult, isn't it!'

'Carly thinks Mum's done very well for herself,' I said. 'Do you think so, Cam?'

She paused. 'Most people would think she has,' she said eventually.

'Yes, but do *you* think so?' I persisted.

'She's got the house of her dreams – and the car – and her own swimming pool. *You* must love the swimming pool, Jess. And  I think it's ridiculous, a perfectly fit man having a housekeeper, but Rosalie seems lovely.'

'And do you think Sean Godfrey's lovely? Carly thinks he's a hunk.'

Cam snorted. 'I think he's probably more Carly's

type than your mum's,' she said. 'But Tracy seems very fond of him. Much fonder than she's been of anyone else.'

'*I'm* not fond of him,' I whispered.

'I know that, chickie. I can't say I am either. I wasn't that keen on him when he was a kid, though it wasn't really his fault. He'd had to grow up tough. I admire the way he's worked hard and done so well. And I suppose he's kind in his own way. Very protective. He's been good to lots of kids with the football training. And Carly's right, he *is* a hunk. It's just . . .' She pulled a face.

It was my turn to say, 'I know.'

Cam laughed, and I did too. Alfie made snuffly sounds as if he was joining in.

'I'm so happy I've got Alfie,' I said.

'I'm glad. I was dreadfully irresponsible, taking you to choose a dog before you were even living here – but I'm so pleased I did, even so,' said Cam.

'Do you think Mum's really going to *marry* Sean Godfrey?' I asked.

'It looks like it.'

'And I'll have to be the bridesmaid?'

'Your mum will be really upset if you're not,' said Cam.

'I'll be really upset if I *am*,' I replied. 'But I suppose I'll have to. So long as the dress isn't pink.'

'Just hope and pray your mum doesn't go shopping for it with Carly,' said Cam, and we both laughed again.

'Imagine what *she'll* wear to the wedding!' I said.

'Oh goodness yes. The mother-of-the-bride outfit!'

'What will you wear for your foster-mother-of-the-bride outfit?'

'Don't! Oh help – what will I wear? Even *I* can see that a T-shirt and jeans won't hack it.'

'Will you wear a dress and a fancy hat?'

'No! I wore posh trousers and a silk shirt when Liz and Jane had their ceremony. They'll do. But definitely no hat.'

'Not even one of those little fiddly ones you wear on the side of your head?'

'A fascinator? Oh goodness, imagine me in one of those!' said Cam.

We were still laughing when Mum came into the room.

'You feeling better, Jess?' she asked. 'What are you two giggling about, eh?'

'We're just wondering what Cam will look like when she wears a fascinator to your wedding,' I said.

'Oh Lord, I can't wait!' said Mum, laughing too.

'What are you going to wear, Tracy?' Cam asked.

'Definitely not a white meringue. And nothing too low cut or tight. I don't know. I haven't even got a ring yet,' said Mum. She did a twirl. 'Imagine, Tracy Beaker the blushing bride!'

13

MUM WENT OUT to choose the ring with Sean Godfrey the following Saturday morning. She wanted me to come and help her decide, but I thought that would be a bit weird. So the two of them went off together, while Alfie and I stayed home with Rosalie. We helped her with the housework. She gave me a clean j-cloth to do the dusting. She gave one to Alfie too, but he mistook it for a ball and kept wanting me to throw it for him.

'You and that dog!' she said.

'You don't mind him, do you?' I asked.

'Of course not! He's my furry pal, aren't you, Alfie?' and she made a fuss of him.

'I know Sean Godfrey doesn't really want him here.'

'Oh, Mr Sean is very particular,' said Rosalie. 'He likes everything kept immaculate. No mess, no smells.'

'Alfie's had a few little accidents, but he doesn't mean to,' I said anxiously.

'I know, dear. Don't worry.'

'And *I* was sick on the floor! I'll be ever so careful *this* teatime. My friend Alice is coming to tea, with her sister, Ava, and her mum, Marina. If they bring a big cake I'll just have one bite, I promise,' I said.

'And one bite of *my* cake too. I'm making a coffee-and-walnut,' said Rosalie. 'And Miss Tracy told me she'd make fairy cakes for the children.'

'Will you call her *Mrs* Tracy when she marries Sean Godfrey?'

'I expect she'll want to be called Mrs Sean.'

'Mm, maybe not. It does seem odd, you calling people Mr and Miss and doing all their work for them. Like we're in olden times,' I said. 'Still, maybe you'll find a rich man like Mum found Sean Godfrey.'

Rosalie laughed. 'I think my husband might have something to say about that!'

'You have a husband!' I said, surprised.

'Yes, of course I have. I told you, I have two children, Nick and Jane. Here!' She took her mobile out of her pocket and showed me their photos. They were smiling and waving.

'They look lovely,' I said.

'Wave back!' said Rosalie. 'I do every time I take a peep! And this is my husband, Eric.'

'You don't *need* a husband to have children,' I said. 'My mum's not married to my dad.'

'Yes, I know, but we're stricter in the Philippines. We're all good Catholics.' Rosalie was smiling and waving at Eric too, so I copied, just to be polite.

'Is he in the Philippines too?'

'No, he's here, but we don't see each other much. He's a nurse – he often works night shifts and gets up at midday, when I'm here at Mr Sean's.'

'You have a hard life, Rosalie,' I said seriously, but it made her burst out laughing again.

'You're a funny child, Jess,' she said.

'Don't you have a wedding ring?' I asked, looking at her bare left hand.

'Yes, *and* an engagement ring, but I don't wear them when I'm working. I'll show you.' Rosalie unbuttoned the top of her shirt and showed me the two rings on a thin chain around her neck, a plain gold band and one set with a little diamond.

'I wonder if my mum will choose a diamond too,' I said.

229

'Mr Sean will want it to be big and flashy,' said Rosalie.

She was right. Mum came home with a big diamond solitaire sparkling on her finger. Her eyes were sparkling too.

'Oh, Jess, isn't it gorgeous?' she said. 'And it fits me beautifully so I can wear it straight away. You'll never, ever guess what it cost!'

'A hundred pounds?'

'Much, much, much more!' Mum whispered the amount in my ear and I gasped. Sean Godfrey was seriously rich!

He swaggered about proudly, and kept asking Mum if she really liked the ring and was absolutely sure it was the one she wanted.

'Well, it's not quite as nice as the one I got out of last year's Christmas cracker, but I suppose it will do,' said Mum.

He stared at her, stricken.

'I'm *joking*, silly. It's the most beautiful ring in all the world!'

'And you're the most beautiful girl,' he said.

Alfie and I rolled our eyes. Rosalie seemed genuinely pleased and gave them both a hug. She made me feel a bit guilty. When Sean Godfrey drove off to check on things in the gym, I gave Mum a hug too.

'Congratulations,' I mumbled.

'Thanks, Jess! I couldn't be happier, really. Imagine, I'm actually *engaged*. I'm the only girl Sean's ever proposed to. He's had heaps of girlfriends in the past, but I can't object to that, can I, because I've had my fair share of  boyfriends. And all right, I think he was pretty serious about Sandy Forthright, but he's sworn to me that it's all over now. I watched her on i-player the other evening, and she might have a pretty face but she's the most terrible actress. Her voice! She's sounds like a Munchkin, all high and squeaky.'

Mum had to take her ring off to make the fairy cakes for Ava and Alice and me. She put it carefully on the kitchen windowsill. It was still there when Sean came back from the gym.

'Hey, what's this? You haven't taken it off already! I thought you promised to wear it for ever and ever.' He looked genuinely upset.

'And I *will* wear it for ever and ever, but I can't keep it on when I'm making cakes, stupid – it would get all gungy with cake mix,' said Mum, carefully piping a red 'J' on the white iced fairy cake. She'd already piped two 'A's on two others.

'Don't call me stupid,' said Sean Godfrey, with an edge to his voice.

Mum flushed. 'Don't be like that, Sean. I didn't mean it. I was just joking again.'

'Yeah, well, I get a bit fed up of your jokes at times,' he said, and he marched out of the kitchen.

Mum called out to him, but he went on down the hall, out of the front door, back to his car. We heard him driving off.

'Oh, help,' said Mum.

'Don't worry, Miss Tracy. Mr Sean flares up like that sometimes, but it doesn't last long,' said Rosalie comfortingly, opening the oven to check on her coffee-and-walnut cake.

'I shouldn't have called him stupid. I know he hates it, because his mum always said he was stupid. And how could I have said it today of all days, when he's just forked out a fortune on my amazing ring.' Mum was near tears.

My tummy was squeezed tight. I wondered if this was going to be another awkward tea session, even though Mum's fairy cakes had turned out perfectly, and Rosalie's coffee-and-walnut cake smelled amazing.

Sean Godfrey stayed out for hours. He still wasn't back when Marina drove up with Ava and Alice. They'd brought us a little potted palm for a house-warming present.

'Thank you so much! It will look great in the conservatory,' said Mum.

'You have a conservatory!' said Marina. 'I've always fancied one, but we haven't really got room at the back of our house.'

'Shall I show you round?' Mum offered.

She gave them a grand tour of the house and the grounds and the conservatory and the swimming-pool extension.

Even Ava was impressed. 'You are *so* lucky,' she said to me. 'Your house is a million miles better than ours. I wish *my* dad was a footballer with his own gym. Mine's just a boring old lawyer.'

'Sean Godfrey's not my dad,' I said quickly.

'Yes, but he will be soon,' said Alice. 'Can we come to your mum's wedding? Can I be a bridesmaid as I'm your best friend?'

'Can I be a bridesmaid too?' Ava begged. 'What colour will the bridesmaids' dresses be?'

'I thought slime-green would look cool,' said Mum, which was *my* joke.

Ava took her seriously. 'Well, it's your choice of course, but don't you think blue would be prettier? Blue suits me, doesn't it, Mum? It's because I have blue eyes.'

'Tracy's kidding you, silly,' said Marina. She caught hold of Mum's hand. 'Oh my Lord! Look at your *ring*! It's huge – and so sparkly! So where *is* this fantastic guy, eh? Aren't we going to get to meet him?'

I looked at Mum.

'Well, he's had to go to his gym. I'm not quite sure when he'll be back,' she said.

But just as she was saying this we heard the car coming up the driveway, and within seconds Sean Godfrey was in the sitting room. I held my breath, wondering if he would have a go at Mum in front of Marina and Ava and Alice – but he was smiling.

'Hi there! You must be Marina. Pleased to meet you. And you two gorgeous girls have to be Ava and Alice,' he said, giving them a kiss on the cheek. All three went pink and giggled.

Then he kissed Mum, and held her close. 'How's my lovely fiancée?' he said.

Then he looked in my direction. I rushed back to the kitchen, mumbling that I had to help Rosalie because I wanted to avoid him giving *me* a kiss. Rosalie was setting out the cakes on pretty plates, a red rose one for the fairy cakes and a jade-green leaf one for the coffee-and-walnut.

'They haven't brought a cake too, have they?' she whispered.

234

'No, a potted palm,' I said.

'And I see Mr Sean's back. Is he still in a mood?'

'He's all smiley and chatty.'

'There! I said he'd cheer up soon,' said Rosalie. She put her arm round me. 'So you can relax now and enjoy having your friends to tea.'

I *did* enjoy it, but I was starting to wish that Sean Godfrey had stayed away. He was being Mr Charm, and Marina and Ava and Alice were practically fluttering their eyelashes at him. I had hoped that *Alice* at least would find him creepy – then we could have had a secret session dissing him upstairs in my bedroom – but she hung on his every word. Ava told him that the girls in her year at school all did football, and asked if he could give her any tips. Marina asked him about the nightclubs and posh restaurants he'd been to, and marvelled at all the celebrities he'd met. He showed off horribly, but had enough sense not to mention Sandy Forthright.

'My, Tracy, you're going to be in all the magazines soon!' said Marina. 'In fact, you could do a rags-to-riches story for us! How do you feel about that? I'll find the right person to ghost it for you.'

'Why can't I write it myself?' Mum asked.

'It's a matter of getting the tone right. And knowing how to pace things. And of course we'll want Sean's side of the story too. I love the childhood-sweethearts angle. And Sean's deprived background and his fight to get recognized as a footballer.'

'I'll think about it.' Mum looked indignant, and no wonder. Why would she need anyone to *help* her write? And why did it have to be Sean Godfrey's story too?

'I'm sorry Tracy can't work for you lovely ladies any more,' said Sean Godfrey.

'Oh, we understand,' said Marina.

'I'll carry on looking after the girls until you find someone else,' Mum said quickly.

'It's OK, Tracy. I've already found someone. Julie, one of the girls at work, employed this lovely French girl, Marie-Thérèse, who's over here studying. Julie's moving to the country now, so Marie-Thérèse is free to come to us,' said Marina. 'She's starting on Monday.'

I gasped.

'Oh goodness, so soon?' said Mum.

'Well, I knew how awkward it was for you, having to trail over to the girls' school and the house when you live miles away now.'

'Marie-Thérèse came to meet us this morning and she's lovely,' said Ava. 'She did my hair for me. Doesn't it look cool?

And Mummy's ever so pleased because she's going to teach us French and we'll have the right accent.'

'Marie-Thérèse sang us a song about French elephants, and it was ever so funny. She showed us how to wave our arms around like elephant trunks,' said Alice, demonstrating. 'And guess what! She's got a dog too – a weeny little fluffy one called Pommy. She showed me a photo on her phone. She's so cute! She can do tricks too. She can shake hands with her tiny paw. Marie-Thérèse says she'll bring her next week, and then she can shake hands with me! I just love Pommy already.'

I stared at her, betrayed. She loved *Alfie*! And what about me? Didn't she want to be my best friend any more?

'She's not called Pommy, she's *Pomme*. That's French for apple. See, we've learned heaps already,' said Ava.

Marina must have seen Mum looking crestfallen. 'But of course it won't be the same as having you, Tracy. You've been marvellous. You've been like a real friend,' she said. 'I've paid your wages into your bank account, with a special bonus as a thank-you.'

'You didn't need to do that,' Mum said stiffly.

'Well, I suppose not, seeing as you're much better off than me now! But you've earned it, darling. And of course you must come round to tea soon. And supper. All of you,' Marina said, glancing at Sean Godfrey.

'I'll get Marie-Thérèse to do your hair, Jess, but I don't think it will work because it's so curly-wurly,' said Ava.

'And Alfie can meet Pomme, and then they can be best friends too,' said Alice, seeing how much she'd upset me.

Mum said thank you to Marina. I said thank you to Ava and Alice. Alfie gave a little bark to say thank you too. But none of us sounded enthusiastic.

'At least that visit went well,' said Sean Godfrey when they'd gone.

I suppose it did, though I felt unsettled and fidgety afterwards. I think Mum did as well. Still, she was relieved that Sean Godfrey wasn't cross about being called stupid any more. Though he *is*, he *is*, he *is*.

They got all lovey-dovey again, so I took Alfie for a long walk, round and round the grounds.

'Sean Godfrey *is* stupid,' I said. I muttered *stupid* again and again as I walked – left, right, left, right, *stu-pid, stu-pid* – with Alfie trotting along in time. Then I told him that I wasn't sure I liked Marina any more, and I thought Ava a terrible show-off. Alice was still OK, and I was

238

very glad when she insisted that I was still her best friend, but I wished she wasn't so keen on this little apple dog. Alfie agreed that she sounded silly. I tried teaching him to shake my hand with his paw, but he looked scornful and said he wasn't a cutesie-pie little dog who did party tricks, thanks very much.

It started to rain a bit, so Alfie and I trailed inside. We didn't feel like joining Mum and Sean Godfrey, who were down in the cinema room, so we went to find Rosalie instead. She'd already made every-where immaculate, and was sitting down reading *Glossip* and eating a slice of her coffee-and-walnut cake.

'Sean Godfrey isn't in that magazine, is he?' I asked anxiously. 'Or that actress Sandy Forthright?'

'No, sweetheart. Don't worry – he doesn't see her any more,' said Rosalie.

'You promise?'

'Darling, I know everything about Mr Sean.'

I sat down beside Rosalie and helped myself to a slice of cake too.

'Not too big a slice!' she warned me. 'We don't want you being sick again.'

'I'm fine now,' I said, munching. I fed Alfie a couple of doggy treats from my pocket so he didn't feel left out. 'Rosalie, tell me honestly – what do you *really* think of Sean Godfrey?'

'He's very good to me.'

'I know, you keep saying that, and maybe he is, I don't know – but do you *like* him?'

Rosalie shrugged her shoulders. 'He's my employer, not my boyfriend. I don't have to think whether I like him or not.'

'Do you think he's stupid?'

Rosalie looked anxious and listened hard, her head on one side.

'It's all right, he can't hear – he's down in the cinema room,' I said.

Rosalie relaxed. 'Of course he's stupid!' she said, chuckling. 'But try to show him some respect, Jess. He's doing his best to be good to you too.'

I suppose he was, in his own way. The next day he took Mum and me to Chessington World of Adventures. It was Mum's idea – Cam took her there when she was a little girl. I got quite excited – but then they said I couldn't take Alfie because they don't allow dogs.

'I won't go then,' I said. 'Alfie and me will stay with Rosalie.'

'Rosalie doesn't work on Sundays,' said Mum.

'Then we'll stay by ourselves.'

'Don't be silly. As if I'd let you stay by yourself!'

'As if I'd let Alfie stay by *him*self!' I retaliated. 'I

can't leave him all day long. He won't understand – he'll think I'm never, ever coming back!' I started to get tearful at the very thought of it.

'It's OK, Jess,' said Sean Godfrey. 'I've asked Trev, one of the lads at the gym, to come round. He'll take Alfie for a walk and give him something to eat.'

'Alfie won't want some stranger taking him for a walk. He'll want *me*,' I said.

But when Trev came to the house, Alfie seemed to like him a lot. Trev bent down and held out his arms, and Alfie went rushing up and licked him joyfully, as if he'd been dying to meet him all his life.

'Let's go for a little walk right away, mate,' said Trev.

Alfie bounced about, barking, clearly thinking this an excellent idea. He went off with Trev without even looking back.

'There!' said Sean Godfrey. 'Come on then, girls.'

Mum squeezed my hand. 'Alfie will be fine, Jess, I promise.'

So I had to leave him. Chessington World of Adventures *was* exciting, and we went on lots of the rides. We didn't even have to queue. This guy in charge was a big football fan, and when he recognized Sean Godfrey he came round with us as if we were royalty. No one seemed to mind. Lots of people wanted selfies with Sean Godfrey. Some wanted photos of

Mum and me with him too. Mum didn't seem to mind a bit. She hung on Sean's arm and grinned. I expect I was scowling.

Sean Godfrey tried to make me cosy up to him too. He kept fussing over me and telling me daft jokes and buying me ice cream. He insisted on taking me into the souvenir shop and buying me a great big toy wolf – 'Because you like dogs, Jess.'

 The shop assistant said I was a very lucky girl. I had to lug it round with me all day, until I was boiling hot and my arms ached. I didn't like the wolf. It had a sly face, and a lolling pink tongue that turned my stomach. It looked like it wanted to eat me up.

I just couldn't make myself act grateful to Sean Godfrey. When we had quite a crowd around us, he seized hold of the wolf and pretended to make him bite a little kid, who squealed in fearful delight. Then he did the wolf act on me, but I clamped my lips shut to stop myself squealing too. I expect I looked surly, because I heard an old lady say, 'Sean's daughter looks like a spoiled little madam.'

I kept fretting about Alfie, wondering if Trev had

cleared off the moment we left – but
when, at long, long last, we got home,
he was still there, watching
football, with Alfie curled
up by his side, looking very
happy and relaxed.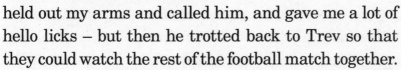

He did come running
when I dropped the wolf and
held out my arms and called him, and gave me a lot of
hello licks – but then he trotted back to Trev so that
they could watch the rest of the football match together.

Sean Godfrey burst out laughing. 'There now,
Jess! No need to make a fuss about leaving the dog
any more. He's clearly got a friend for life in young
Trev here.'

'I'll look after Alfie any time, boss. He's a cracker,'
said Trev.

I was pleased that Alfie had made a new friend –
but a little bit hurt that he hadn't missed me at all.

'Someone's nose has been put out of joint!' said
Sean Godfrey, pulling a face at me.

I couldn't wait to go to bed to get away from him.
I had to take the wolf up with me too. Woofer didn't
like him one bit and cowered under my pillow. Alfie
seemed keener, and played tug with him. Alfie's teeth
were stronger and sharper, and the wolf's face got a
bit chewed.

Mum was shocked when she came into my room. 'For pity's sake, Jess, don't let Alfie savage that wolf like that. It cost Sean a fortune!' she said.

'I didn't ask for it. I don't even like it,' I said sulkily.

'Why are you being such a brat?' Mum asked. 'You're usually such a sweet kid. Sean's trying so hard to get on with you, but he can't seem to do anything right.'

'He doesn't like me one bit. He was just making a fuss of me to show off to everyone. He can't fool me, even if he can fool you,' I said.

Mum sighed. She twisted her flash ring round and round her finger. 'Couldn't you try just a little bit, Jess? Please?'

When Mum left, I cried into my pillow. I burned all over, hating Sean Godfrey. I knew I seemed spoiled, but *he* was the one who had spoiled everything. I ended up thumping my pillow hard. If Miss Oliver had seen me she'd have said I had Anger Issues too.

Or perhaps she wouldn't. Miss Oliver seemed surprisingly understanding nowadays when people at school treated me so differently. All the girls in my class wanted to be my best friend, especially Aleysha Roberts, and the boys wanted to be my mate. In fact, Piotr asked me if I'd be his girlfriend!

'Shove off out of it,' said Tyrone. 'Jess is *my* girlfriend.'

'No I'm not! I'm not *any-one's* girlfriend!' I insisted.

'Yes, but if you *were* you'd choose me, wouldn't you, because we've been mates for ages, since before 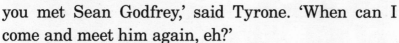 you met Sean Godfrey,' said Tyrone. 'When can I come and meet him again, eh?'

'This Saturday,' I said. I knew that Tyrone's mum wouldn't bring him so I said we'd come and pick him up.

'You promise?' he said.

'Promise.'

'You're not having me on?'

'No, I *said*. I promise promise promise.'

'Wow! Hey, you lot, listen!' Tyrone went rushing all round the playground stopping every child to tell them he was going to Sean Godfrey's house.

They all started begging for an invitation too. It was all a bit much. I didn't know what to do. I didn't want to hurt anyone's feelings, but I couldn't have the entire school to tea.

Luckily Miss Oliver was on playground duty. She came over and tapped me on the shoulder. 'Can I have a word, Jess?'

The children melted away.

'Let's go to the Peace Garden. It looks as if you could do with a bit of peace!' said Miss Oliver.

I nodded. I hadn't been to the Peace Garden for ages. Miss Oliver and I sat on the little wooden bench and listened to the trickle of the fountain.

'It's lovely here, isn't it?' she said.

'I used to hide here,' I said shyly. 'I was scared of Tyrone then.'

'But then you made his nose bleed!' said Miss Oliver.

'It was an accident!'

'I know. I bet you never thought you'd end up friends.'

'I never thought a lot of things,' I said, sighing.

Miss Oliver looked at me carefully. 'How's life now then?'

'I've got a dog!'

'Yes, I've seen him when your mum picks you up from school in her amazing car. He looks like a lovely dog,' said Miss Oliver.

'He's called Alfie. He's the best dog in all the world. I'm ever so lucky,' I told her.

'I know you are. Dogs are wonderful companions.'

'Alfie's my best friend,' I said. 'Actually, everyone wants to be my best friend these days.'

'Everyone thinks you're ever so lucky because you

and your mum are living with a famous footballer. Even the staff are in awe!'

I snorted. 'They don't know what he's like,' I mumbled.

Miss Oliver was suddenly on red alert. 'Isn't he kind to you then?' she asked.

It was tremendously tempting to tell a story and say he was really mean and horrible to me. Then Miss Oliver would be sorry for me and it would be bliss. But she might report it and talk to Mum, and Sean Godfrey might get into trouble, and I *certainly* would.

'He's OK,' I said reluctantly. 'He's kind to me, I suppose. Yesterday he took me to Chessington World of Adventures and bought me a wolf.'

'From the zoo?' Miss Oliver asked, startled.

'Not a real wolf, a toy one. He's forever buying things. He bought Mum that pink Cadillac, just like she wanted, and a big flashy diamond ring.'

'Goodness. And your mum's happy?'

'Yes. Ever so.'

'But you're not?'

'Well. I am sometimes. But I don't like living in that huge house. I like Rosalie – she does the housework and the cooking – and I like the swimming pool, but it's not like *home*,' I said. 'I wish we could go back to our old flat, but Mum's going to tell the council we don't need it any more.'

'I can see that your whole life's been turned upside down, Jess. Even at school,' said Miss Oliver.

'And that's another thing,' I wailed. 'Mum wants me to go to a posh school now, like my friends Ava and Alice.'

'Oh dear. Yes, I suppose she would.'

'But I don't want to.'

'Well, I shall miss you if you change schools. You've been a joy to teach, Jess,' said Miss Oliver.

I was taken aback. Miss Oliver often told me off, and she didn't always give me top marks for my work, and Mum had *shouted* at her. I hadn't always been sure that I liked Miss Oliver, but now I was totally certain.

'I shall miss you too, Miss Oliver. Ever so,' I said fervently.

WE PICKED TYRONE up after lunch on Saturday. It was so strange being back on the Duke Estate. We'd only been living at Sean Godfrey's for a few weeks but it already seemed a lifetime.

'Dear goodness, it's a right old dump here, isn't it?' said Mum, looking around at the abandoned mattress and the burned-out car and the mess of paper and boxes strewn everywhere from the chippy and the Chinese and the KFC.

I could see that Sean Godfrey agreed, but I was peering up at the windows of the fourteenth floor of Marlborough Tower. There was our living-room window with the velvet curtains and the mother-and-baby china dogs walking along the windowsill. Well,

I couldn't actually *see* the ornaments, but I knew they were there.

'Mum, can we go and get the china dogs?' I asked urgently. 'And the balloon ladies and the birds and the teddy bear's picnic and—?'

'Oh, Jess,' said Mum, but I could see that she was missing them dreadfully too. 'Well, we could take the china dogs – and you could have the teddy bear's picnic in your bedroom. Hang on, let's see if I've got the door key in my bag.'

'No!' said Sean Godfrey, snapping her bag shut again. The cheek of it! 'For God's sake, I thought we agreed. You don't need any of that old junk. We'll get you some brand-new ornaments if you're desperate to clutter up the house.'

'Yes, but I think Jess really wants some of our *old* stuff,' said Mum.

'Don't let's start an argument now. We're late as it is. We'd better find this kid Tyrone. Where does he live?'

I thought I'd somehow have to summon up the courage to go into Devonshire Tower and walk along the balcony and knock on the door and face the scary mum, but Tyrone was waiting for us downstairs.

'*There* you are!' he yelled, charging up to the car. 'I've been waiting *ages*. I was sure you weren't coming. I didn't think you'd *really* come for me, Sean Godfrey!'

'Call me Sean. Hop in, son,' he said.

Tyrone got in the back of the car with me. 'Sean Godfrey just called me *son!*' he mouthed.

It didn't seem like such a big deal to me. I'd have absolutely hated it if Sean Godfrey had called me *daughter*. But Tyrone was over the moon. When we got to the house he was over the stars as well. We took him on a tour, and he walked on tiptoe across the pale rugs, though I saw he'd tried to scrub his ancient trainers clean. He went into the glass extension and circled the swimming pool in awe, but shook his head determinedly when Sean Godfrey invited him to try it out.

'Ain't got no swimming gear,' he said.

'I'll fix you up. I've got some shorts that will do you.'

Tyrone still shook his head.

'Can't you swim, Tyrone?' I asked.

'Course I can. Right to the end and back, easy-peasy. Don't even mind going out of my depth,' he boasted, but he'd gone red.

'I bet you're more of a football guy,' said Sean Godfrey. 'Fancy a kick-around? We'll let the ladies have a little splash in the pool while us guys have fun.'

I decided I *might* like him a little bit after all. He was great with Tyrone, running around and teaching him all kinds of tricks. Tyrone's face got redder and redder. He looked as if he was going to explode with happiness.

'He's a funny kid, but he's quite sweet really,' said Mum. 'Though if he ever knocks you over again I'll still wring his neck.'

'I hope Tyrone's mum won't wring *my* neck if I accidentally knock *him* over again,' I said.

'I bet she's nowhere near as fierce as Sean's mum. It's a huge relief that he's not really in touch with her any more – though he bought her a fantastic house when he first started earning big-time. She'll have to be invited to the wedding! She'll probably throw stones instead of confetti,' said Mum.

I edged up to her. 'Are you really and truly getting married?' I asked.

'What do you think this is all about?' Mum held out her left hand and wiggled her fingers so the diamond sparkled in the sunlight.

'Couldn't you just stay engaged?' I asked. 'If you don't marry, then we won't be stuck with Sean Godfrey for ever and ever, until death do you part.'

'I *want* to be stuck with him, Jess,' said Mum.

'But you often have rows,' I said.

'I often have rows with everyone. Even you.'

'Yes, but we only started having rows when you hooked up with Sean Godfrey,' I pointed out.

'Yes, because you're so blooming difficult with him!' said Mum. 'Like you keep calling him Sean Godfrey all the time.'

'Tyrone does too,' I said.

'Yes, but he says it in a hero-worshipping sort of way. *You* certainly don't.' Mum gently tweaked my nose. 'Look, you'll *like* the wedding, I promise. I fancy having the ceremony in a castle. What do you think? Then you could have a fairy-princess kind of brides-maid's dress.'

'But not pink,' I said. 'Ava wants the bridesmaids' dresses to be blue.'

'Yes, but Ava isn't going to be a bridesmaid, so it's what *you* want that counts,' said Mum.

'Well, you know what *I* want. No wedding at all,' I said.

'We're going round in circles here. You're the most obstinate kid I've ever known!'

'And I wonder who I take after?'

'Shut it, Miss Lippy,' said Mum, putting her hand over my mouth.

'No, *you* shut it,' I said, putting my hand over *her* mouth.

We started wrestling. We were

only mucking about, playing at fighting, but Alfie took it seriously. He rushed over, barking anxiously, trying to protect me. Sean Godfrey came running over too.

'What are you two *doing*?' he said, trying to pull us apart.

'Stop it – we're just having a bit of fun,' said Mum.

'What . . . ? *Women!*' he said, turning to Tyrone.

'Yeah, *women!*' Tyrone echoed happily. 'Can we go on playing footie for a bit, Sean Godfrey?'

'Course we can,' he said – but Alfie had got so worked up he wanted to play too, and kept trying to catch the ball, though his mouth was much too small.

So we had tea instead. Rosalie had baked a lemon meringue pie this time, and Mum made her fairy cakes again.

'*Fairy* cakes?' Tyrone said doubtfully – but when he saw that Mum had iced each one with a football he thought they were seriously cool, and ate two,

 *and* two big slices of Rosalie's pie. Then he asked for yet another slice, plus a third fairy cake.

'Don't you make yourself sick now, Tyrone,' said Rosalie warily.

'I could scoff a whole pie and it still wouldn't make me sick,' said Tyrone. He looked at me. 'Do you get pies and cakes like this for tea every day? I'd give anything in the whole world to swap places with you, even though you're a girl.'

That made me feel ashamed. I was forever bleating about my life, but everyone else thought I was the luckiest girl alive. Except Cam.

When we had taken Tyrone home and were driving back, I asked Mum if Cam could come to tea next.

'I miss her so. We haven't seen her for ages. And she hasn't really had a proper visit. She had to share it with Granny Carly,' I said.

Mum blew through her bottom lip, remembering. 'Yes, I'd love her to come,' she said. 'Though I get the feeling she doesn't really like it at Sean's.'

'She's probably jealous,' said Sean Godfrey smugly. 'Didn't you say she lives in this scruffy little house with a lot of mad teenage girls?'

'Cam's not the type of woman to be jealous. And *I* was a mad teenage girl once,' said Mum, giving him a dig in the ribs.

'You're still mad now, babe,' he said. 'Tell you what. Why don't you and me go off castle hunting for the wedding next weekend, while Jess goes to stay with Cam?'

'Oh yes!' I said.

'Don't you want to come and check out the castles too, Jess?' Mum asked, disappointed. 'We might even find one with a tower, and then you can look out the window and pretend you're Rapunzel.'

'Mum! I'm not a little kid any more,' I said. '*Please* let me stay at Cam's.'

So I went, and had a lovely weekend. It was like I'd slipped back into my old life, though it was much better because I had Alfie. I even had my own room – one of the girls was on a home visit so her bed was going spare.

All the girls thought that Alfie was marvellous, even big scary Jax. She squatted down and held out her arms, and Alfie rushed up to her and licked her face. I'd never seen her smile before.

We had a cosy morning, all hanging out together in the kitchen, baking.

'Though maybe we'll steer clear of muffins this time,' said Cam.

We chose cornflake crispy cakes. They were ever so simple to make, and yet they tasted really good. I loved Rosalie's cakes, but they sometimes filled me up too much and made my teeth feel funny.

Then all the girls lounged about posting stuff on their phones while Cam caught up with her writing. I'd brought my felt-tip pens, so she found me some A4 paper for me to draw on. I drew a castle, but there was no wedding. I was looking out of the tower window, and my hair had suddenly grown long and straight and golden, and I was letting it hang down like Rapunzel. Alfie was beside me, and his ears had grown too, almost as long as my hair.

Then I drew four more windows in the main part of the castle. Mum had the biggest. Cam had a big window too. Alice had a little window under the turrets. Even Tyrone had a window. I didn't include

Sean Godfrey, but I drew an arrow pointing underneath the castle and wrote: To the dungeon

I reckoned he was down there. Not locked up in chains like a prisoner – he hadn't actually done anything really wicked. There might even be a gym so that he could keep fit. He just wasn't allowed to come out. There was probably a big strong door with an enormous lock. I drew a big key on a gold chain hanging around my neck.

After lunch – sausage and mash – Cam and I took Alfie for a long walk. She had brought him some packets of expensive dog food, but he politely made it clear he'd

much rather share my sausages. After he'd come back from his walk he ate the dog food too, and then he curled up on some cushions and went fast asleep, even though the girls were playing loud music and dancing around the living room.

I did a little dance too, but I felt a bit silly. Jax laughed at me, but not nastily. I expect I'd have laughed at me too. Cam and I went off to her room for a bit of peace, and she read me *The Hundred and One Dalmatians*, which was absolute bliss as she did all the voices.

'Shall we go back to Battersea and find

a Mrs Alfie, and then my two Alfies could have lots of puppies like Pongo and Missis?' I suggested hopefully.

'In your dreams,' said Cam. 'One Alfie is quite enough. And anyway, all the dogs at Battersea have a little operation to make sure they can't have any puppies.'

'Poor Alfie. Well, maybe one day we could adopt just one little puppy from Battersea and Alfie could be a foster dog,' I said.

'That's a better idea,' said Cam. 'Though you'd better get Alfie a hundred per cent house-trained and obedient first.'

'Did you have to be house-trained and obedient before they let you foster?' I giggled.

'Very funny,' said Cam dryly.

'Do you really like fostering?' I asked.

'Well, I seem to be doing an awful lot of it at the moment. It gets a bit much sometimes! I never, ever thought this is what I'd end up doing. It all started because I met your mum when I was writing an article about life in a children's home.'

'And she was having a royal strop.' I loved hearing this story.

'Yes, she was. She had a lot of them in those days,' said Cam.

'She still does,' I said. 'But not with me. Well, not much. She gets a bit narked if I moan about Sean Godfrey.'

'Do you think Tracy really *is* happy with Sean?' Cam asked, suddenly serious.

I thought about it, screwing my face up to concentrate. 'I *think* she is. I mean, she seems happy most of the time, and she gets all lovey-dovey with him, which is revolting – though sometimes I think she's just acting. She wants to have a nice husband and a big house and all the rest of it, but she can't *really* want to be stuck with Sean Godfrey for ever, can she?'

Cam sighed. 'I don't know. Is she going to get another job now that she's not looking after Ava and Alice?'

'There's a job going as a receptionist at Sean Godfrey's gym. She found out when she went to her kick-boxing class. She thought she could do that, but he went bananas and said he wasn't having his fiancée working there. He couldn't understand why she wanted to work when he could buy her anything she needed.'

'I hope your mum went into one of her famous strops!' said Cam.

'Yes, she did! But he still wouldn't let her take the job.'

'He sounds like a dinosaur from the past. What does he expect her to do – waste her time shopping

260

and going to the hairdresser's and having her nails done?'

'Pretty much.'

'Tracy's not that sort of person at all,' said Cam.

'Maybe she's turning into Granny Carly.' I meant it as a joke, but my voice wobbled. What if she really *was*?

'Look, I know your mum better than anyone. She's gone a bit bonkers just at the moment, but she'll soon snap back into her old self.' Cam meant it to sound reassuring, but her voice went a bit funny too.

'She did try to get the china dogs and the teddies and all our other stuff back – though Sean Godfrey stopped her,' I said.

'What? Didn't he let you take all your special things?' This time Cam was outraged.

'He says he'll get Mum *new* things. He doesn't like anything second-hand. Mum and I don't even go to Sunday boot fairs any more,' I said. 'She just has a long lie-in with *him*.'

Cam pulled a face. 'Well, tell you what we're going to do,' she said, scrabbling in her bag and bringing out a set of keys. 'Aha! Look! Your mum gave me a spare key to your flat ages ago. Let's go there right this minute and collect some of your stuff. And then tomorrow morning we'll go to a boot fair, you and me.

If Sean creates, you can always keep your treasures here, OK?'

'Oh, Cam, I do love you,' I said, throwing my arms around her neck. 'I'm so, so glad you came along to the children's home and met Mum!'

The girls were all going out bowling. Cam and Alfie and I went to Marlborough Tower.

When we got inside the flat I burst into tears. It seemed to have shrunk, and I saw that the sofa was a bit saggy and the curtains uneven and the damp patch on the wall much bigger – but it was still *home*. Alfie liked it too, and bounded around, trying the sofa and the chairs and the beds for size. He barked happily at everything, though I kept trying to shush him because dogs weren't allowed. I kept imagining some scary dog catcher creeping along the balcony with a big net and a cage, all set to capture him.

'Calm down, Alfie! We won't be long, I promise. Please stop barking,' I begged.

 I went around the flat giving everything a little stroke, even the kettle and the toilet-roll holder and the wastepaper basket.

'So what do you want to take, Jess?' Cam asked. She'd brought two big bags-for-life and some bubble wrap.

I gave the flat another quick circuit. 'Everything!' I declared.

'I know. I understand. But we can't shrink it all down so it fits into two bags. Pick out the things you like best, and we'll take them now. We can always come back for more before the council gives the flat to someone else,' said Cam.

'Nobody else should be allowed to come and live in our flat!' I declared.

'I know. I felt like that about *my* old flat,' said Cam. 'It was small and shabby but it was *my* flat, and I thought it looked lovely, with all my books and plants, and my pictures on the wall. I was very happy there, especially when your mum came to live with me. Still, I think she always hoped I'd write a best-seller and we'd move somewhere really swish.'

'Yeah – and now she has,' I said, sighing.

'Come on now, Jess, let's get your favourite things. Alfie's looking fidgety. We don't want him weeing on the carpet,' said Cam.

I picked out the china dogs, and the teddies, and the Toby jugs, and the balloon ladies, and the bluebirds, and the plaster ducks, and the parrot in the cage. I wanted the bookcase as well, but Cam

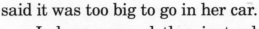

said it was too big to go in her car.

I chose some clothes instead
– my cosy dressing gown, and
last year's jacket with the
silky red lining, and my
shorts, and my green swimming costume and my
matching green flip-flops with
big daisies on the toe-straps.

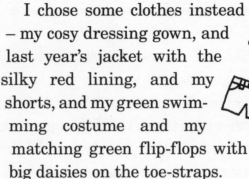

'Excellent choices,' said Cam. 'What about your
mum's clothes? Do you think she'll want any?'

'I know!' I went to Mum's wardrobe and burrowed
my way through her jeans and jackets and found the
child's outfit right at the back, on a special
little hanger. It was a red jumper and a
blue skirt. They were very old and had
a musty wardrobe smell, but several
times I'd caught Mum getting them
out and looking at them.

I'd wondered if she'd bought them at a boot fair
and was keeping them for me. I rather hoped not
because I didn't really like them. For ages they were
too big for me, but now they seemed exactly the right
size – though she hadn't made me wear them. She
hadn't chucked them out either. She'd just kept them
in the wardrobe, as if they were special.

Cam saw me holding them. 'Oh my goodness.' She

held the old woolly jumper to her cheek and then smoothed the crumpled skirt. 'I had no idea your mum still had these. They were her clothes – the ones she always wore at the children's home. She was wearing them the day we met. Yes, let's take them too. *I* want them, even if your mum doesn't!'

We set off with the two bulging bags, Alfie capering along the balcony, barking his head off. I kept looking back, wishing I'd been able to take more. I even wondered about our doormat, the one that said *Home Sweet Home.*

When we got back to Cam's I felt all shaken up and sad, but she made us hot chocolate with whippy cream on top, and we watched a DVD, and I cheered up. Mum sent me a funny goodnight text via Cam's phone, saying she was staying the night in a fairy-tale castle that I would absolutely love. She signed it *Cinderella.* Did she really think Sean Godfrey was the handsome prince? I went to sleep in my borrowed bed surprisingly quickly – but I woke up very early, wide awake.

I kept thinking about our flat. Even if I smuggled all our precious things into Sean Godfrey's house, it still wouldn't be *home*. Mum might be planning to marry in a fairy-tale castle, but I didn't see how our story could possibly end *happily ever after*.

My tummy felt tight. I got up to go to the loo. I tried to walk on tiptoe so I wouldn't disturb Alfie. He was curled up at the end of my bed, thankfully not stirring, but Cam must have heard me pattering up and down the landing. Her door opened.

'Jess? Are you all right?' she whispered.

'Not really,' I mumbled. 'I've got tummy ache.'

'Come in here then.'

I got into bed with her. It wasn't really cold but I seemed to be shivering.

'There now,' said Cam, giving me a cuddle.

I gradually got warmer and the knots in my tummy loosened.

'Bit better?' she asked.

'A lot better. Sorry if I woke you.'

'I was actually awake myself.'

'Were you worrying too?'

'I suppose I was.'

'About Mum or me?'

'That's the problem. I want you both to be happy.'

'And there's Alfie too,' I said.

'Yep, and he's all my fault. I've just made things even more complicated,' said Cam.

'But in a good way,' I said. 'I absolutely love Alfie.

I love him just as much as you and Mum. You're my top three equal people.'

'And I want all three of you to be living in the right place, and I can't work out how to do it. When I was at school there was this horrible intelligence test where some poor man had to ferry a fox and a chicken and a sack of corn across to an island and he didn't know how to do it, because the fox would eat the chicken and the chicken would eat the corn if they were put together. It made my head spin. I was never much good at that kind of test,' said Cam.

'Me neither. I'm glad Miss Oliver doesn't give us tests like that. So what's the answer?'

'Oh, the man rows them over two at a time, and then leaves only one on the island, going back for the next. Something like that,' said Cam vaguely. She was quiet for a minute or two. 'I don't know! Now I've *really* woken up. How's that poorly tummy of yours? Might you be ready for a spot of early breakfast, just us two?'

It seemed like a good idea. We crept downstairs and had a bowl of cornflakes each. Jax came creeping down too, wearing big pyjamas with a teddy-bear pattern. She looked a lot less scary in them.

'Come and have some breakfast, Jax,' said Cam.

Jax had two bowls of cornflakes and a banana and a huge jam sandwich. 'Is this proper breakfast or is it just an early snack?' she asked.

'Whatever.' Cam stretched. 'You know what I sometimes do on Sunday mornings when the girls are still asleep? I go for a swim. Do you fancy that, Jess?'

'A swim in Sean Godfrey's pool?'

'No! Down the leisure centre. It always opens early, even on a Sunday. Let's do it. You've got your costume with you. What about you, Jax – do you feel like it?'

'No thanks! I'm going back to bed,' she said, yawning.

'Will you keep an eye on Alfie for us – he'll probably need a wee soon?' Cam asked.

'If I must,' said Jax, but she grinned. 'He's a cute dog.'

I worried about leaving Alfie all the same, but Cam reassured me.

'Jax is great,' she said as we set off for the leisure centre.

'Great as in a great big girl?' I said.

'Well, she's that, and she can be a bit gruff at times – but she's utterly reliable. And she's good at looking after people. She's got a lot of little brothers and sisters, who sometimes come on a family visit, and they all adore her,' said Cam.

I still wasn't quite convinced, and couldn't help worrying when we were getting changed in the leisure centre.

'Alfie's still in my head,' I complained through the cubicle wall. 'I keep worrying that he's woken up and is desperately trying to find me. I think I'm going to have to go back for him.'

'You have to leave him sometimes,' said Cam. 'You said he was fine with Trev.'

'Yes, but that was just a one-off.'

'What about when you go to school?'

'I can leave him with Mum then,' I said.

'Well, what are you going to do if you and your mum have a day out shopping? Dogs aren't allowed in shopping centres.'

'Not going to happen. Mum hates that kind of shopping. And anyway, if we do have to go somewhere stupid where dogs aren't allowed, then I'll leave Alfie with you. Not Jax.'

'Suppose it's a day when I have a meeting with a social worker or I've got to take one of the girls for a medical appointment? *I'd* leave him with Jax then,' said Cam. 'Have you got your swimming cossie on yet?'

'I've just taken it off to go back to your place.'

'Well, put it on again! I know you're worried about Alfie, but you have to learn to put up with it. It's what happens when you love someone. You worry about them,' said Cam.

'Do you worry about me?'

'Of course I do, you jam pot. And your mum. And all my girls, even the ones who've grown up and gone their own way.'

'Mum thinks you're mad looking after so many girls,' I said, stepping back into my costume.

'It was more worry looking after your mum when she was little than all my current girls squashed together,' said Cam. 'Only better not tell her that! Come on! Let's hold hands and jump in together.'

As soon as I was in the water I found the Alfie-thoughts had shrunk to a little worried face emoji in my head, and I could enjoy myself after all. There weren't too many people in the pool, so we could swim up and down to get warm. Then we had a rest floating on our backs. We played around doing handstands in the shallow end, and then we swam underwater. I pretended I was a dolphin, and Cam laughed.

'That's exactly what your mum used to do when we went swimming together,' she said.

'She still does it now,' I told her. 'She's actually better at it than me.'

Cam knew several of the swimmers. They all said hello to me as well.

'Who's this little mite then? Is she your grand-daughter?' one old man asked, putting his goggles on his forehead to have a good peer at me.

'Yes, she is,' said Cam. 'This is my Jess.' She sounded so proud of me.

Next we did a few lengths of freestyle. Cam got a bit out of puff, so she leaned against the side in the shallow end while I did some more lengths and then swam back to her. She was chatting to a lady of about her age wearing a black swimming hat. There was something  strangely familiar about her pale face and her smile. She had little pink marks on her nose, as if she normally wore glasses.

'Mary, this is my Jess,' said Cam, putting her arm round me. 'Jess, this is Mary. She's giving Sunday-morning swimming a whirl.'

'Hello, Jess.' I *knew* that voice! 'We're friends already, aren't we?'

I nodded uncertainly, still not quite able to place her – I couldn't see her very clearly without my glasses. I didn't think I'd met any Marys – so how did I know her?

She laughed. 'Don't tell me you've forgotten who I am! We meet up five days a week.'

'Oh my goodness, you're *Miss Oliver*! Cam, this is Miss Oliver, my teacher!' It was so surprising to see her in the swimming pool, with her hat covering up her blonde hair.

'Well, what a lovely coincidence,' said Cam.

'So *you're* Tracy Beaker's mother!' said Miss Oliver.

'Well, I was her foster mother – and we're certainly a family now. So I suppose you've met Tracy at parents' evenings?'

'Yes, I've met her,' said Miss Oliver. 'She's . . . unforgettable.'

'Miss Oliver says Mum has Anger Issues,' I said.

Miss Oliver went as red as a peony. 'That was very rude of me,' she said apologetically.

'But accurate,' said Cam, grinning. 'Oh dear, I hope Tracy didn't have a royal strop.'

'She was just concerned about Jess – she thought she'd been bullied by one of the boys,' said Miss Oliver quickly. 'She's a very caring mother.'

'Yes, she is,' Cam and I said in unison.

'And of course her circumstances have now changed considerably,' Miss Oliver added.

'Yes, worst luck,' I said.

'You're starting to shiver, Jess. Why don't you do another couple of lengths to warm up? You're such a good swimmer!' said Miss Oliver.

So I swam off, and Cam and Miss Oliver went on nattering. I think it was about me.

Then we all got out of the pool and showered. I couldn't help peeping at Miss Oliver in her black swimsuit, though I knew it was very rude of me. You don't often get a chance to see your teacher with hardly any clothes on. It was surprising seeing Miss Oliver *with* her clothes on too, because she was wearing jeans and a jumper, and she didn't look a bit like a teacher any more.

Cam and Miss Oliver were acting like they were old friends. They suggested we go and have coffee in the café. I wanted to get back to Alfie, but I had to go too. I didn't have coffee, I had a strawberry milkshake, my favourite.

'It was always your mum's favourite too,' said Cam.

'Still is,' I said.

I concentrated on my milkshake, and then I played around with the dregs at the bottom of the glass, sucking them into my straw and then blowing them out again. Normally both Cam and Miss Oliver would have told me off, but they were too busy talking to each other. They weren't chatting about me now, they were talking about the badminton sessions at the leisure centre, and then about Miss Oliver's rambling club, then some history series on television, and then they got on to some box set they'd both been watching, and *then* their favourite books.

I grew more and more anxious about Alfie. It was getting too much for me.

'I'm sorry to interrupt, Cam, but please can we go soon? Alfie's bound to be awake now, and maybe Jax won't remember that he needs to be taken out for his wee,' I gabbled.

'Yes, OK, sorry. And stop dribbling into your milkshake, it's revolting! We'd better get going, Mary,' said Cam.

'Maybe see you next Sunday?' said Miss Oliver. 'And I'll see *you* tomorrow, Jess.'

'I really like Mary,' said Cam when we were driving back. 'What's she like as a teacher?'

'She's nice – though very strict. You can't mess around in her class. Even Tyrone does as he's told,' I said.

'Quite right too,' said Cam.

When we got home Alfie was wide awake, and it turned out that Jax had taken him out into the garden twice already, and given him a very large breakfast with extra treats. Alfie liked Jax so much that he just gave me a quick hello lick and then bounded back to her, staring up at her lovingly.

I love Alfie to bits, but I wish he wasn't quite so fickle.

15

I **TOLD MUM** that Cam and I had met Miss Oliver at the leisure centre.

She pulled a face. 'Poor you!'

She's never really liked my teachers. She didn't get on with any of *her* teachers when she was young. She especially disliked the one called Mrs Vomit Bagley – though surely that can't have been her real name. I think Mum has Teacher Issues.

I've always liked my teachers. I liked Miss Oliver even more now. I felt weirdly shy going to school on Monday. I wasn't sure how to talk to her any more. Was she a friend? But Miss Oliver greeted me in her usual cool, calm way, making it perfectly plain that at school she had to be treated like a teacher.

I decided not to tell Tyrone about our encounter at the leisure centre, even though I knew he'd be interested – he'd probably fall about laughing if I told him I'd seen her in her swimsuit. I knew he'd blab to all his mates, and soon everyone would be sniggering and it would be awful for Miss Oliver.

So I held my tongue and felt very grown up and discreet. At the end of school Miss Oliver gave me a secret little nod to show that she was pleased with me. She also asked if I'd be interested in going to swimming training on Tuesday evenings after school.

'But I already know how to swim, Miss Oliver,' I said, rather put out. Hadn't she seen me flashing up and down the pool?

'I know you can swim, Jess. That's the point. This is proper training for children with potential. The girls go to the leisure centre at five o'clock on Tuesdays. It's called the Ariel Club.'

The Little Mermaid had always been my favourite Disney film. Suddenly I badly wanted to join the Ariel Club. I wondered if you pretended to be a mermaid. Maybe you had to wear a mermaid costume!

'Please please please can I go, Mum?' I asked when she collected me.

'I suppose so. Yes, I'll take you. Though I hope your Miss Oliver isn't involved,' said Mum. 'Oh, hang on a minute – Tuesdays?'

I suddenly remembered. That was the day Mum went kick-boxing at Sean Godfrey's gym.

'Maybe Cam could take me?' I suggested hopefully. Then she might get me another strawberry milkshake afterwards.

'*I'll* take you,' said Mum.

'*I'm* your mum.'

'But what about your kick-boxing?'

'Well, I can practise with Sean any old time. I'm getting good at it. Watch!' She demonstrated, kicking her leg right up at an imaginary opponent on the pavement. The other mums gasped and giggled, and all the kids stared in awe.

'*Mum!*' I hissed, horribly embarrassed.

Of course I wouldn't swap my mum Tracy Beaker for the world, but sometimes I wish she'd act more like ordinary mums. Still, I was touched that she was giving up her kick-boxing to go to the leisure centre with me.

I was really excited about going to the Ariel Club – but it wasn't a bit how I'd imagined. We didn't dress

up as mermaids – everyone wore regulation black swimsuits. We didn't sit on the edge of the pool pretending to comb our long hair, and then dive deep into the water to our palace. We just swam up and down, up and down, doing front crawl and breaststroke and backstroke and butterfly. It was exhausting! And I wasn't the best, as I'd hoped. I was one of the worst. There was one tubby little girl of about six who flashed past me and finished half a length in front.

It wasn't fun in the changing rooms either. The other girls all knew each other, and chatted about some special swimming gala, totally ignoring me. Stevie, the swimming instructor, came striding past in her tracksuit, and gave me a Sean Godfrey-type wink.

'How are you doing, kid?' she asked. 'Don't worry, you'll soon catch up. I can see you've got potential. If you train really hard, by the end of the year you might make the B team.'

I was used to being top at most things at school. I couldn't help feeling humiliated.

'Did you like it?' Mum asked when I went up to the viewing balcony to find her.

'Not much,' I muttered.

'Maybe we'll find something else to do, just you

and me,' she said. 'Or you and me and Alfie. Shall we see about those dog-training courses?'

'Oh *yes*! But do you think Alfie would get along OK? He doesn't seem to like doing what he's told. I'm not sure he's very trainable. I wouldn't want *him* to be bottom of the class,' I said.

'Everyone can be trained. When I was a kid Cam even managed to train *me*. I used to be a holy terror, but now look at me. Little Miss Perfect!' said Mum.

When we got back to Sean Godfrey's we saw there were two cars outside. The red Porsche – and a little white car.

Mum wrinkled her nose. 'Sean must have brought one of his lads back from the gym,' she said.

'I'm not sure it's a lad,' I said, peering at the white car. There was a little white lucky-mascot unicorn dangling from the driving mirror – and a copy of *Glossip* on the front passenger seat.

My heart started thumping. I'd been a bit shivery after swimming but now I went hot all over.

'Do you think that's Sandy Forthright's car?' I whispered.

'It had better not be,' said Mum, 'or I'll be practising my kick-boxing on her!'

We let ourselves into the house. We could hear Sean Godfrey's voice in the living room – and a woman's voice answering. Then they both laughed.

'Sean?' Mum called, her hand on my shoulder.

'Hey, babe!' he said, coming out into the hall. He was wearing a tight white T-shirt that showed off his toned muscles, and white trackie bottoms. I thought he looked a right prat, but he strutted about as if he was drop-dead gorgeous. 'I've got a surprise for you!'

'I'm not sure I like surprises,' said Mum.

'Chill, darling! It's an old friend.'

'I'm not sure I want to meet any of your old friends.' Mum's fingers were digging into my shoulder now.

'She's not *my* old friend, babe. She's *your* old friend, back when you were kids,' said Sean Godfrey. 'Come and say hello.'

Mum walked into the living room, still holding onto me. A woman in a slinky black top, very tight jeans and black high heels was sitting back on the sofa, a glass in her hand. She was wearing a lot of make-up and her hair was ultra-styled. The whole room smelled of her musky perfume.

Mum stared.

The woman raised her glass. 'Hi, Tracy. Remember me?'

'Justine Littlewood!'

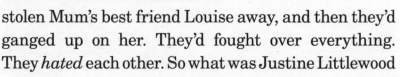

The name made the back of my neck prickle. I knew that name so well, even though I'd never met her. Justine Little-wood, my mum's arch enemy at the children's home. She'd stolen Mum's best friend Louise away, and then they'd ganged up on her. They'd fought over everything. They *hated* each other. So what was Justine Littlewood doing here, lounging in the living room as if she belonged there?

'Long time no see,' she said. 'Oh, Tracy, you haven't changed a bit! I'd have known you anywhere!'

'I'd have known you too,' said Mum.

They looked each other up and down. Mum ran her hand through her wild curls. One leg of her jeans was rucked up from sitting in the car – she stood like a stork to push it down with her high-top.

'So, you know Sean then?' she said.

'I do now,' said Justine, smiling.

'She came to the gym.' Sean Godfrey was smiling too. 'We got talking, and she said you two used to be best friends at the children's home.'

'Best friends?' said Mum.

'Well. Frenemies,' said Justine.  'Oh my God, the laughs we had then, Tracy. Remember our Dare Game? I couldn't believe it when you ate that worm and then were sick in the bushes!'

'I wasn't sick,' said Mum, jutting her chin.

'That's my girl!' said Sean Godfrey, putting his arm round her. He winked at me. 'They'll be daring each other again any time now!'

I saw that Mum was completely rigid, her fists clenched. Then she moved closer to Sean Godfrey, nestling in to him. 'We're not kids any more. A lot has changed since then,' she said.

'I'll say!' said Justine.

'Show Justine your ring, Trace,' said Sean Godfrey.

Mum held out her hand and the diamond flashed.

'Oh my, that's a rock and a half!' said Justine. 'Congratulations, you two. And you have a family already?' She looked at me. 'Dear goodness – apart from the glasses you're the spitting image of your mum!'

'Jess isn't mine – but I treat her just like my own daughter,' said Sean Godfrey.

I wanted to spit.

'And, of course, Tracy and I want our own kids too,' he went on.

That thought made the saliva actually rush into my mouth.

He poured Mum a glass of wine and me an apple juice. We were still standing there as if we were the guests.

'I've asked Justine to stay for supper,' said Sean Godfrey. 'I thought you two would like to catch up on old times. Don't look so worried, Tracy – *I'll* do the cooking! You girls have a good natter while I go big-game hunting in the kitchen for a steak or three.'

He went off whistling. Mum sat down on the sofa opposite Justine. I sat close beside her.

'This is so spooky,' said Justine, crossing her legs. 'Big Tracy and little Tracy!'

'So how come you just happened to wander into Sean's gym?' asked Mum, gulping her drink. 'You don't look ready to do a stint on the tread-mill in those shoes.'

'I've got my gym

kit in the car,' said Justine. 'But you're right of course, Tracy. I tracked you down! I saw your photos of the house on Instagram. And my God, the pool! I thought you were just having a laugh, pretending you lived like that. And then I saw a photo in the "Fun Day Out" column in *Glossip*. You were at Chessington World of Adventures, you and Sean and little Tracy here.'

'My name's Jess,' I told her.

'And you were hanging on Sean Godfrey's arm!' said Justine, ignoring me. 'My God, Tracy Beaker, you've done all right for yourself, haven't you! So I was just itching with curiosity. I googled Sean, and there was stuff about his gym, so I thought I'd toddle along and see the big man for myself.'

'*My* big man,' said Mum.

'So however did you pull it off?' Justine asked. 'I mean – no offence, but according to his past history he usually goes for gorgeous little blondes, twenty if they're a day.'

'Sean and I go way back,' said Mum. 'We knew each other when we were kids.'

'What? You're never telling me he was at the Dumping Ground too! I don't remember him.'

'This was after I got fostered,' said Mum. 'Sean and I were mates. We lost touch because we both moved. And then we met up again. When I went to the gym.'

'It's like a little dating agency, that gym.' Justine stood up, stretched, and started stalking around the living room, looking at the framed cuttings on the walls, the photos, the giant portrait. 'And this is the Sean Godfrey museum! Sweet! I don't see any photos of you though, Tracy – or any of his other WAGs.'

'Mum's not a WAG,' I said indignantly.

'Yes she is. She's one of Sean's girlfriends,' said Justine.

'I'm his *only* girlfriend.' Mum fiddled with her diamond. 'And pretty soon I'll be his wife.'

'Well, I hope I get an invite to the wedding, seeing as we're such old friends.'

'Worst enemies, more like,' said Mum.

'Still, as you said, we're not silly little kids any more,' said Justine. 'We're two successful women. Stars of the Fostering Network! Does Cam still write magazine articles? She should write about you and me.'

'So what have you done that's so great, Justine?' Mum asked.

'I'm a business woman now – doing very nicely, thank you. I did business studies at uni.'

'You went to university?' Mum's always saying she wants me to study hard and go to university. She left school early and says she's always regretted it.

'Of course I did. You can't get on without a good degree nowadays,' said Justine. 'I've always been ambitious. I was nearly picked for *The Apprentice* – I made the shortlist out of thousands. I was in sales and marketing in several big companies, and then I started up my own business. Beauty products – a whole range. They were called *Justine*, all very classy looking – dark navy with a white lotus-flower motif – Superdrug stocked them. Maybe you used to buy them, Tracy – though you don't really look like you're into beauty products.'

'Do you do hand cream?' I asked. Mum never lets me wear make-up, but she sometimes gives me some of her hand cream, which smells almost as good as perfume.

'I used to. But I've stopped producing the range now,' said Justine.

'Did you go bust?' Mum asked.

'Oh, that's business for you,' said Justine airily. 'Even Simon Cowell went bust once upon a time. You have to learn to take the rough with the smooth. So what about *your* career, Tracy?'

'I've done this and that,' said Mum. 'I worked with Marina Grey recently. She's in publishing.'

'Really? In what capacity? Editing? Or were you in sales too?' Justine asked.

'Mum wrote a book,' I said proudly.

'Oh yes. You were always going *scribble-scribble-scribble* when we were kids, weren't you, Tracy? Your life story? Don't tell me you're really getting it published at last!'

'I've still got some work to do on it.'

'Mm!' said Justine meaningfully.

'And Mum's Marina's best friend now. She used to look after her children, Ava and Alice. Alice's *my* best friend, actually,' I said, though I hadn't seen her for a while now.

'Oh! So, you were this Marina's nanny, were you, Tracy? That's a laugh, you looking after someone else's kids!'

'Why is that a laugh, exactly?' Mum asked, her eyes narrowing.

'Well, you were only the worst-behaved kid ever. You were famous for it. You drove Mike and Jenny mad – and what was the name of that care worker . . . ? Elaine! And you called her Elaine the Pain. She always ended up in tears when she had to deal with you!'

Mum was scowling.

'Uh-oh! Look at the face on you! You're about to throw one of your famous wobblies!' Justine pulled a silly face at me. 'What's it like, having Tracy Beaker for a mum? I bet she's pretty embarrassing at times.'

288

'No she's not,' I lied fiercely. 'She's the best mum ever.'

'Ah, isn't that sweet?' said Justine. 'Have you got a bit of a temper like your mum?'

'No, she hasn't,' said Mum. 'She's a great kid. Very well behaved. And she's doing brilliantly. Next term we'll be sending her to a girls' prep school where she'll do all sorts of extras like drama and music. She'll love it.'

I wasn't so sure. I quite liked the sound of drama and music – but I wanted to keep Miss Oliver as my teacher and Tyrone for a mate.

Justine still had that stupid smirk on her face. 'I'd have thought she'd experience enough drama living with you, Tracy,' she said.

'Why don't you finish your drink and then clear off,' said Mum.

'Oh, don't be like that! Can't you take a bit of banter? And I'm invited to dinner, aren't I? Your chap's cooking me a steak,' said Justine. 'You've got a gem there all right, Tracy. He's a real hunk – he cooks too, bless him. And, of course, he's rich and famous. You've really hit the jackpot.'

'Why are you so interested in *my* chap. Haven't you got a man of your own?'

'Oh, I've got a very nice boyfriend, thanks very much. He's crazy about me,' said Justine. 'Want to see him?' She flicked through the images on her mobile phone and then held it out.

I saw a man sitting at a great big desk, good-looking, but quite old.

'He looks more like your boss than your boyfriend,' said Mum.

'It just so happens that he is my boss at the moment. But I'm thinking of starting up my own business again,' said Justine. 'We'll have to see if the big romance lasts.'

'Is he married?' Mum asked.

'Well – technically. *I* was married before actually. Hundreds of years ago. In a long white dress sewn with crystals, walking down the aisle on my dad's arm. He told me I looked beautiful.' Her voice wobbled suddenly.

'We were always waiting for them to come and see us at the home – your dad and my mum,' said Mum. 'Only they hardly ever turned up.'

'My dad came practically every week,' said Justine. 'We were ever so close. We still are, even though he doesn't always recognize me. He's got dementia. He's in a home now, so *I* go and visit *him*. Funny, that.'

'Oh,' said Mum. 'I'm sorry, Justine.'

There was a little pause.

'Life doesn't always work out the way you want,' said Justine.

'And the husband isn't around any more?' Mum asked.

'Nope. And there weren't any children either, though we tried. No little Justines for me,' she said.

Mum poured her another drink – and by the time Sean Godfrey came to say the steaks were ready they were chatting like real old friends.

'There! Isn't it great for you two to catch up!' he said delightedly.

He'd cooked chips as well as steak, and he'd even done a couple of fish fingers for me. Alfie was most put out because the smell of steak was making him drool, and I was the only one likely to slip him some.

Mum and Justine went on talking about their childhood, telling stories about the pranks they'd played in the children's home, making it all sound fun.

'Are you still in touch with Louise?' Mum asked.

'Louise? Which one was she?' Justine asked vaguely.

'You really don't remember? She was my best friend – until she palled up with you! She was the very pretty one with long blonde hair.'

'Oh, *her*! Haven't seen her for donkey's years. We met up when we were teenagers but we didn't really have a thing in common,' said Justine. She looked at Sean Godfrey. 'So I hear you and Tracy were mates when you were kids. *We* never met up, did we?'

'Well, if we did, I was the big fat kid with the bad attitude,' he said, laughing. 'I was a right tough nut, wasn't I, Trace?'

'Still are,' said Mum, and she gave his arm a squeeze.

'Please may I leave the table?' I asked, because I'd finished my fish fingers and I hated it when the two of them got all lovey-dovey.

I could tell Justine didn't think much of it either, though she kept smiling.

'Sure, Jess,' said Sean Godfrey, as if he was my father.

I went off to take Alfie for a walk in the dark. When we came back, Mum and Sean Godfrey and Justine were having coffee in the living room. I nipped into the kitchen and scooped up little leftover bits of steak. Alfie had a royal feast.

Then we went upstairs and I got into my pyjamas

and Alfie curled up in his bed. We were nearly asleep when Mum came upstairs to check on us.

'Is she still here?' I asked sleepily.

'Yes – I wish she'd clear off too,' said Mum.

'I bet she's dead jealous of you now, Mum.'

'Yes, I think she is. It's weird – I thought I'd feel like gloating because everything's worked out so well for me, but I just feel a bit sorry for her now. Funny if we end up friends after all!'

SEAN GODFREY THOUGHT that Mum would be
thrilled to be reunited with Justine. He said so at
breakfast the next day.

'Er – *no!*' she said.

'But you seemed to be getting on so well last night,'
he said.

'Sean, we really, really, really have nothing in
common, apart from the fact that we once lived in the
same children's home.' Mum rolled her eyes.

'OK, no need to snap at me,' he said. 'I thought she
was a nice girl, anyway – and it's clear she wants to
be friends with you, Trace.'

'No, I think she maybe wants to be friends with
you, Sean,' said Mum.

'Do you think she likes me then?' he asked, preening.

'Yep – clearly another paid-up member of the Sean Godfrey fan club.'

Rosalie chuckled as she stirred the scrambled egg and cut strips of smoked salmon.

'Are you ladies ganging up on me?' Sean Godfrey asked, draining his murky green juice. He was on a health kick now. 'Here, I wish you'd try this, Tracy, it's absolutely brimming with vitamins. It would do *you* good too, Jess. Put some roses in your cheeks.'

'It looks like witch's wee-wee,' I murmured.

Mum laughed. 'Yes, it does!'

'You shouldn't encourage her,' said Sean Godfrey. 'She's cheeky enough as it is. My mum would have knocked my block off if I'd come out with stuff like that. You button your lip, young Jess. And stop that wretched dog making such a stupid noise! He shouldn't even be allowed in the kitchen.'

Alfie was butting his head against Rosalie's legs, whimpering hopefully. He'd discovered that smoked salmon was the most heavenly treat in the world.

'Quit nagging her, Sean,' said Mum. 'I don't see why Alfie can't be in here with us. He's part of the family.'

Rosalie dished up our breakfasts – and gave Alfie a big strip of salmon when Sean Godfrey wasn't looking.

'What are your plans for today, babe?' He ruffled Mum's hair. 'How about going to the hair salon, eh?'

'No thanks,' said Mum, jerking her head away. 'What's the matter with my hair anyway?'

'Nothing! I love your curly mop. I just wondered if you might like it more . . .' He gestured vaguely with his hand. 'You know. Styled.'

'I'm not that sort of woman,' said Mum. 'I don't want to waste my day sitting in a hairdresser's.'

'It would give you something to do. I thought you said you were bored.'

'I'm bored because I'm used to rushing around working. I'm going to have to get a job, Sean, whether you like it or not.'

'You don't need to do some crappy job,' he said. 'Especially not looking after someone else's kids. Look, tell you what. Why don't you work for yourself? Start up your own business like Justine. Yeah, that's a great idea. She could give you some tips.'

'I thought her business had gone bust,' said Mum.

'She's got new ideas now, hasn't she? Why don't you have a think about it, Trace?' said Sean Godfrey, getting up from the table and checking his watch.

'OK, I'll think about it. Do I want to start my own

beauty product business? Now, let me
see . . . It could be called *Tracy* – with a
dinky little deadly-nightshade motif. Do I
think it a good idea? Probably *not.*'

'OK, OK, no need to take the mick. It doesn't have
to be a beauty product. What about some kind of
sporty thing?' Sean Godfrey peered at the green
dregs in his glass. 'A special health juice, say. I like
that idea! Or ladies sportswear – little crop tops and
leggings? I could sell them at the gym. Hey, I'm on a
roll here!'

'Well, try your ideas out on Justine then,' said Mum.

She was joking, but he took her seriously. 'I might
just do that!' he said.

Mum pushed her plate away and
stood up. 'You'd better not.'

'Ooh-er!' Sean Godfrey said, in a
pantomime squeal. 'Don't say you're
just a teeny bit jealous of her.' He
was grinning, lapping it up.

Mum walked over to him. She
only comes up to his chest, but he
took a step backwards.

'You have anything more to do
with Justine, and I walk,' she said,
in a calm but deadly voice. Then
she swept out of the kitchen.

There was a little silence.

'She's only joking,' said Sean Godfrey.

'I think she means it, Mr Sean,' said Rosalie.

'I *know* she means it,' I said.

'She knows which side her bread's buttered,' he muttered. 'No one bosses me around and tells me what to do like that. Not even my Trace.'

I glared at him. 'She's not *yours*!' I shouted. 'And she's called *Tracy*, not Trace.' I ran out of the room too, with Alfie following behind.

Mum was putting on her jacket in the hall. 'Come on, or you'll be late for school,' she said. She was trying to sound casual, but her voice was higher than usual and her face was very red.

'Are you going to lose your temper, Mum?' I asked tentatively.

'Nope.'

'But you mean it about Justine Littlewood?'

'Yep.'

She didn't say anything else all the way to school. She drew up near the gate, where parents aren't supposed to park. Miss Oliver was walking across the playground. She looked up and saw us.

I thought she'd come charging over and tell us off – but she just shook her head slightly, then waved and smiled.

'Wave back, Mum!' I said. 'She's not just my teacher now, she's Cam's friend.'

'There's no accounting for taste,' Mum muttered, but she waved apologetically and mouthed 'Sorry' about parking in the wrong place. 'Jump out quick, Jess.'

'Are you going to be all right, Mum?' I asked anxiously.

'Of course I am,' she said.

I wasn't so sure, but the bell went and I had to go into school. I hoped Alfie would be as good as gold. It wasn't a great time for him to chew a cushion or make a puddle on the rug.

Tyrone got on my nerves all day. He was still going on about his Monday session at Sean Godfrey's gym, and he was not just over the moon, he was somersaulting over the entire Milky Way. It was Sean Godfrey this, Sean Godfrey that, and at lunchtime he kept demonstrating for me all the things Sean Godfrey had showed him in his training session. By the end of the day he'd dropped the Godfrey part and was calling him *my mate Sean*.

Mum was still in a weird mood when she came to pick me up.

'Are you OK, Mum?' I asked, giving Alfie a cuddle.

He seemed a bit subdued too.

'Of course I am,' she said. 'So, what did you make of Justine, Jess?'

'I hated her,' I said.

'That's my girl.' Mum was quiet for a bit and then said, 'But she's attractive, isn't she? In an obvious kind of way.'

I wrinkled my nose.

'I was wondering – do you think I should start wearing high heels? They're dead uncomfortable but they'd make me look taller.'

'I think they look stupid,' I said, though I couldn't wait until I was old enough to wear them myself. I sometimes walked around the bedroom on tippy toes, pretending.

'Yes, I suppose. But you know Carly's always nagging at me to stop wearing jeans? Do you think she's right? I suppose I always look a bit of a scruff.'

'Mum! Have you gone nuts? Do you want to look like Granny Carly?'

'No!' said Mum. But she still wasn't finished. She glanced at herself in the driving mirror and then tried tucking her hair behind her ears. It sprang out again immediately. 'I can't do anything with it,' she groaned.

'We *like* having curly hair,' I said, although that was a total fib too.

'I suppose I could get it straightened,' said Mum.

'But then you wouldn't look like you.'

'That's true.'

'And you're Tracy Beaker,' I said.

'Yes, I'm the only Tracy Beaker in the world. And you're the only Jess Beaker. We're unique,' Mum declared, cheering up. She put her foot down on the accelerator and we swooped off in our pink Cadillac.

Sean was so late home that we'd already had our supper. Rosalie had bought chops and sausages and bacon and black pudding and mushrooms and tomatoes for a mixed grill – 'one of Mr Sean's favourites', she told us before she went home. We were sick of eating so much meat, so Mum made us mushroom and tomato omelettes instead.

They were very good, but my tummy was so tight I could only manage half of mine. Mum ate even less, and she kept looking at the kitchen clock. We didn't even say Sean Godfrey's name out loud, but we were both wondering where on earth he was.

Then we heard the Porsche draw up outside. Mum

was nibbling her lip, looking very pale. I hated seeing her so anxious. I wanted to fly at Sean Godfrey and yell at him – but he came waltzing in with a simply enormous bunch of red roses in one hand and a posy of pink rosebuds in the other.

'Sorry I'm so late, girls,' he said. 'Problems at the gym – someone injured themselves and blamed the equipment – but it's all sorted now. Huge apologies.' He gave Mum her red roses with a flourish and then presented me with the posy.

I couldn't help feeling a little bit pleased. No one had ever given me flowers before. And they were so pretty. Mum's roses had to be split up into four huge glass vases, but she put my posy into our lady Toby jug, where they looked beautiful.

'What's that lovely smell?' said Sean Godfrey, wrinkling his nose like a rabbit.

'The roses, stupid!' said Mum. Then she looked anxious again because Sean Godfrey goes weird if you call him that – but he didn't react at all.

'Not the roses – there's a lovely savoury smell. Have you been cooking, Trace?'

'I just made Jess and me an omelette, that's all,' she said, shrugging.

'How about making one for me, darling?' he said, putting his arm round her.

'OK. With some chops and stuff?'

'I'll skip the meat tonight. The medic at the gym said I should vary my sources of protein and not rely so heavily on red meat,' said Sean Godfrey.

So Mum made him an enormous omelette and he ate it enthusiastically, smacking his lips.

'It's really tasty, babe,' he said. 'Your mum's a great cook, Jess.'

'I know,' I said. I paused. 'She looks great too, doesn't she?'

Sean Godfrey did a pantomime peer, his hand over his eyebrows and his eyes scrunched up. 'Yes, I think you're right, kid. Your mum looks G-R-E-A-T!'

'She'd look weird in a tight skirt and high heels, wouldn't she?'

'Well, she'd look great in anything – but I love her most in her funny jeans and T-shirts.'

'Me too,' I said, amazed that he was managing to say all the right stuff.

'Have you two started up the Tracy Beaker fan club?' said Mum.

'We could!' said Sean Godfrey. 'Jess could be the number-one founder member. And I can be the number-two fan – with benefits.'

Mum laughed, and I laughed too because I was so happy for her.

Sean Godfrey carried on being lovely all through the Easter holidays. He stopped nagging about Alfie and started giving him little treats. And he even gave me my very own mobile phone!

'But I said I didn't want her to have one just yet,' said Mum. 'Maybe for her next birthday. And just a little pay-as-you-go one, not a proper smartphone.'

'Well, I was in the shop anyway upgrading mine, and I just thought she'd like it. It'll be useful. She can text all her friends now, be one of the in crowd,' said Sean Godfrey. 'It'll be great, eh, Jess?'

'You bet!' I said. 'Thank you very much, Sean.' I thought it would seem very rude and ungrateful if I called him Sean Godfrey then. I just added it mentally.

I tapped in the numbers of my favourite people, but Alice didn't have a mobile phone so I couldn't text her. I texted Mum, even though she was in the same room. I also texted a smiley emoji to Sean Godfrey, who was actually sitting beside me, showing me how to do it.

The person I texted most was Cam. I sent her lots

of messages and she replied – and if I couldn't go to sleep at night I sometimes curled up with the duvet over my head and called her. It was lovely having a private chat with her. Though sometimes her phone was engaged.

One night I tried and tried for nearly an hour before I got through.

'Cam, you've been talking to someone for *ages*,' I complained. 'Were you on the phone to Mum?'

'No, I don't phone her in the evenings now, when she's with Sean.'

'Were you phoning Jane and Liz?'

'No,' said Cam. She sounded a bit cagey.

'Were you phoning a care worker about one of your girls?'

'*No!*'

'So who was it?'

'Honestly, Jess, stop being so nosy. I was simply chatting to a friend,' said Cam.

'Which friend?'

'Well, it was Mary, if you must know.'

'Mary? *Miss Oliver?* Why were you phoning her? Were you having a chat about me?' I demanded.

'Jess, you're my favourite girl in all the world, but you're not my only topic of conversation, you know. We were talking about all sorts of stuff. Mary was asking me about this book I'm writing. And I wanted the recipe for her ace banana cake – she made it when I went round to hers for tea.'

'You went to *tea* with Miss Oliver?' I asked, astonished. 'At her house?'

'No, we sat and had afternoon tea in a bus shelter,' said Cam. 'Of *course* we had tea at her place. *Anyway,* why have you phoned? Are you OK, Jess? And Mum? And Alfie?'

'Yes, we're fine.'

'And things are OK with Sean?'

'Well, they're better than OK actually. He's being ever so nice.'

'That's good,' said Cam.

'I might even have started liking him, just a little bit,' I said.

'So you're settling down and it's all working out just like a fairy tale? And the wicked ogre has turned into the handsome prince?'

'I wouldn't go that far!' I said. 'Cam, weren't you and Miss Oliver talking about me even a bit?'

'Perhaps just a tiny bit.'

'She does like me, doesn't she?'

'I think you're probably her favourite, though she's too professional to admit it,' said Cam.

'Mum keeps going on about sending me to this school where you do drama and music,' I said. 'And it's got its own swimming pool.'

'Goodness! Well, maybe you'd like that.'

'Yes, but I don't want to leave *my* school. And maybe I wouldn't like the swimming-pool part much. I'm one of the worst swimmers at the Ariel Club. I don't think I'm going any more,' I said.

'Well, talk it over with your mum,' said Cam. 'It's late now, sweetheart. Snuggle down and go to sleep. Night night.'

I curled up, with Alfie on the end of my bed like a big furry hot-water bottle, and Woofer tucked into the crook of my neck.

As I didn't want to be in the Ariel Club any more Mum decided to go back to her kick-boxing class the next Tuesday.

'I'll just turn up at the gym and give Sean a surprise!' she said. 'I'm sure the kick-boxing is good for me. I hardly ever lose my temper nowadays. This is the brand-new Tracy Beaker – c-a-l-m!'

Rosalie stayed late and looked after Alfie and me. She made a big fuss of us. We went for a walk all round the garden and threw the ball for Alfie and played tug with him. Then we had our tea – a lovely chicken-and-vegetable stew that had been simmering on the stove for ages.

'Yum yum, Rosalie. I like it,' I said.

'It's a special Filipino dish, Jess. Jane and Nick love it too – though he prefers McDonald's,' she said.

'It must be so weird for you, not being with them,' I said.

Rosalie nodded. 'I just have to be patient. When they're a little older we hope they can come here. My husband is expecting a promotion soon. And Mr Sean is always very generous to me.'

'But it's not fair! He's got so much money and you've got hardly any! Don't you ever get fed up?' I asked, running my finger around my plate to scoop up the last of the sauce.

'Don't do that! Use a spoon. There's no point thinking about what's fair and what isn't. Anyway, if I'd been a famous footballer, *I'd* have lots of money. Maybe I'd better start practising!' Rosalie aimed a kick at Alfie's ball and sent it skidding across the kitchen floor. It went right into the open cupboard. 'Goal!' she shouted, laughing.

Mum came home looking a bit anxious. Rosalie had saved her a portion of chicken stew, but she said she didn't feel like eating.

'So why didn't you come home with Sean Godfrey?' I asked.

'He wasn't at the gym.'

'So where was he?'

'How do I know?' said Mum. 'He's not answering his mobile either.'

She didn't sound very calm now. It looked like there was going to be a big row. A very, very, very big row.

'Where on earth have you been?' Mum demanded when Sean Godfrey came home at half past eight. 'And don't tell me you were down the gym because I know for a fact that you weren't.'

'Sorry, babe,' he said, bending down and giving her curls a kiss, though Mum jerked away angrily. 'I wasn't at *my* gym, I was checking out another gym up west. It looks like it's going to be up for sale soon, and I'm considering buying it. I'm thinking of starting up a whole chain of Sean Godfrey gyms. What do you think, eh?'

'Why didn't you answer your mobile?'

'Because I was working out. See – my hair's still wet from the shower. Lighten up, Trace! You've got a face like thunder,' he said.

'Well, you could have told me! The guy at the kick-boxing class didn't know where you were either,' said Mum.

'I thought you'd given up going – weren't you taking Jess swimming or something?' said Sean Godfrey. 'Anyway, I don't go round gassing to my staff, telling them all my plans. Shame I missed you though. I love seeing you aiming kicks and getting all red in the face.'

'I'll practise on you if you like,' said Mum.

They started play-fighting. Mum was quite fierce at first, but soon they were just larking about. They didn't have a row. They ended up getting all lovey-dovey. Again.

I wondered about asking Mum to teach me to kick-box. I could try it out on Tyrone when he started to annoy me. He was still going on and on and *on* about Sean Godfrey. He even started writing his biography!

Miss Oliver said we all had to choose a person we admired and then find out all sorts of information about them and write it up in our own words.

'And if they're famous I don't want you copying Wikipedia word for word,' she warned. 'I want you each to write something really original and interesting.'

Half the class thought *I'd* write about Sean Godfrey!

'You're so lucky, Jess. You can find out all sorts of stuff, easy-peasy, and get photos and old football programmes and newspaper cuttings,' said Aleysha.

'I'm not doing Sean Godfrey,' I told her. 'I'm doing my mum Tracy Beaker.'

'But your mum's not famous!'

'Miss Oliver said we should write about someone we admire. And I admire my mum,' I said.

I spent ages working on my biography.

MY MUM TRACY BEAKER

I think my mum Tracy Beaker is a little bit famous. She's had the most interesting life too. She didn't have a very happy childhood. Her own mum couldn't always look after her so she had to live in a children's home. She didn't like it much. She got very fed up. I think she was quite naughty but it wasn't really her fault. She was missing her mum. She wrote about it in her own story. It's called an autobiography when you write about your own life.

But then – guess what! A lovely kind lady called Cam came to the children's home and she fostered my mum Tracy Beaker. And Mum was much happier, though she was still quite naughty. She made friends with a boy nicknamed Football and they hung out together.

When Mum grew up she worked in a children's home for a while because she wanted to help other children like her. She did all kinds of other jobs too. I especially liked it when she was a dog walker. I was a dog walker too. I am very good with dogs, and when I grow up I'm going to work at Battersea Dogs and Cats Home. Mum says if I work very, very hard I might get to be a vet. Mum didn't always work hard when she was at school but she wants me to do better.

Mum is the best mum in all the world to me. She can get a bit cross at times, but she's never, ever cross with me and she always sticks up for me, no matter what. Now she's going to marry that boy she once knew, only now he's called Sean Godfrey and he turned into a famous footballer. I think he's very lucky to be marrying my mum.

I drew lots of pictures of Mum and me – in our Marlborough Tower flat, and going round a boot fair, and walking Alfie, and riding in our pink Cadillac.

I was one of the first to hand their work in to Miss Oliver. She read it immediately, while I was still standing at her desk.

'Well done, Jess,' she said when she'd got to the end. 'It's a lovely piece of work, and I like all the drawings too.'

'Did you see I mentioned your friend Cam?' I asked.

'Yes, I did,' said Miss Oliver, smiling.

'I admire her too. I'll do a biography of her if we have to do another one,' I said. 'I like writing biographies of people.'

Tyrone was finding writing a biography of Sean Godfrey hard work. He'd filled one side of paper, but it was just a load of match results he'd copied out. He'd added stars for each goal Sean Godfrey had scored.

'It looks rather like the sky at night,' said Miss Oliver, glancing at it. 'I can see you've put a lot of effort into this, Tyrone, but I'd like you to do some writing too, at least a couple of pages. Tell me about Sean Godfrey the person. Imagine what it feels like to be Sean Godfrey.'

Tyrone rolled his eyes. 'It must feel terrific, Miss!'

'Well, that's a start.'

So Tyrone wrote that down. Then he got stuck. 'I don't know what else to put,' he said.

I remembered what Aleysha had said about using football programmes and newspaper cuttings.

'Shall I see if I can find something at Sean Godfrey's for you, Tyrone? Newspaper cuttings and stuff? He's got all sorts in his study. I've had a peep.'

'Oh, wow! *Would* you? That would be magic!' he said.

When we got back from school Sean Godfrey was already there.

'How's my girls?' he asked. 'And my boy,' he added, squatting down and making a big fuss of Alfie.

'You're in a good mood!' said Mum.

'I'm always in a good mood when you're around, Trace,' said Sean Godfrey. 'I thought I'd come home early and take us all out for a meal tonight. What do you fancy? Italian, signora? A beeg plate of spagi boli? Or French, mademoiselle? Steak frites and beaucoup de plonk?' He put on dreadful silly accents to make Mum laugh.

'How about Indian? I fancy a curry,' she said.

'Then I will whisk you off to the Taj Mahal, memsahib. I'll nip out for a run first so the calories won't stick. Coming with me, Trace?'

'As if!' said Mum. 'I'll have a cup of tea with Rosalie before she goes home.'

I wondered about asking Sean Godfrey for an old football programme and a cutting or two as he was in such a good mood, but he was so weird about all his football stuff. He didn't just have it framed on the walls in the living room. The study was like a Sean Godfrey shrine. I wasn't allowed in there. He didn't even let Rosalie dust – he did it once a week with a special feather duster, and polished all his trophies.

I thought he'd probably say no, good mood or not. I decided not to risk asking. I'd just borrow some little token and hope he'd never notice. I knew I'd be in serious trouble if he caught me in his precious study, but he wouldn't be back from his run for ages. It wasn't just a jog around the garden. He changed into a vest and silly little shorts and set off for a proper run to the local park. He'd be gone for an hour or more.

So I crept into the study and tiptoed around, keeping a careful eye on Alfie, who

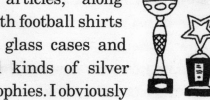

had followed me in. He padded softly, as if he knew we had to be stealthy. All around the room there were framed newspaper cuttings and magazine articles, along with football shirts in glass cases and all kinds of silver trophies. I obviously

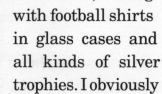

couldn't sneak *them* away. But there was heaps more stuff filed away in cabinets and in the drawers of the big desk. Sean Godfrey surely wouldn't miss

a couple of little souvenirs.

My heart was beating fast even so. Was it a crime if you took something from your own home? I knew it probably was. And it all clearly meant so much to Sean Godfrey. I didn't like him much, but now that I was in his study I found I didn't want to steal from him, even just a piece of newspaper.

Maybe I'd better wait to ask, and risk him saying no, I thought. Perhaps he'd not mind too much. After all, he liked Tyrone. He'd like the idea of being picked for Miss Oliver's biography project. And Tyrone could return everything afterwards.

I stood there dithering, wondering what to do. Alfie got a bit bored, and stuck his nose into the open desk drawers, sorting through the papers himself.

'Alfie! Don't! You'll crumple them,' I said, panicking.

I bent down, pushed him away, and took out all the things he had rumpled, hoping I could smooth them out. Underneath, at the bottom of the drawer, I saw a phone.

It was like my new one, but a different colour. Was it another present for someone? I wondered. But it was already out of its box – it looked as if it had been used.

Why did Sean Godfrey have it hidden away in a drawer? He already had a phone, so why did he need this spare one? I picked it up, puzzled. I touched the screen and stared at the screensaver. His other phone

had a photo of Mum. This one just had a
deep blue sky scene. I touched the screen
again, and was asked for a password. I
wondered what Sean Godfrey's was.

I'd chosen mine carefully. It was 170830.
My birthday's on 17 January, Mum's is on 8
May, and Cam's is on 30 October. Birthdays are very
important in our family. It makes the number easy
for me to remember. I wondered when Sean Godfrey's
birthday was. Or had he chosen some other number
combination? What was important to him?

I looked up at a framed newspaper cutting with
the headline PREMIERSHIP SEAN! There was a big photo

of him leaping into the air in
triumph. Tyrone had told me all
about this match. According to him,
it was legendary. Sean Godfrey had
scored a hat-trick, and the third
goal meant that the team won the
Premier League.

I looked at the number 7 on his football shirt. I
squinted at the date on the newspaper: 2008. I tapped
in 372008 – but it didn't work. I tried reversing the 3
and the 7 – and the phone opened up! I felt like a
genius, though it had taken the simplest deduction.

I pressed the messages symbol. Then I stopped
dead, staring at the latest little box.

Hi, Big Guy! It's gr8 doing business with u, lol!
Ur the best. Better than the best. Luv and more,
ur bad girl J xxx

My hands started shaking. I scrolled upwards.
I saw Sean Godfrey's last message.

Ur one hot babe, my J. Can't wait to see you!
Ur S xxx

They were texting several times every day. Some
of the stuff they said made me feel sick. It was obvious
what was going on. She never used her full name, but
she had sent photos. I stared at her triumphant smile.
It was Justine Littlewood.

'Jess!' Mum came bursting into the study.
'I've been looking for you everywhere! What
on earth are you doing? You know you're
not allowed in here. What are all those
programmes doing jumbled up on the floor?
Alfie, leave! Jess, how could you? Sean will go nuts if
he finds out. Come and help clear it all up – don't just
stand there texting like a moron,' she said furiously.

I stood there helplessly, the words still dancing in
front of me. 'It's not my phone, Mum,' I mumbled.

'What? What's the matter? Why are you looking
so worried?'

I didn't know what to do. If I showed Mum those texts, she'd see for herself what Sean Godfrey was really like. But it would destroy her.

'Whose phone is it?' she asked.

I shook my head helplessly. I had a mad thought that I should hurl the phone out of the window so she couldn't see it, or dash it against the desk to break it, or run to the nearest loo to drown it . . . But Mum already had her hand on it. The photo of Justine Littlewood was still showing.

Mum looked at it. She flicked through the messages. Then she dropped the phone and sat down in a heap on the carpet.

'**M**UM? OH. MUM. I'm sorry,' I said. 'I wish wish wish I hadn't found the stupid phone.'

Mum said nothing. Her head was bent so I couldn't see her face.

'Please, Mum. Say something. Look, we don't know that all those stupid messages really mean anything.'

I knelt down and put my arm round her. She didn't cuddle into me. She didn't shrug me off. She just sat there, utterly lifeless. I put my head against hers and tried to tuck her curls behind her ears so I could see her face. She was crying. She wasn't making any

sound at all, but tears were slowly rolling down her cheeks.

'Mum! Don't cry! You never cry!' I said.

'I'm not crying. It's hay fever,' said Mum, in a tiny voice. Then she screwed up her face. 'That's what I always used to say when I howled back at the Dumping Ground. Especially when Justine Littlewood took my best friend Louise away. And now she's done it all over again. It's like I'm on a roundabout and I keep going round and round and everything repeats itself. I can't get off, no matter how hard I try.'

'But you like roundabouts, Mum,' I said stupidly.

'I thought I'd made it this time. I've mucked up so much. I didn't try hard enough at school, I've never had a proper job, I've never had a long-term relationship – not even with your dad – I've never been able to give you a nice home, I've just messed up royally time after time. Then I met Sean, and there I was, suddenly in cloud-cuckoo-land, believing it was all coming right at last. Only now it's all messed up again. What's the matter with me, Jess? What's the *matter* with me?' She clenched her fist and punched the end of the desk really hard.

'Mum! Stop it – you'll hurt your hand!' I grabbed hold of it. The knuckles were starting to bleed. I started to sob. 'Please don't! You're frightening me!'

'Oh, Jess! I'm sorry,' she said, wringing her poor hand.

'Don't punch the desk! What about punching Sean Godfrey instead?' I said.

'I'll punch Justine Littlewood! She obviously couldn't bear it when she saw the photo in the magazine and realized that everything had gone right for me at last. She had to come slinking along to take him away.'

'But he hasn't gone, Mum. He's still here. With you. And he's bought you a great big diamond engagement ring and he's going to marry you in a fairy-tale castle,' I said.

'No he's not,' said Mum. 'I'm leaving.'

'But what will we do?'

'We'll go back to Marlborough Tower. Thank goodness the council hasn't re-let it yet.'

'But what about Alfie?' I said desperately.

'Oh God, *Alfie*,' said Mum.

Alfie had been cowering in a corner, frightened by all the tears, but now he thought Mum was calling him. He came bounding up and gently licked her damp face.

'I can't bear it if I can't keep Alfie,' I said.

'You can keep him, Jess. We'll have to ask someone else to look after him – just for a few weeks until I get things sorted – but I'll find somewhere we can all live together, you, me and Alfie,' said Mum.

'But how?' I asked.

'I don't know yet, but I'll do it, I promise. I never break a promise to you, do I?' Mum stood up shakily and then pulled me up too. She dropped the phone with its horrible messages back in the drawer. Then she shoved all the programmes on top of it.

'Do you think I might have just one programme for Tyrone?' I asked.

'What? Here!' Mum thrust several at me. 'Take them!'

Rosalie was hovering in the hallway anxiously. She'd clearly been listening.

'Oh, Miss Tracy! Come and have another cup of tea,' she said sorrowfully.

'I don't think tea's going to help,' said Mum, but she went into the kitchen and let Rosalie make another pot of tea. Rosalie got out the cake tin too, but Mum shook her head.

'Give Jess some though,' she said.

Rosalie cut me a large slice of coffee-and-walnut. It was as creamy and moist and delicious as always, but it didn't seem to taste right any more. There was something wrong with my throat – I couldn't swallow.

'You're not really leaving, are you?' Rosalie said.

Mum nodded.

'Because Mr Sean's got some secret lady?'

'I wouldn't call her a lady.'

'It won't mean anything though. He can't help himself – he loves the ladies. But I've never seen him so happy with anyone as he is with you. He's like a little boy again. It's you he wants. The other one won't last five minutes. They never do. Can't you just ignore it?'

'I wish I could,' said Mum.'

'*I* would,' said Rosalie. 'It's not as if you're married yet. And when you are, Mr Sean might take his vows seriously. He's not a bad man at heart. He's just used to doing what he wants. All that money and fame from his football has gone to his head. He's made such a fuss of you too. Look at your ring! And the funny pink car. He adores you. You can ask for anything you want and he'll give you it, you know that.' She paused. 'Do you want to be poor again?'

Mum shook her head.

'And what about little Jess? And Mr Alfie dog? Don't go! It's been so good having you here, just like a proper family,' said Rosalie.

'That's all I've ever wanted for Jess,' Mum whispered.

'Think about it,' Rosalie begged, putting on her coat to go home. 'Please, Miss Tracy.'

'Please just call me Tracy.'

'I wish I could call you Mrs Sean,' said Rosalie.

She gave Mum a big hug, and then me.

It was very quiet in the kitchen when she'd gone. Mum sat at the table staring into space. I hauled Alfie onto my lap and held him tight. We waited. I licked my finger and dabbed at all the cake crumbs on my plate, counting them. I decided that if I ended up with an even number, we'd go. If it was an odd number, we'd stay. But there were too many crumbs and they all smeared into each other.

'What are you going to do, Mum?' I asked.

'I don't know,' she said.

We waited some more. Then Alfie started barking and jumped down off my lap. He'd heard Sean Godfrey running up the driveway. The front door opened, and I looked at Mum and she looked at me, and then Sean Godfrey burst through the kitchen door, grinning and sweaty, jogging on the spot now.

'There!' he puffed. 'I reckon I've made room for a massive chicken vindaloo now! I'll just have a shower. Why are you two looking so serious, eh? Go and put your glad rags on, girls!'

Mum shook her head. 'I don't think it's a good idea after all, Sean,' she mumbled.

'What's up? Don't you feel well, Trace?' He sat down beside Mum and peered at her face. 'You're very white. Have you got a headache, babe?'

'I'm not ill. I've had a shock.' Mum looked at me. 'Maybe you'd better go to your room, Jess. Take Alfie with you.'

'But, Mum—'

'Jess!'

So I went out, but I stayed in the hall, sitting cross-legged just the other side of the door, my arms round Alfie.

'What shock, Trace?' Sean Godfrey sounded so concerned. I wound my fingers through Alfie's fur, waiting for Mum's reply.

'I know about you and Justine,' she said, so quietly I barely heard her.

'What you on about?'

'You. And. Justine,' Mum said, much louder, spitting each word out.

'Well?' said Sean Godfrey. 'What about her?'

'You've been seeing her.'

'Yes. She came round the gym. And I invited her back here for a meal.'

'And you've been seeing her ever since,' Mum said.

'No I haven't. You're getting your knickers in a twist for nothing. I know you were a bit jealous of her that night, but there's no need to torture yourself imagining things, babe. I only have eyes for you – you know that.'

'The liar!' I whispered into Alfie's ear.

Mum called him something much worse. Then, 'Don't you dare take that tone with me. I *know* you've been seeing her.'

'You're so insecure, Trace. Remember you thought I was still seeing Sandy?'

'You're probably seeing *her* too. But this isn't about her. It's about Justine Littlewood. And what the hell makes you think I'm *jealous* of her?'

'Well, I don't know what she was like when she was a kid, but you have to admit she's quite a looker now. And a clever little business woman too. Shame you can't stand her – I fancy a line of her health and beauty products for the gym,' said Sean Godfrey.

'And you fancy her too,' said Mum.

'Here you go with those beady green eyes again! It's you I fancy, babe. Why can't you get it into that silly little noddle of yours?'

'Because my beady green eyes have read every disgusting message on that secret phone of yours.'

There was a tiny pause. I held Alfie so tightly he whimpered.

'You've been ferreting around in my study, reading my *phone*?' said Sean Godfrey. He sounded furious now. 'How could you be so despicable? And how did you know my password anyway?'

I swallowed hard.

'Any fool could work it out,' said Mum. 'And how dare you call *me* despicable? You've been seeing her ever since you brought her here! You have the cheek to act the Mr Nice Guy with Jess and me, and yet, now I've found you out, you make out it's somehow *my* fault!'

They went on and on yelling at each other, while I hung onto Alfie, shivering. I hated it when they were all lovey-dovey together – but this was far worse.

'You're a liar and a cheat, Sean. I can't bear it. I'm leaving you,' said Mum.

'Don't be stupid, Trace. We're getting married!'

'No we're not. Here!'

I knew what Mum was doing. She was pulling that big diamond off her ring finger and giving it back to him.

'Tracy, Tracy, Tracy. Don't be like this, babe,' said Sean Godfrey, wheedling now. 'OK, hands up, I had a little fling with Justine. It was all her doing. I'd have had to be a man of steel to resist her. But it was totally meaningless, babe – surely you can see that. *She* doesn't mean anything to me. *You* mean all the world.'

'And you meant all the world to me,' said Mum. 'I thought you were the man of my dreams.'

'And I still am! Look, I never dreamed you'd be so straight-laced about one little fling. You should see some of my football pals! You've given me the grief – now I'll make it up to you. We'll put it behind us, eh?'

'I can't,' said Mum. 'Perhaps if it was any other girl ... but you had to go and choose Justine Littlewood. If you can't see why that hurts so much, then you're more of a fool than I thought. I'm leaving, I tell you.'

'Then *you're* the fool, Tracy Beaker,' said Sean Godfrey. 'Go on then, get out. Go back to your grotty little flat and your sad little life, Miss Nobody.'

There was the sound of a very hard slap – and then Mum came rushing out of the door. I caught a glimpse of Sean Godfrey looking dazed, one side of his face bright red.

'Come on, Jess,' said Mum. 'We're getting our things.'

We got the laundry bags from the back of the cupboard and started packing. We didn't stop to search for bubble wrap – we simply wrapped the Mickey Mouse alarm clock and the china dogs and the Toby jugs and all the other breakables in our clothes. Then I pulled the mother-and-daughter picture out of the wardrobe. Alfie kept circling us, whimpering, wondering what on earth was going on.

When we dragged everything downstairs, we found Sean Godfrey in the sitting room, drinking a glass of whisky.

'We're off now,' said Mum. 'I'll phone for a taxi.'

'For pity's sake, Trace, use your car,' said Sean Godfrey.

'I'm not taking it. It's not mine any more.'

'Look, you idiot, I don't want that ancient piece of pink metal, and I can't see anyone else being mug enough to take it either. If you don't keep it, it'll just get crunched in the scrapyard.' Sean Godfrey took another gulp of his drink.

'All right. I'll take it. Thank you,' said Mum. She paused. 'Thank you for everything, Sean.'

He didn't answer her, so we left. I didn't say goodbye to him, and I held Alfie on a tight lead so he couldn't either. But as Mum started up the car he came running out.

'Trace! Stop this nonsense! I can't believe you're really going through with it!' he shouted.

'I can't believe it either,' said Mum. 'But I am.'

'Well, don't think you can come crawling back in a couple of days when you come to your senses. You drive away now and that's it. Finished. For ever. No one turns their back on Sean Godfrey.'

'And no one cheats on Tracy Beaker, especially not with Justine Slimebag Littlewood,' said Mum, putting her foot down on the accelerator.

'Good for you, Mum,' I said as we drove off. I waited a few seconds. 'Where are we going?'

'Home.'

'But—'

'We'll smuggle Alfie in somehow. Even if someone reports us, it'll be a while before the council sends one of their snippy letters. And by that time we'll be gone. Starting our new life,' said Mum.

'Right,' I said. I wished she would say what our new life was going to be. It felt like we'd jumped off a cliff, Mum and Alfie and me, and were frantically running through thin air like cartoon characters, not sure where we were going to land.

The Duke Estate looked grimmer than ever. Someone had spray-painted more tags all around Marlborough Tower. There was another old stained mattress dumped on the asphalt, and the rubbish chutes were blocked, so reeking plastic bags spilled their contents everywhere. Our old car was still in its place, but they'd sprayed tags on that too, and stolen

331

all four wheels. Mum said a few very rude words about the kids who'd done it and then looked at me.

'You didn't hear that, did you, Jess?'

'Good job you kept the Cadillac, Mum,' I said.

'I'm not leaving it here five minutes,' said Mum. 'I'll take our stuff up, and you and Alfie stay here to guard the car, and then we'll go and park it somewhere safe and walk back, OK?'

Mum staggered off with the bags and disappeared into the lift. Lots of kids came up, gawping at the Cadillac.

'What sort of car's that then, Jess Beaker?'

'It's a Barbie Doll car!'

They all laughed. How dare they mock Mum's dream car!

'Get them, Alfie,' I hissed.

Alfie didn't understand. He stood up on his seat, tail wagging, trying to lick them, desperate to make friends.

'Come to gloat over us, have you? Slumming it for five minutes before you go back to your posh mansion, eh?'

I was shocked at how horrid they were – and a little bit scared. Very scared, actually. Especially when one of the big boys got out a knife. It was only a penknife, but it could still do a lot of harm.

'Shall I write your mum's name on it for her?' he said, grinning.

'You make one scratch and I'll punch your teeth in,' I said, as fiercely as I could.

That made them all laugh, because the boy was twice my size. I sat up as tall as I could and screwed my face up in a scowl, my fists clenched, though I was actually very nearly wetting myself. Then I heard a chorus of 'Hey, Jess!' and it was Tyrone and his gang from Devonshire Tower come to see what was going on.

'Oh, Tyrone!' I called, thrilled to see him.

Even the biggest boy on our block was wary of Tyrone. They backed away uneasily, pretending they'd just remembered they had some place else to be.

'What you doing back here then? Hey, Alfie, boy! Good dog! That's right, lick me all over, I could do with a little wash,' said Tyrone, laughing. He stroked the shiny pink of the Cadillac regretfully. 'What on earth was your mum thinking, choosing this old wreck? You gonna take me for a spin in it then, Jess?'

'Ha ha,' I said.

'Tell you what – I'll take *you* for one,' he offered, jumping into the driver's seat.

'No! You can't drive for starters!' I said.

'I know how. And any fool can steer. We won't go very fast, just round the block. No one will know,' he said.

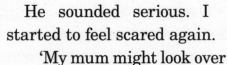

He sounded serious. I started to feel scared again. 'My mum might look over the balcony and see us and she'd go mad,' I said, truthfully enough.

'Well, maybe we'd better stay put,' said Tyrone. 'Is Sean with her? Hey, guess what, Jess – he says I'm his lucky discovery. Truly. I get to stay at the club half an hour longer than the others, and he gives me special intensive training. He does, I'm not kidding. Isn't he fantastic?'

'No,' I said shortly.

'Yes he is!'

'No he's *not*! He's a pig,' I insisted.

'You'd better not let your mum hear you say that – especially as Sean's going to be your stepdad soon!'

'No he's not.'

'Yes he *is*. He told me he was getting married in

this big castle place, see. He tells me all sorts of things. It's like we're mates,' said Tyrone, beaming.

'Well, next time you see him, your mate Sean Godfrey will drop you a hint that he's *not* getting married in a big castle after all. Not to my mum anyway,' I said.

'So where are they getting married then?' Tyrone asked. 'Are they going to have a beach wedding?'

'They're not having *any* wedding. They're not together any more. They've split up,' I said.

'*What?*' Tyrone exclaimed, and there was a little explosion of *what-what-what*s from the gang of boys surrounding the Cadillac.

'It's no big deal,' I said. 'Mum's much better off without him.'

'So he's dumped her.' Tyrone looked appalled. 'I thought it was too good to last. I mean, he's Sean Godfrey, and he's been out with TV stars and models. He could have anyone. I mean, your mum's OK, but it's not like she's special.'

'Yes she is! She's ever so special! Sean Godfrey was blooming lucky to get her! Only she's gone off him now. *She's* dumped *him*!' I declared.

'*Never!*' said Tyrone, and all the gang *never-never-never*ed like a stupid chorus.

'Look, shut up, you lot!' I said. 'Sean Godfrey's a big flash pig and we're heaps better off without him.'

'Tracy Beaker dumped *Sean Godfrey*? Has she gone crazy!' said Tyrone, screwing his finger into the side of his head to indicate loopiness. 'He *must* have dumped her. I bet he's got some other woman.' He saw me flinch. 'He *has*, hasn't he!'

'OK, he's been seeing someone else, who just happens to be my mum's worst enemy.'

'Who's that then? I reckon she's got a lot to choose from,' said Piotr, and they all sniggered.

'Just clear off, the lot of you!' I said, fighting back tears.

'Yeah, scram!' said Tyrone, looking fierce. 'It does my head in the way you hang around me all the time. Go on, get lost!'

They backed away, looking disgruntled.

'He just wants to be with his tatty little *girlfriend*,' said one, and they all made stupid kissing noises.

'Take no notice of them,' Tyrone told me.

'I'm not your girlfriend,' I said. 'As if!'

Tyrone looked hurt. 'No need to be so huffy! Especially as I've been sticking up for you!'

'Sorry,' I said, craning round to look at the lift entrance, wishing Mum would hurry up.

'So what's your mum going to do about it?' Tyrone asked anxiously.

'What do you mean?'

'To get him back!'

'She's not going to do anything. She doesn't *want* him back, not now,' I said.

'Then she's mad,' said Tyrone.

'No she's not! Don't you dare say she's mad!'

'But she *is*. It's obvious. You could live in that fantastic house with the pool and everything and have whatever you wanted – or live in this dump. Come *on*, Jess! It's not fair on you, is it?'

'Yes it is. It's what I want. You just shut up about it,' I said.

'And it's not fair on me,' Tyrone persisted. 'Sean Godfrey only started taking me to his club because I'm friends with you. And now he won't bother. And it was so great.' He sounded so sad that Alfie nudged up against him and started licking him sympathetically. 'And that's another thing. You'll have to send Alfie back to Battersea.'

'No I won't. Mum says we're going to find a way to keep him,' I said.

'And you believe her?' Tyrone asked.

'*Yes!*' I said, though my voice wavered.

At last Mum came out of the lift. When she got nearer I saw that her eyes were red.

'Hey, Tracy Beaker. I'm sorry about Sean. Jess told me all about it. But maybe he'll take you back if you play your cards right,' said Tyrone.

337

Mum glared at him. So did I.

'Hop it, kid.' Mum used the voice that makes you do what she says, pronto.

Tyrone scrambled out of the car. Mum got in and switched on the ignition.

'That's it – go back to him,' said Tyrone.

'We're not going back, are we?' I asked Mum as we drove off.

'No, we're not. I *said*, we're just going to park the car somewhere safer, that's all,' she said. 'Away from all these no-good kids.'

It was hard to find anywhere. We had to drive all the way up to the park and leave it there, and even then Mum kept looking back anxiously. Alfie had a sniff of the grass and trees, and tugged desperately at his lead, wanting to explore.

'Could he have just a little walk, Mum?' I asked.

'All right,' she said.

So we wandered around the park. I didn't dare let Alfie off his lead because he still didn't always understand about coming back to me. I had to run quite quickly to keep up with him. We zig-zagged in and out of trees and dived under bushes while Mum trudged along behind us.

'You OK, Mum?' I asked stupidly.

'Not really,' she said. She was crying again.

I stood still, so Alfie had to stop abruptly too.

'Mum – Mum, I'm so sorry,' I said. 'It's all my fault, isn't it? I should never have looked at Sean Godfrey's phone, and then you wouldn't have known about him and Justine, and we'd be having supper out with him, and you'd still be fine.'

'Of course it's not your fault, Jess. I'd have found out sooner or later,' Mum said wearily. 'Supper! We haven't got any food in at the flat.'

'Can we have fish and chips then?' I asked.

'I suppose so,' said Mum.

'Alfie likes fish,' I said. 'He can share mine. We can buy him some proper dog food tomorrow, can't we?'

Mum nodded.

'It's going to be all right, Mum, isn't it?' I said, putting my arm round her. 'You *said*.'

'Yes,' she said, though she didn't sound at all sure.

I HOPED THAT WHEN we were back in our cosy flat
we would feel better. But somehow it didn't feel cosy
any more. For a start it was so small. We'd got used to
Sean Godfrey's spacious rooms. It was almost as if
the flat had shrunk. Something had happened to the
furniture too. Had it always been quite so shabby?
Had the sofa always sagged so badly? Had the table
always been so scratched and stained?

And what was the matter with the walls? We'd
always had a damp patch on the ceiling, but it seemed
to have spread, and there were little black dots of
mould everywhere. The windowsills were stained and
the doors were stiff and wouldn't shut properly. Half
the posters and drawings we'd Blu-Tacked to the walls

had slipped, and either hung at drunken angles or lay crumpled on the floor.

Mum and I stood holding hands, breathing heavily. The flat smelled mouldy. Alfie padded around the flat warily, and then bounded back to my side, giving little enquiring woofs. It was clear as day he was asking when we were going home. He didn't know that this *was* home.

'Oh God,' said Mum.

'It'll look better when we put all our ornaments back,' I said.

'The whole place will have to be scrubbed from top to bottom. We ought to open all the windows too, but it's so *cold*.'

It was a lovely spring evening, but somehow it felt like the dead of winter. Mum switched on the electric fire, and then found two plates and a couple of forks.

'We'd better eat our fish and chips before *they* go cold too,' she said. She switched on the television 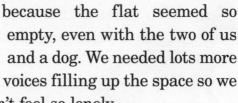 because the flat seemed so empty, even with the two of us and a dog. We needed lots more voices filling up the space so we didn't feel so lonely.

We ate the fish and chips, and Mum made us a mug of tea, though we had to have it black because we hadn't bought any milk. We warmed up a little.

'I suppose I'd better get started on the cleaning,' said Mum wearily, but she flopped on the sofa instead.

I flopped beside her, and then Alfie came and nestled up to me. At last it started to feel cosier.

'Maybe I'll do the cleaning first thing tomorrow,' said Mum, putting hot-water bottles in our beds to air them.

I went into Mum's bed anyway, and Alfie lay on a cushion at the end. I was so worried about him. I'd sneaked him out after dark so he could have a wee. I told him over and over again that he had to be quiet, but he was so happy to get out of the flat he started barking joyously, and when the grumpy old man at the end of our balcony peered out, Alfie lifted his leg and watered an empty KFC carton left near the rubbish chute.

'Filthy beast! I'm telling the

council you've got a dog, Jess Beaker. Dogs aren't allowed, you know that,' the man said.

'Please don't tell! He's only here for a little while. I promise I won't let him wee all over the place any more,' I gabbled, but he wouldn't listen.

'Alfie, you have to learn to be *quiet*,' I said – but he barked in the lift, he barked running around Marlborough Tower, and he did three more wees and a poo.

I did my best to clean up after him, but several ladies from the ground floor leaned out of their windows and shouted at us. I didn't understand their language, but it was plain they'd seen and were complaining bitterly.

It was no use getting cross with Alfie for being noisy and making a mess. He couldn't help it. He was a dog, and all dogs behave like that. He just seemed a bit noisier and messier than most. And try as I might to keep him a secret, it looked as if quite a lot of people would be emailing the council about him.

In the middle of the night he started whimpering in his sleep – just tiny noises, and I knew he was probably just dreaming of chasing squirrels – but the sad sound broke my heart. I crawled carefully out of bed, worried about waking Mum because she'd been tossing and turning, and it had taken her a very long time to fall asleep. I scrunched up really small and lay down on the cushion with Alfie, curling myself right round him. He licked my hand happily, squirmed into the comfiest position possible and went back to sleep. *I* wasn't at all comfortable, but Alfie had stopped whimpering. It was cold without any covers, but Alfie was as warm as a hot-water bottle so I cuddled him close.

Perhaps I whimpered in my dreams too because much later I woke up to find Mum tucking the duvet over me and then stroking my hair.

'Go back to sleep, darling,' she whispered.

'Sing to me, Mum,' I begged sleepily. She always used to sing when I couldn't sleep.

'Baby,' she teased, but she quietly sang all my favourites: 'How Much Is That Doggie in the Window?', 'Hound Dog' and 'Who Let the Dogs Out?'

I drifted off to sleep. When I woke up again, I could hardly move because I was so stiff. I had to shuffle to the bathroom like a little old woman. Mum was already up and washed and dressed, sitting at the table with a mug of black coffee, tapping away on her phone.

'You're not texting Sean Godfrey, are you?' I asked.

'No! I'm texting Cam to let her know we're back

here,' said Mum. 'And I'm asking if she'll have Alfie today, while I go job hunting. I've checked our bank account and we're OK for a bit, but I need to start earning now. Still, we'll manage, you'll see. Come here, sweetheart, let me give those shoulders a rub.'

I wriggled as Mum massaged me. She soothed most of the outside aches, but she couldn't make all the knots of worry inside unravel. I hadn't thought about money.

'Maybe you should have kept your diamond ring. It was probably worth a lot of money.'

'Yep, I could have sold it and had enough money to keep us going for ages,' said Mum. 'I've still got the keys to Sean's house. Shall I sneak back and grab it?'

'Yes, do it!' I said – but she was only joking.

'No, we're going to manage by ourselves,' she said. 'Right, let's make you and Alfie some breakfast. It'll be a bit weird because I haven't been to the shops yet.'

It was actually quite a good breakfast. I had dry cornflakes because we didn't have any milk, but Mum let me sprinkle raisins on them for a treat. Then she found a tin of peaches and shared them with me.

'I'm not having my girl going to school hungry,' she said.

She didn't let her Alfie go hungry either. At the back of the cupboard she found an old can of mince and gave him a few spoonfuls. Alfie was very appreciative and wolfed it down quickly.

'He loves it, Mum! Could he have a little bit more?' I asked.

'No, that's enough for now. I'll make a cottage pie for our supper with the rest. We have to be dead economical until I get a job.'

'Can't you just go back to looking after Ava and Alice?' I asked.

'I texted Marina earlier,' said Mum, 'but she said she was ever so sorry but she wanted to keep Marie-Thérèse now.'

'That's so mean when you had the job first!' I said. '*And* you're her friend.'

'She tried to be kind. She offered me some money to keep me going.'

'Did you say yes?'

'No, of course not! We don't need anyone else to keep us going, Jess. We're Beakers. We're going to stand proud and be independent,' said Mum.

I didn't feel I was standing proud when I went into school. My legs were so wobbly I wasn't sure they could support me. Everyone was staring – they all knew already. Some were nudging each other and whispering stuff about me, their eyes gleaming. Some looked concerned, and several of the girls actually came and put their arms round me. That was somehow worse.

'It's OK,' I kept saying. 'We're fine. It's good to be back home. It wasn't that great at Sean Godfrey's.'

They rolled their eyes pityingly, not believing a word of it.

Even Miss Oliver knew. Maybe Cam had texted her. She didn't say much, but she patted me lightly on the shoulder as she walked past my desk, and at lunchtime she beckoned me over for a little word.

'How are you doing, Jess?' she asked.

'I'm fine, Miss Oliver,' I said.

'That's good. And Mum?'

'She's fine too. She's going to sort everything out and show Sean Godfrey that we're fine without him.'

'I'm sure she will. She's a woman of great character, your mum,' said Miss Oliver.

She looked out for me in the playground too. The other kids kept going on about Sean Godfrey, asking why he'd broken it off with Mum.

'He didn't! *She* dumped *him*!' I insisted, but they wouldn't believe me.

Tyrone still didn't believe me either, which was dead irritating seeing as he was supposed to be my friend. He went on and on about Sean Godfrey until my ears shrivelled at the sound of his voice.

'Will you *stop* it!' I burst out, and ran off to the Peace Garden. I sat on the bench by myself, wondering how Mum was getting on. I was worrying about Alfie too, though I knew Cam would make a fuss of him. I was missing him dreadfully. I tried to summon up Wolfie and Faithful and Pom-Pom and Snapchat for comfort, but they wouldn't come alive properly. They were pale shadows of themselves, scarcely visible in the sunlight. I tried whistling their magic tune. That had always made them come running, but now they stayed as still as statues, not a bark, not a lick from any of them.

'That's a pretty tune,' said Miss Oliver, coming into the garden and sitting down beside me. 'I didn't know you could whistle, Jess.'

'Mum taught me,' I said. 'I can do a wolf-whistle too. Want to hear it?'

'Maybe not just now,' she said.

We didn't say very much more, but it was comforting sitting together all the same. I wasn't the slightest bit scared of Miss Oliver now. You can't really be in awe of anyone once you've seen them in their swimsuit.

Mum was late coming to collect me. Not just five minutes late – more like fifteen. I stood there by the school gate, nibbling the skin on my bottom lip, wondering where she was. What else had gone wrong? Had Alfie run away? Had our flat been vandalized as well as our old car? Had Mum gone back to Sean Godfrey?

I fidgeted from one foot to the other, banging my thighs with my clenched fists. I closed my eyes and counted to a hundred, but when I looked at the road again, I couldn't see the Cadillac. What if Mum had had an accident? Maybe she'd started crying again and her eyes were too blurry to see properly and she'd smashed the car.

My tummy was so tight and painful I had to bend over.

'Jess?' Miss Oliver was standing beside me.

'My tummy hurts,' I said, straightening up gingerly.

'You poor thing. Try taking a few deep breaths.'

'Mum's late,' I said, sucking in my breath.

'Breathe through your nose, not your mouth! Don't worry, I'm sure she'll be fine. She's probably just got held up in traffic.'

And just as Miss Oliver was saying this I saw a gleam of pink in the distance. I breathed in, I breathed out, my tummy unknotted, and Mum drew up beside us.

She was looking anxious. 'I'm so sorry, Jess. Was she getting in a state, Miss Oliver? I know I shouldn't park here, but I needed to get to her as soon as possible.'

'That's all right, Ms Beaker – Tracy. I was just keeping Jess company.' Miss Oliver paused. 'I'm sorry things didn't work out,' she added softly.

'Oh well,' said Mum, shrugging. 'That's life. You're dancing along on a gold pavement, and then suddenly – whoops – there's the banana skin.'

'I'm sure you'll be dancing again soon,' said Miss Oliver. 'You and Jess, doing your own two-step.'

I didn't quite follow all this dancing stuff, but they smiled at each other.

'Thanks for staying with Jess anyway, Miss Oliver,' said Mum.

'I'm Mary out of school,' she said.

'Thanks, Mary,' said Mum, and she nodded at Miss Oliver, while I blinked in surprise.

'Are you making friends with Miss Oliver, Mum?' I asked when we drove off.

'Looks like it,' she said.

'She's Cam's friend as well.'

'I know. Cam told me.'

'She's my friend too. Out of school.'

'Hey, guess what, Jess,' said Mum. 'I've got a job already! I told you I would, didn't I?'

'Oh, Mum, you're brilliant! What is it?'

'It's not *that* brilliant. I'm going to be working in a café near the bus station – it's called the Silver Spoon. As opposed to Greasy. I went there for a cup of coffee at lunchtime, as I'd been all round the shopping centre looking for jobs without any luck at all. It was a bit humiliating really. One clothes shop was advertising for an assistant – and this girl half my age looked me up and down and said, "Oh dear, I don't think you're really the right type for this sort of work."'

'What a cheek!' I said loyally.

'Well, she's probably right,' said Mum. 'I tried two shoe shops and a Waterstones and a Paperchase, with no luck, and then I started tramping the High Street. I saw an advert on the back of a bus saying they needed more drivers, and I thought it might be cool to be a bus driver – but when I went to the station they said that once I'd been trained I'd have to do shift work, and I explained I couldn't do that with a child at home. So then I felt a bit fed up and went to the café, and they were rushed off their feet, and I said to the old guy behind the counter that it looked like they needed more staff, and what about taking me on. And he has, just like that! That's why I'm so late picking you up – I've been working the last three hours! They've taken me on for a month's trial. The money's not great, but it'll keep us going – and I dare say I'll get a few leftover sandwiches to take home for our tea.'

'And leftover cake?' I asked hopefully. 'Oh, Mum, well done!'

Cam gave Mum a big hug when we got to her place. She gave me a hug too. We sat on the sofa, one on either side of her, and she put an arm round each of us.

'My girls,' she said.

'Oh, Cam,' said Mum. 'Do you think I'm crazy leaving Sean?'

'No, I think *he's* the crazy one, playing around behind your back.'

'I've got a job in a café,' said Mum, 'but the hours are eight till four. How will I manage with Jess and school? And what about Alfie? I can't take him to the café, and the council are going to come after us soon anyway, because we're not allowed pets – but it will break Jess's heart if we can't keep him.'

'Yes, it will,' I said, and I clutched Alfie close. I had a tight pain in my chest, as if my heart had started cracking already.

'Hey, stop the wailing, you two,' said Cam. 'You know perfectly well we'll get everything sorted out. Perhaps there's a breakfast club at Jess's school. And some kind of homework club? I'll look after Alfie. He's been no trouble at all today. Well, apart from a little accident. And a sneaky bite of my cheese and onion pasty. Still, he made our sad Rosie laugh, and that was marvellous.'

'You're a star, Cam,' said Mum.

'That's ever so kind of you, Cam – but he would still be *my* dog, wouldn't he?' I asked.

'Of course. I'll just be his foster mum. I'm good at that,' she said.

I hung onto Alfie as long as I could, but when the dreaded letter from the council came saying we were in breach of our tenancy and had to get rid of our dog, I packed his cushion and ball and tuggy toy and all his food, and we took him to Cam's.

I cried all the way home, though I knew I was going to see him the very next day. It was all fixed. After school Mum took me to Cam's, and I made a gigantic fuss of Alfie, and then took him for a long walk and gave him his supper.

'You do know you're still *my* dog, Alfie?' I said.

353

Alfie bounded round me and licked my knees to show me that of course he knew.

I didn't go to the breakfast club, even though Mum had to drop me off at school at half past seven. I went to my own *private* breakfast club with Miss Oliver! She always liked to come into school early to prepare all her lessons, so I sat in the classroom with her. I helped tidy the stationery cupboard, and sharpen all the crayons, and check that the library books were in alphabetical order, and feed Sweetcorn, the class hamster. Then Miss Oliver made a cup of tea for both of us, and we had marmalade sandwiches, just like Paddington.

During class time Miss Oliver was my teacher, but before school she was my friend, and on Sunday morning, while Mum was having a lie-in, I went swimming with Miss Oliver and Cam.

Tyrone jeered at me for being a teacher's pet, but I didn't care. We weren't really friends any more now – he just went on about Sean Godfrey all the time, which was really annoying.

'Can't you get it into your head that I can't stick Sean Godfrey?' I said. 'And neither can my mum. We're *much* better off without him.'

'You're mad, Jess Beaker,' said Tyrone. 'Sean says you're mad too, you and Tracy Beaker. He says he's better off without *you*. Sean's my mate now. He calls me Buddy. He doesn't call any of the other boys that.'

It was probably because Sean Godfrey couldn't remember his real name, but I was pleased to hear that Tyrone still went to his club. However, that didn't mean I wanted to hear him showing off about it all the time.

Fred and Margie at the Silver Spoon wanted Mum to work on Saturdays too. I went to Cam's, where I could spend all day with Alfie, and that was bliss. Alfie followed me around everywhere. He even insisted on coming into the loo with me. He made it plain that he was OK living with Cam and the girls, but he'd much, much rather be with me.

But then, the next Saturday, Miss Oliver asked Cam if she'd like to join her at her rambling club.

'Rambling?' said Mum. 'With a lot of old folk with bobble hats and socks outside their trousers and pointy sticks?'

'Yes, and when I get my own pointy stick I'll give you a good poke with it,' said Cam. 'OK, OK, don't tease. I just fancied the idea, that's all.'

'I don't think it's the rambling you fancy,' said Mum, and Cam went pink.

'We were thinking Jess and Alfie could come too. It'll be too far for Jess – they walk all day – but we could come home on the bus at lunchtime.'

'No, Jess can come to the Silver Spoon with me.

She can be our Saturday girl. Margie won't mind, she loves kids,' said Mum, 'but she draws the line at dogs.'

So on Saturday Alfie went off hiking with Cam and Miss Oliver, and I went to the Silver Spoon with Mum.

'You don't mind Jess, do you? She's a good little kid and great at helping out,' said Mum. 'She can butter the bread for the sandwiches and spread the fillings and do a bit of waitressing. She never spills anything.'

'What a little love!' said Margie, giving me a hug. 'Look at you! Spitting image of your mum. You've even got her lovely curly hair.'

I decided I liked Margie. She was an old lady with a flowery apron over her jumper and trousers. Her own hair was rather thin and straggly, but she wore a lot of bright red lipstick to look cheerful.

I didn't like Fred anywhere near as much. He could wear all the lipstick in the world and he'd never look cheerful. He was small and thin, with a frowny, pinched face. He frowned even more when he peered at me.

'She can't help out. Child labour's not allowed. We'll be reported to Health and Safety,' he said.

'Well, OK, she can sit at a table and read

a book or do some drawing,' said Mum. 'She's brought a satchel of stuff with her.'

'Oh, the pet!' said Margie.

'Tables are for customers,' said Fred.

'Well, Jess can be a blooming customer,' said Mum, starting to get angry. 'I'll buy her a cup of tea every hour – how about that?'

'It's still not right. You can't take a kiddie in to work with you.'

'Well, I have, so you'll have to put up with it.'

'You watch your tone, Tracy. You're only here on trial, you know.'

'Lighten up, Fred,' said Margie. 'Little Jess won't be no trouble.'

I tried to squash myself into a corner and look harmless. I was scared Fred might sack Mum on the spot and it would all be my fault. None of the customers seemed to mind me being there. Margie had a little cluster of regulars, mostly old ladies like her, and they made a beeline for my little table at the back and talked to me. One of them even insisted on buying me a big jam doughnut.

When I didn't have anyone to talk to I read *The Hundred and One Dalmatians*, and then I did some drawing. I copied one of the Dalmatian pictures – though I didn't attempt a hundred and one of them. Next I drew Alfie running, Alfie sitting up and begging, Alfie lying on his back, Alfie asleep. I hoped he wasn't getting tired out on his long ramble.

By this time I was getting a bit tired of drawing, so I just sat and watched people. I liked seeing Mum dashing around chatting to the customers as she served them. She was very popular with the bus drivers when they popped in for a fry-up and a cup of tea. She was always quick with the banter – and she piled their plates up high: three rashers, two eggs, two sausages, fried tomatoes, baked beans, black pudding and hash browns. They cheered when they saw their plates – but Fred frowned.

'You're giving them far too much!' he growled to Mum.

'But if they feel their plateful's good value, they'll keep coming back, and they'll tell their mates too,' said Mum.

She was great with the mums when they came in with their huge buggies. She always made a fuss of the babies and todd-lers, and was happy to warm up their food from home. She slipped the children free toasted soldiers to keep them quiet while their mums drank their coffee and shared a chocolate brownie.

'They take up half the caff and sit there nattering a full hour or more for the price of two coffees and one cake,' Fred complained. 'Where's the profit in that, Tracy Beaker?'

'Quit nagging her, Fred, she's doing a grand job,' said Margie – but she wasn't too happy when Mum started chatting to all her old lady friends, refilling their teapots for nothing and letting them show her photos of their grandchildren.

'It's lovely that she's such a friendly person, but I'm having to do most of the serving here while she's sitting down with Susan and Kath and Marilyn,' Margie murmured to Fred.

I signalled to Mum, but she just winked at me, happy to be so popular. I tried not to worry, and wandered over to the window to distract myself. I started counting all the passers-by, but there were far too many – people dashing to and fro to catch buses, and ladies hurrying towards the shopping centre. So many ladies – in jeans and T-shirts and denim jackets, in loose tops and leggings, in smart suits and kitten heels, in slinky dresses and stilettos . . . A lady with ultra-styled hair, a slinky dress showing off her figure, and high heels that made her wiggle as she walked. I blinked behind my glasses. I knew that lady. I'd seen her before. It was Justine Littlewood.

'Who are you staring at, Jess?' Mum asked, rushing past with a fry-up in either hand.

'Oh, no one in particular,' I said quickly.

But Mum was looking through the window herself now. With a flick of her fancy hair, Justine Littlewood turned her head and saw us standing there, staring out. For a moment she looked shocked. Then she started smiling. She stood there, hands on her hips, shaking her head. She looked Mum up and down, clearly taking in her shiny face and tousled hair, her apron, the two fry-ups. She mouthed one word at Mum. *Loser.*

There was a crash. Two crashes, as both plates of food landed on the floor, tomatoes and baked beans and egg yolk spraying our legs. I'm not sure Mum even noticed she'd dropped them. She ran outside, though I yelled at her to come back. She ran right up to Justine Littlewood, who took a couple of steps backwards, looking alarmed. She wasn't quick enough.

Mum's leg shot out and up. Her foot flew through the air. Justine Littlewood wobbled in her high heels and landed slap-bang on her bottom. Mum's kick-boxing classes hadn't been in vain.

FRED SAID MUM had to go right that minute. He said he didn't want members of his staff brawling with the general public, thank you very much.

'It's not Mum's fault. That lady is her worst enemy – she stole her fiancé,' I explained, but he wouldn't listen.

Fred counted out Mum's small wage packet in an insulting fashion and thrust it at her. 'Come on, get out of here, and take your bratty daughter with you,' he said.

When we got outside, both of us bright red in the face, Justine Littlewood came tottering up.

'I've dialled 999! I'm going to have you for assault, Tracy Beaker. I've got witnesses, haven't I?' She

appealed to various gawping passers-by. 'They all saw you attack me. It's a wonder I didn't break my legs. I'm going to A and E to get myself X-rayed, just to make sure. As it is I'm going to be bruised all over! In fact, I bet the police will go for grievous bodily harm. How *dare* you!'

'Just shut your face, you scheming little toad,' said Mum, taking my hand. 'Come on, Jess.'

'I didn't have to scheme much! Sean just fell into my arms,' Justine Littlewood called after us. 'He's so glad to be rid of you – do you know that? We're blissfully happy, him and me. *And* we're going into business together. I've made a success of my life, Tracy Beaker. It looks like you've messed things up every which way. Loser! *Loser!*'

I felt Mum twitch. 'Come away, Mum. Please please please don't kick her again!' I begged, pulling at her. 'Quick, before a policeman comes! Oh, Mum, don't get arrested!'

Mum saw that I was frantic so she let me lead her away, while Justine Littlewood screamed abuse after us.

'Hurry, Mum!' I kept urging her.

'She won't have called the police. She's just bluffing. And I didn't kick her, I didn't even touch her – she just fell over because she lost her balance. I wish to goodness I *had* kicked her now,' Mum said furiously, but she kept pace with me.

All the way home I was terrified the police were after us. I couldn't even relax when we were in the car because it was so terribly distinctive. I kept hearing sirens behind us. We had to leave the car miles away from the Duke Estate. As we were trudging along the pavement I heard a wailing noise coming along the road.

'Oh, Mum! Run! Let's hide in the park! *Quick!*' I yelled.

'It's not the police, Jess, it's an ambulance. See? It's OK,' she said.

I breathed out so hard I felt dizzy.

'Here.' Mum took my bag and gave me a quick hug. 'I'm sorry, Jess. I didn't mean to frighten you so. I'm a terrible mother.'

'No you're not, you're the best mother in the world,' I insisted.

I went on saying it when we were back in our flat, but Mum couldn't seem to take it in. She sat on the sofa and kept shaking her head.

'She called me a loser, Jess. And she's right. I *am* a loser. I've made a mess of everything. I've never had a proper job or relationship. I always thought the one thing I could be proud of was being a good mum – and then I go scaring you to death every time I lose my temper,' she said.

'It's not your fault you've got Anger Issues, Mum. It's because *you* didn't have a proper mum looking after you,' I said, sitting beside her.

'Neither did Justine. And Sean certainly didn't have a proper mum. Yet they've both made a big success of their lives. It's just me,' said Mum, and she hid her face in her hands.

She stayed sad no matter how hard I tried to cheer her up. She got a Monday-to-Friday job in a big coffee shop straight away, but she didn't like it because she had to make coffees all day and didn't get a chance to talk to the customers.

'But it's a job. And I get paid, even though it's a pittance,' she said.

She tried to be friends with the girls who worked there, but they were both in their teens and very giggly.

'They're OK, but they treat me like I'm an old lady,' said Mum. 'I suppose I am in their eyes.'

'Don't be daft, Mum. You're still young. Well, young*ish*,' I said. 'You look young anyway.'

'No I don't. I look like an old bag,' she said.

She wasn't looking that great actually. All her sparkle had gone. She was very pale and she was getting thinner, so that her T-shirts hung off her and her jeans were baggy round the bottom. Even her hair lost its spring and drooped limply.

'Tell you what,' said Cam when we paid our daily visit to Alfie. 'How would you like to go to a spa and have a lovely massage? I went with Mary – I thought I'd hate it but it was absolute heaven. You could get your hair done and your nails painted.'

Cam was certainly looking great.

'It's not my sort of thing,' said Mum. 'And however much would it cost?'

'I'm not sure. Mary paid for me. But it could be my birthday treat to you.'

'No thanks,' said Mum.

'So what *would* you like for your birthday?' Cam persisted.

'I'm not bothering with my birthday this year.'

'Don't be daft – you always love it when it's your birthday,' said Cam. 'What shall we do next Saturday? Shall I throw you a party?'

'Oh yes!' I said.

'Oh no!' said Mum. 'And don't even *think* of a surprise party, because the surprise will be the birthday girl walking straight out. How many times do I have to say it? I'm ignoring all birthdays from now on.'

'No celebrations whatsoever?' Cam asked.

'What's there to celebrate?'

'Not even any cards or presents?' I asked in a tiny voice. I'd already spent ages secretly making Mum a card – a picture of the Earth, a round blue and green globe. It was right at the bottom, and quite small like all my drawings, but I'd drawn a giant Mum standing on top of it and taking up the rest of the space. In my best handwriting I'd written: *Happy Birthday to the Best Mum in the World.*

I'd also made her a present out of an old cornflake packet. It was a little house with cardboard furniture, where Mum and Alfie and I might live in the future.

Cam saw my face. 'Maybe other people want to celebrate your birthday, Tracy,' she said sharply.

'So what? It's *my* birthday and I can do what I want on the eighth of May. And I want to do a big fat nothing.'

Cam sighed. 'I learned long ago that there's no arguing with you when you're in this mood. Let's drop it.'

However, when we came to take
Alfie for his walk on Friday 7 May,
Cam invited us to stay for tea –
and she'd made a cake. It was a
lovely jam and cream sponge with
white icing on top. She'd decorated

it with strawberries and written in red icing: *This is
not a birthday cake, Tracy!*

'Oh, Cam!' said Mum. 'You don't give up, do you?'

'You know I don't,' she said.

'It's an absolutely beautiful not-a-birthday cake,
Cam,' I said.

'And you don't have to share it with . . . what was
the name of that little kid with the same birthday as
you?' Cam asked.

'He was called Weedy Peter!' I said.

'That's right. You didn't want to share
your cake with him. You were so mean to
him, poor little devil, yet he thought the
world of you, Tracy.'

'It was because Mum didn't want to share the
birthday wish,' I said.

'Well, this cake doesn't have candles, obviously,
but I dare say Mum can have a wish if she cuts the
first slice,' said Cam.

'For goodness' sake, I'm not a little kid any more,'
Mum snapped.

'OK, *you* have a wish instead, Jess.'

So I cut the cake, closing my eyes tight and wishing with all my might. *I wish wish wish Mum would cheer up and we could go back to being happy again!*

The cake was delicious, the best cake ever – even better than Rosalie's coffee-and-walnut. I ate two big slices, but Mum only had a very small slice and then she left half.

'It's lovely, isn't it, Mum?' I said.

'Yes. Thank you very much, Cam. But really, you shouldn't have bothered,' said Mum, in a very flat voice.

'I rather wish I hadn't bothered either,' said Cam, her cheeks pink.

She was getting angry with Mum – and yet when we said goodbye she pressed an envelope into Mum's hand.

'I said no birthday cards,' said Mum.

'It's not a card.'

'Look inside, Mum!' I said.

'You look,' she said, shrugging.

It was fifty whole pounds!

'Buy yourself something special,' Cam said.

'Stop it, Cam. You'll make me cry,' said Mum.

'You're Tracy Beaker. You never cry.'

I cried a bit when I had to say goodbye to Alfie, like I did nearly every time. I just couldn't help it, especially when he whimpered. Cam promised me that he only cried for a minute or so, and then he cheered up and ate his supper and played with the girls and slept all night curled up on his cushion – but I still worried about him dreadfully.

Still, the next day was Saturday, so I could be with him all day long. I woke up early and lay curled up tight in bed, wondering if my wish had come true. I decided to make Mum breakfast in bed for a special surprise. I so so so wanted to make her happy. I made tea, being very careful with the kettle, and I made toast too, cutting Mum's two slices into heart shapes. They were a bit lopsided, but they looked quite good once I'd spread them with butter and strawberry jam.

'Wakey wakey, Mum,' I said, carrying the tray carefully into her bedroom.

'Shh, Jess! It's Saturday. We don't have to get up early,' Mum mumbled from under her duvet.

'But, Mum—'

'Let me go back to sleep.'

'But I've made you breakfast!'

'What? Oh, Jess, I'm not really hungry. I'm too tired.'

'I turned your toast into a special surprise,' I muttered.

Mum sighed and sat up. 'Show me,' she said.

I put the tray on her lap. 'Do you see – I've made you little hearts,' I said.

'Yes. Thank you.' Mum didn't sound surprised – or even pleased – but she sipped her tea and nibbled half of one piece of toast.

'Does it taste better like that?' I asked.

'I suppose so.'

'And I know you don't want anyone to go on about your b-i-r-t-h-d-a-y, but I've got you a card *and* a present,' I said. 'Can I show you?'

'If you must.'

I ran to fetch them. I showed Mum the card of her and the world. It didn't look quite as good as I'd hoped. Mum nodded at it and gave a weird sort of smile, but she didn't seem to like it. Then I showed her the little cardboard house. It was a bit wobbly so I stood it on the tray.

'See, it's our house, Mum,' I said.

'What do you mean, our house?' she said dully.

'The house we'll have later on, you, me and Alfie. I've drawn all three of us.'

'And how are we going to get this house, eh?' Mum asked. 'Will we pay for it with cardboard money?'

'Don't be like that, Mum. We'll get a house one day, you'll see. A little one, where we can have Alfie with us.'

'No we won't,' she said. 'It's never going to happen, Jess. We're going to stay stuck here, in this hateful mouldy dump.' She said it despairingly and thumped the duvet hard. The tray jerked, her mug toppled over and the cardboard house was flooded with brown liquid. It started buckling.

'Our house!' I started crying.

'Oh, for goodness' sake – it's only cardboard. You can make another one,' said Mum.

'No I can't!' I shouted suddenly. 'There's no point! I made it specially for you, and I tried so hard to make it look good, and you don't even like it. You won't even pretend. Well, I'm not pretending any more either. You're spoiling everything. You were horrid to Cam last night, and now you're being horrid to *me*. It's not *my* fault Sean Godfrey cheated on you! We were so happy before you met him, so why can't you be happy again now? You won't even try! You've just given up! You're meant to be the great Tracy Beaker who gets the better of everyone, but you're just hopeless and mean and sorry for yourself. Look, I've written on your card that you're the best mum in the world, but it's not true, not any more! You're a *rubbish* mum!' I took hold of the card and ripped it in two, and then I ran out of the bedroom.

I went to my room and pushed my chair hard against the door so it couldn't be opened, and then I threw myself on the bed, and cried and cried. I was clutching Woofer, and I cried so hard I made him soggy. Every now and then I stopped sobbing to catch my breath and heard I Mum moving about, and then the sound of the bath running.

I cried some more, and then curled up tight in a ball, my chin on my knees. I couldn't believe I'd said all that. I'd never, ever said anything as bad to Mum. I felt like my whole head might explode.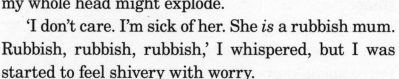

'I don't care. I'm sick of her. She *is* a rubbish mum. Rubbish, rubbish, rubbish,' I whispered, but I was started to feel shivery with worry.

I listened again. I couldn't hear anything now. Was Mum all right? It was a big relief when I heard her coming out of the bathroom. I stayed in bed, hiccupping, though I'd stopped crying now. Then there was a little knock on my bedroom door.

'Jess? Can I come in?'

I didn't answer. I heard Mum joggling the door handle.

'Jess, are you all right?' she called. She sounded anxious.

I pressed my lips together.

'Jess!' Mum was pushing at the door now. The chair suddenly toppled over and the door opened, and she came over to my bed.

'Hey, Jess?' She lifted up the duvet and peered in at me. 'I'm sorry, baby. I *am* a rubbish mum.'

'Not really,' I whispered.

'No, really. I deserve a good kick up the bum. Yes, I'll kick-box myself, OK. Watch!'

She jumped off the bed. I watched as she leaped into the air, doing a couple of crazy back kicks, aiming at her bottom.

'Mum! You'll hurt yourself, you mad thing!'

'Good! Jess, I'm so sorry, sweetheart. I've been so selfish and pathetic – but I'm going to pull myself together now. See!' She pulled at her own arms and legs. 'There, that's better. Now let's find some sellotape to see if we can stick your beautiful card together – and maybe I can blow-dry the little house with my hair dryer and make it as good as new. I love it, I really do. Please forgive me.'

'Of course I do,' I said.

We had a big, big hug. Mum's hair was still wet from her bath and my cheeks were still wet with tears, but neither of us minded. When I was washed and dressed we had another cup of tea, and Mum insisted on eating up her other strawberry heart-shaped slice of toast, even though it had gone cold.

'It's totally yummy,' she said. 'Hey, Jess, I think I want to celebrate my birthday after all. We could spend Cam's present. Let's have a day out together, you and me!'

'Oh yes! And Alfie?'

'Definitely Alfie. Let's go and collect him.'

It was still only eight o'clock when we drove round to Cam's. All the girls were still fast asleep, but Cam and Alfie were up – and Miss Oliver was already there.

'We're going on another hike,' said Cam.

'You're not taking Alfie again, are you?' I asked anxiously. He had come back *exhausted* from his first one.

'Who do you want to spend the day with, Alfie – Mary and me, or Jess and Tracy?' said Cam.

Alfie came bounding over to me!

'Oh, Alfie, you clever dog,' I said, making a huge fuss of him.

Mum and I took him for a walk in the park first so he could have a wee and stretch his legs, and then we secured him safely in the back of the Cadillac.

'So where are we going, Mum?' I asked.

'I don't really know!' she said. 'You choose, Jess.'

'No, it's *your* birthday. You have to say where.'

'I can't think. Not a town. What about the country somewhere? Alfie would like that. Or . . . I know! The seaside. It's not very sunny, but it might brighten up later. Do you fancy a trip to the sea?'

'Yes please! Alfie's never seen the sea. He'll be so excited.'

'I remember the first time *I* saw the sea. Mike took all us kids from the Dumping Ground camping for a week. It was magic. I couldn't believe the sea was so huge. I went charging into the water for a paddle without even bothering to take off my shoes and socks! I was a right nutter when I was little. Still am!'

'Shall we go there then. That same beach?' I suggested.

'Good idea!' Mum looked at a map of the coast on her phone. 'Aha! This is it. Cooksea. It's only a little place. It hasn't got a pier or a big amusement arcade or anything like that – is that still OK?'

'Let's go for it,' I said.

So we did.

MUM PUT ON her shades, and we pretended we were movie stars driving along in our pink Cadillac. Mum drove fast so our hair tangled in mad curls, and our cheeks grew pink. We started singing daft old pop songs. Mum often forgot the words and I didn't know them anyway, but it didn't matter – we made up new crazy words or la-la-la'd.

People stared at us, singing away in our flamingo-pink car. Some of the drivers tooted and people on the pavement waved. We tooted and waved back.

'Watch out, the Beaker Babes are in your area,' Mum yelled. 'We're here to have fun!'

'We *are* having fun, aren't we, Mum?' I asked.

'You bet we are,' she said. 'Let's make the most of it. We might have to sell the car to keep us going.'

'But it's your special car, Mum, the kind you always wanted right from when you were a little girl,' I reminded her.

'I'm a big girl now, and I have to think of boring things like the rent and new shoes for you and school trips – and I think you need new glasses because you're always frowning nowadays,' said Mum.

'My shoes still fit, sort of, but anyway my feet will soon be big enough to wear *your* shoes – the red sparkly high-tops! I don't want to go on any stupid school trips because I haven't got any proper friends now, not even Tyrone, not that I care – and I don't need new glasses, honest. I've been frowning because I was worried, but I'm not worried any more because my unbirthday wish came true. I wished you'd be happy again, and you are!'

'Yes, I am,' said Mum, and she put her foot down and we zoomed along even faster.

'Not *too* fast, Mum!'

Alfie started whimpering and fidgeting in the back.

'I think he needs a wee,' I said, craning round anxiously.

Mum stopped at the next lay-by, and I walked Alfie along the grass verge, where he did *lots* of wees. There were several lorries parked there – the drivers were having breakfast at the refreshment hut. They all gathered round to admire the Cadillac as they munched their bacon rolls.

We'd already had our strawberry hearts, but the bacon rolls smelled so delicious we had a second breakfast while Mum chatted to the lorry drivers. They all wanted to peer inside the bonnet, and stroked the Cadillac's shiny pink sides the way I stroke Alfie.

'Lovely car you've got there,' said one of the drivers. He had big blue eyes and a big white smile. 'And a lovely little girl and a lovely dog. And you're quite lovely too. What's your name, Mrs?'

'Tracy Beaker,' said Mum. 'And it's *Miss*, not Mrs. It's going to stay Miss too. Come on, Jess. Back in the car. See you, guys.'

'That man fancied you,' I said as we set off again.

'Yep,' said Mum.

'But you didn't fancy him?'

'Nope. I'm not going to get involved with any more men. We're fine just as we are, you and me . . .' Mum paused, waiting for me to open my mouth. 'And Alfie,' we said in unison.

There was country all around us now, rolling green hills as far as you could see. The sky seemed much bigger and bluer than it was in London, and the sun made everything look so bright it was as if we had landed in Munchkinland.

'We couldn't have picked a better day for the seaside,' said Mum. 'Not far now. I remember this hilly part from when I was a little kid. Mike took us hiking, and we were all completely knackered by the time we got to the top of that big hill over there. Then, on the way back, we walked across a meadow and Justine stepped in a cowpat and we all fell about laughing.'

'Are you sure you didn't push her, Mum?' I asked.

'Me?' she said, grinning. 'Maybe I gave her just a little shove. Accidentally on purpose.'

'You're bad, Mum. When are we going to see the sea then?'

'Soon soon soon!' said Mum.

We drove through a little village.

'Oh yes, Mike took us to have cake in a teashop here, and we had to swear we'd be on our best behaviour so as not to show him up!' said Mum.

'Hey, shall we stop now and have a cake, Mum? A birthday cake?' I suggested.

'I'm still too full of bacon roll,' said Mum. 'And I'm not sure about Alfie's manners in a teashop. He might play tug with the tablecloths and slobber on the scones. Anyway, we're nearly there. We'll see the sea in a minute.'

We drove up such a steep hill that the car juddered in protest, but when we got to the top there was a wonderful view of fields stretching out to the sky, with the sea glittering silver in front of us.

'Is this Cooksea?' I cried. 'Oh, Mum, it looks lovely!'

'*Oh, I do like to be beside the seaside!*' Mum sang, and pretended to be a trumpet for the *tiddely-om-pom pom* part.

I sang, '*My Bonnie lies over the ocean, my Bonnie lies over the sea*', and did all the hand gestures too.

'Very good,' said Mum. 'Are you making up all those gestures?'

'No, Miss Oliver taught us,' I said. 'I *do* like her, especially now she's Cam's friend.'

'I like her too,' said Mum. 'How could I ever have called her a bossy old bag?'

'You were awful, Mum!'

'I know. That was a terrible thing to say, even for me.'

'I'm so glad you like her now.'

'She's different when she's not being a teacher. Anyway, it doesn't matter what I think. It just matters that *Cam* likes her.'

'So long as she doesn't like her more than us! She's *our* Cam, isn't she, Mum?"

'Of course she is. Fancy her getting into this rambling lark! They were going on a twelve-mile hike today – imagine!'

'Alfie's *much* happier being with us. He doesn't have walking boots like Cam and Miss Oliver. I'm sure his paws must have ached dreadfully after all that hiking,' I said.

When we parked the car on the seafront and let Alfie loose on the beach, he bounded about like a puppy. He gambolled over the pebbles, sniffing ecstatically, ran to meet all the other dogs on the beach, and then dashed towards the sea. He leaped over the tiny waves at the edge, barking with joy.

I took off my shoes and socks and paddled with him. Mum did too, rolling up her jeans and splashing about like a little kid. She got quite wet but she didn't seem to mind.

We sat down on the pebbles for a while and threw stones into the sea. Mum was good at finding flat ones that skimmed the water three or four times before sinking. I searched for shells without much luck, but found a pebble with a perfect round hole in the middle. I peered through it.

'I spy with my little eye something beginning with TB,' I said.

'Um . . . let me see. Terrible Bore? Total Blockhead? Tyrannical Bimbo?' Mum joked.

'It's Tracy Beaker, silly!' I said. 'Are you having a good birthday, Mum?'

'The best ever.'

It was getting rather cloudy and we were still damp, so we went for a walk along the promenade to warm up. We had races. Alfie always came first and laughed at us, his tongue lolling. I came last but I didn't mind.

Near the cliffs we saw a long row of beach huts, all painted different colours.

'Aren't they lovely? If we had one, which colour would you choose, Mum?' I asked.

'Red. *This* one, with the white cockleshell above the door,' she said.

'Yes, it's definitely the best. I wish it wasn't all shut up so we could see inside. Do you think anyone actually lives there?' I asked.

Mum shrugged. 'It looks empty to me.'

'Do you think *we* could live there?' I suddenly felt excited. 'Oh, Mum, it would be wonderful. I know it's very little, but *we're* not very big, are we? I'm sure there would be space for a bed, just about, and during the day we could use it as a sofa. And Alfie could live with us because there are heaps of dogs here. Think how he'd like to have doggy friends to play tug with. And we could go paddling every day. It would be so brilliant!'

'Beach huts don't have toilets, Jess.'

'There's bound to be public toilets somewhere.'

'They don't have proper cooking facilities either.'

'We don't need to cook. We could eat fish and chips every day,' I insisted.

'You can't live in a beach hut for nothing. You have to buy them,' said Mum.

'Couldn't we save up? Maybe sell the car?'

'Beach huts cost thousands and thousands of pounds.'

'Seriously?'

'Yep.'

'Oh.' I thought for a moment. 'I do wish you'd kept Sean Godfrey's engagement ring.'

'Mm, I keep thinking that too,' said Mum. 'Especially if Justine Husband-Snatcher Littlewood's wearing it now.'

'Mum – do you still mind terribly?' I asked in a tiny voice.

She pulled a face. 'I suppose so. I did love him. Maybe I still do, though I hate him now too. And it was so heavenly, everyone envying us, and not having to worry about money. To be honest I miss that the most.'

'I don't miss it one little bit,' I said.

'Well, I'm glad because it was mostly for you. I wanted you to have the home you deserve, Jess.'

'I'm fine, just so long as we're together,' I said.

'It's awful – you always end up having to reassure me,' said Mum. 'That's what *mums* should do, not daughters.'

'Who says? We're the Beaker Babes. We do it *our* way,' I said. 'Race you? Bet I win this time!'

I did – but I think Mum and Alfie let me. Then the sun came back out and we sat on a bench and did some sunbathing.

'Are you still full of bacon roll, Mum?' I asked hopefully.

'No, I'm getting quite peckish now. It must be from all that running,' she said.

'You know I said we could have fish and chips every day if we lived here?' I said. 'Do you think we could have fish and chips *now*?'

'Great idea,' said Mum.

We wandered up into the little town looking for a fish-and-chip shop. Then we took our cardboard boxes into a park and sat on a bench and ate our lovely lunch while Alfie ran around in circles with the other dogs, coming back every few minutes for a morsel of fish or half a chip.

'I think this is the best fish and chips ever,' I said, swinging my legs happily.

'Absolutely,' said Mum. She patted her tummy. 'I'm full to bursting now. Shall we go for a little mooch around the town and see if they've got any junk shops?'

The High Street just had ordinary shops – WHSmith and Boots and pound shops – but there were more interesting ones in the little side streets. There was a jewellery shop that sold second-hand necklaces and bracelets and rings. Mum sighed over the price of the tiny diamonds.

'Mine was such a biggie,' she said. 'Still. I'm not going to keep looking back and dwelling on the past. Maybe that's why I fell for Sean. I got carried away remembering us as kids and how different we were then. It made me feel fond of him right from the start.'

'You didn't feel fond of Justine Littlewood, and she's part of the past too,' I pointed out.

'True. Do you know something? It's time I grew up and stopped harping on about what happened donkey's years ago. I'm going to make a conscious effort to forget all about my childhood. Give me a quick slap about the chops if I ever say the words Dumping Ground again,' said Mum.

We turned a corner, went down another alleyway – and stared open-mouthed at the shop ahead of us.

It was double-fronted and very shabby. The windows were dirty, but we could see that it was packed to the ceiling with all kinds of junk – old wicker chairs and battered suitcases and faded satin eiderdowns and spotted mirrors and

plaster ducks and pictures of ladies with green faces. But we weren't focusing on the things in the shop window. We were looking at the sign above it. It announced its name in scrawly writing:

The Dumping Ground

'Does it *really* say that, Mum,' I said, blinking, 'or are my eyes playing tricks on me? Maybe I *do* need new glasses after all!'

'That's what it says all right. What a weird coincidence! Still, it can't be anything to do with my children's home. It's just a clever name for a junk shop. All the stuff here has been dumped, right? Let's go in and have a rummage, eh?'

We opened the door cautiously and peered into the gloom. The bell above the door tinkled. The huge velvet cushions covering an ancient sofa suddenly moved, and Mum and I stepped back in alarm. The cushions heaved themselves upright – and a head appeared at the top.

'Hello, my darlings!' said the lady, as if we were her best friends and she'd been expecting us for ages.

She was very large and wore a rather grubby long green velvet dress, with a silky yellow shawl round her shoulders, the fringing coming away. She looked as if she'd been reclining on the sofa for many years. When she eased herself up – with the help of two ebony sticks – we saw that she could barely walk, her large feet spilling out of her slippers. She had several ropes of amber beads dangling over her very big front, and a pair of glasses instead of a locket hanging from a gold chain. She propped the specs on her nose and peered at us.

'*Do* come in and have a rummage.' She spoke in a very dramatic way, waving her arms about, though this affected her balance and she nearly toppled over. Mum rushed to help her.

'Thank you so much, darling. I always forget I need these wretched sticks nowadays. Never have a stroke, dear. Total misery. Here I am, day after day, positively marooned, a heap of blubber – though inside I'm still skipping around like a teenager. Settle me back on the sofa or I'll fall bum over bosom and become even more of an old crock,' she declared.

Mum did her best to do as the shop lady suggested, though it was quite a struggle. Alfie watched with interest, and when she was settled again he tried to jump up beside her.

'No, Alfie! Down!' Mum and I shouted.

'Yes, Alfie! *Up!*' said the lady, patting the sofa with her hand. She had a ring squeezed onto every finger and they clattered together.

For once Alfie did as he was told, and jumped up, though there was hardly any space for him on the sagging sofa. He landed mostly on the lady's large tummy, but she didn't seem to mind a bit.

'What a lovely friendly little chap! He *is* a boy, isn't he? From this angle I can't see if he's got a willy,' she said.

I'd never heard an old lady say two rude words in the space of a minute, especially in such a posh fruity voice. I looked round at Mum uncertainly. She was grinning.

'Yes, he's a boy. His name's Alfie – and he's certainly taken a shine to you,' she said.

'Oh, darling, once upon a time *all* chaps made a fuss of me – but now I count myself lucky if a little dog snuggles up to me when customers come into the shop. Not that I get many customers nowadays. And who can blame them? Everything's in such a pickle.'

The shop lady waved her hands dismissively and set her rings clanking.

'Well, we'd love to have a look round,' said Mum.

'Certainly, certainly. Have a good poke. If you don't see anything you fancy – and who could blame you? – there's cupboards and chests and cardboard boxes all crammed fit to bursting, only I haven't got room to display them, and in any case these silly old hands are too clumsy. Last time I tried, I broke the spout off a rare Clarice Cliff teapot and smashed a French porcelain doll to smithereens.'

So Mum and I edged our way through a maze of chairs and tables and trunks and looked at everything while Alfie sat with the lady like a perfect little lap dog.

'Just tip him off if he's squashing you,' Mum said.

'Never! He's such a little treasure,' the lady declared. 'I love dogs. He reminds me of my dear Chin-Chin. He was the love of my life, a black-and-white Japanese Chin – went everywhere with me when I could still get around, and after my stroke he scarcely left my side. It broke my heart when he died. I was desperate for another, but I can't walk a dog in this state, so it wouldn't be fair. Life isn't fair, is it, girls? In fact, life can be a real whatsit!'

'It certainly can,' said Mum, laughing. 'A total whatsit!'

They didn't actually say the word *whatsit*, they said something much ruder. Mum caught my eye. 'Don't ever let me hear you saying that, Jess!' she said.

We went on looking.

'Have you seen anything you want, Mum?' I whispered. 'You should pick yourself a birthday present. We've still got heaps of Cam's money left.'

'*You* must pick something too. Everything's very reasonably priced,' Mum whispered back.

I spent ages rummaging, and eventually decided on a blue china bunny with big ears, just like the one Alice had in her bedroom. One of his paws was a bit broken, but I didn't mind. Mum dithered over an old leather suitcase and a silky kimono and a baseball jacket, but eventually chose an old doll with blue eyes and thinning yellow hair and a torn dress.

'But you don't even like dolls, Mum!' I said, surprised.

'Yes, I know, but this one's a bit like the one I had when I was a little girl, my Bluebell. I loved her,' said Mum. Then she hissed, 'And she's only ten pounds, a total bargain! She's worth heaps more, even though she's so shabby.'

The shop lady seemed delighted when we showed her our choices. She peered at the price tags. 'I'll knock a bit off, seeing as we're like old friends already,' she said. 'You can have the doll for eight, and the little SylvaC bunny for two, seeing as he's got a chip on his paw. That's a tenner, if you please.'

Mum looked at me. I looked at her. We hesitated. They were almost too much of a bargain.

'Is it too much, dears?' the lady asked. 'Are we going to haggle?'

Mum nibbled her lip. 'It's not enough,' she said. 'Not nearly enough.'

'You mean you want to pay *more*?'

'Yes,' said Mum. 'Your prices are far too generous.'

The shop lady shrieked with laughter. 'Oh my, this is interesting haggling! Don't be so silly. Give me the tenner, and take your doll and your bunny and no more nonsense. Tell you what – if you feel really badly you can make me a cup of tea, because I'm gasping.'

'Certainly,' said Mum.

'There's a little room out the back. You'll see the kettle. Excuse all my washing things. I camp down here nowadays. Can't manage the stairs. Make a cup for yourself too – and the kiddie. Do you drink tea, dear?' she asked me.

'Yes please,' I said.

'And what's your name?'

'I'm Jess.'

'Pretty. I used to know a lady called Jessamine Heart. I don't suppose the name rings any bells with you girls, but she was reasonably well known in her day. An actress, though she didn't have much talent, poor dear – just an impressive figure and a way with men. Do you know the type?' she asked.

'Oh yes,' Mum called from the little kitchen.

'I wonder if you've heard of Florence Garland?' the shop lady asked. 'Now she *was* an actress. You might have seen her most famous film on the telly – *Death of a Lady*? She was the lady and she died beautifully, even though I say so myself. She was on the stage too – mostly drawing-room comedies, but she did some Shakespeare too. She once toured as Rosalind and got rave reviews in all the papers. I've got them stuck in a scrapbook somewhere. When she was a little older she did sitcom – she was the comical cleaning lady for seven series of *Life with the Lilliputs*.' She put her head on one side and started talking in a funny Cockney accent. *''Allo, dearies, let me slosh a bit of disinfectant in all your murky corners!* That was my catch line. People used to shout it after me in the street.'

'So *you're* Florence Garland?' said Mum, coming to peer at her.

'I used to be. Now I'm simply poor old Flo who hasn't had a part in years. I had a tough time – had to do some waitressing, which played havoc with my feet. Ever done waitressing, dear?' she asked Mum.

'Yes – it's a killer. I'm working in a coffee shop now, and that's even worse.'

Flo clucked sympathetically. 'And what's *your* name, darling?'

'Tracy Beaker.'

'Now there's a name with a familiar ring. You haven't been on the telly, have you?'

'Oh, there was some documentary about me when I was a kid,' said Mum, going back to make the tea.

'Oooh!' said Flo. 'So why did they feature your mum, pet? She wasn't one of those sickening child phenomenons who speak twenty languages and do advanced algebra when they're five?'

'No! I think it was because she was in a children's home,' I said.

'Yes, and you'll never guess what we used to call it,' said Mum, coming in with a tray and three different china cups with odd saucers, though they all had pretty floral patterns and fancy gold rims. 'The Dumping Ground!'

'Oh, my! Would you believe it! *I* didn't give the shop the name, mind you. It's a bit too basic for my taste. I'd have called it something like Florence's Antique Emporium, only it wasn't mine when it started up. It was run by a dear soul called Arty Williams – Arthur, actually, but he always hated the name. He was in the theatre too. I'd known him for years. He retired and bought himself this little antique shop by the sea, and when I was on my beam ends he helped me out, bless him. I moved in, and we got on like a house on fire, but then poor Arty had a heart attack – and I discovered he'd left me the shop in his will. I went to all the big antique fairs – even bought a van and did house clearances – but a couple of years ago I had my stroke, and now it's a devil of a struggle to keep going.' Flo sighed. 'If only I had someone to help me out, but no one seems interested in working in a junk shop any more.'

Mum looked at me. I looked at her. Alfie looked up at both of us.

'What is it, dears?' Flo asked, sipping. 'Ah, this is the ticket. You make a lovely cup of tea, Tracy Beaker.'

'Look, this is probably a ridiculous suggestion, and you must say no if you're not one hundred per cent keen on the idea, but how about *me* working here with you? I could go around looking for stock and tidy up the shop a bit, and I could help out with the chores. What do you think?' Mum asked.

'What do I think? I think it's a tremendous idea!' said Flo, spilling her tea down her large front. She dabbed at herself with the shawl. 'I couldn't pay you that much, of course – but you could have free accommodation upstairs, if it's just for you and little Jess, though I dare say it's all in a bit of a mess. Hop upstairs and have a look at it, see what you think.'

There was a bedroom and a little box room and a bathroom, all a bit tired and musty.

'But we could scrub all the rooms and paint them and make them look great in no time,' said Mum. 'And just think what we could do with the shop! We could display everything cleverly and make it look great, like a giant version of our flat! It's the job of my dreams, and I think I'd actually be good at it! What do you think, Jess? I know it's completely mad, but shall we give it a go?'

'But how will I get to school, Mum?'

'You could go to a new school. Would you mind?'

'Well . . . I won't like leaving Miss Oliver.'

'Yes, but you'll still see her now she's Cam's friend. And after this term you wouldn't be in her class anyway. This is our chance, Jess! A new start! And Flo likes Alfie, so we could have him here with us all the time,' said Mum.

'Then yes, yes, yes, let's!' I cried.

When we went back downstairs there was a lot more discussion. Alfie started to get a bit fidgety, so I took him for a walk up and down the street, promising not to cross any roads or talk to strangers.

'Will you like living here, Alfie?' I asked him.

Alfie sniffed happily, zigzagging backwards and forwards. It was clear that he thought Cooksea was dog heaven, especially if he could go for a run on the

beach every day. It was *my* idea of heaven too, so long as we could still see Cam lots. We could visit her in the car – and maybe at the weekends she could come and hike along the cliffs with Miss Oliver. Perhaps Marina could bring Ava and Alice and we could all play on the beach together. We could ask Rosalie to come on her day off – she could lie in a deckchair in the sun and have a bit of a rest. I *might* even invite Tyrone, but only if he promised not to go on and on about Sean Godfrey.

Mum and Flo were still making plans when Alfie and I got back, and then they talked for ages afterwards as well. They were both getting so excited, Mum jumping about and Flo rattling her jewellery.

We had lots more cups of tea and some rather stale biscuits, and before we left Mum made Flo her supper. It was a microwave ready-meal for one, so Flo couldn't share it with us, though she wanted to.

'When we come to live here I'll make you lots of lovely freshly cooked meals, Flo,' Mum promised.

'Do you ever make roasts, darling? That's what I miss most of all,' she said.

'You wait till you taste Mum's roast potatoes!' I said.

'I'm positively drooling at the thought,' said Flo. 'Oh, dears, I'm not dreaming, am I? This is all too marvellous for words! You *will* come back, won't you? Promise?'

'Promise promise promise,' said Mum. 'We've got stuff to sort out, but we'll come back next Saturday, and I'll be phoning you heaps in between to let you know how things are going.' She gave Flo a kiss, and I did too.

'Bless you, Jess. You two seem like family already!' said Flo, getting a little weepy. 'The daughter and granddaughter I never had.'

Mum already had two mums and I had two grannies, but we were happy to add Flo to our family.

'I feel we're dreaming too,' said Mum as we walked

back to where we'd parked the Cadillac on the seafront. 'It's just all too good to be true. Let's move in as quick as quick in case Flo changes her mind. It won't matter if you miss a few weeks of school, will it? It would do you good to have a proper holiday, sweetheart.'

'I'm not sure what Miss Oliver is going to say!' I said.

'She'll say I have Responsibility Issues,' said Mum, laughing. 'And she's probably right too. Still, I'm going to *try* to be the best mum in the world. We're going to be so happy here, Jess, I just know it – you, me and Alfie.'

'And no more Sean Godfreys?' I dared ask.

'Absolutely not. I've finished with men. I'm Tracy Beaker. I'm not going to be dependent on any guy. I'm going to make my own way in the world – and be a stonking great success too!' said Mum. 'Hey, it's ages since we had those fish and chips. Shall we have a meal here before we drive back? I'm not sure they'll let Alfie into a restaurant, but we could have a pub meal. You can take dogs into most pubs.'

'Can we afford it?' I asked.

'Probably not – but it *is* my birthday,' said Mum, 'and I feel like celebrating.'

We stopped at the first pub we came to, just round the corner from the seafront. It was called the Spade and Bucket. Along each windowsill they had little

401

 children's buckets planted with red geraniums, and on either side of the door was an umbrella stand full of seaside spades.

'Oh, Mum, it's just the sort of thing *we'd* do!' I said.

The pub was quite full, and when Mum asked the lady behind the bar if we could have a table in the restaurant part, she shook her head doubtfully.

'It's all booked up for a party, dear,' she said.

'Oh please, couldn't you squeeze us in somewhere?' Mum asked. 'This is a really special day for us and we'd love a meal to celebrate.'

We looked at her pleadingly. Alfie looked especially hopeful, giving little expectant whimpers.

The lady's face softened. 'Well, I dare say I could find you a corner at the back,' she said. 'Follow me.'

The restaurant was full of laughing, joshing people, all crowded round a huge table. They didn't even notice us making our way over to a little table, which the lady set specially for us.

Mum pulled a face when she looked at the menu. 'Mm, it's a bit pricier than I thought. Perhaps we should share a main – is that OK? And drink tap water.'

'But we'll pretend it's the very best champagne,' I said.

'Deal,' said Mum.

We ordered spaghetti bolognese because it seemed like the most filling thing, and no one seemed to mind us sharing. In fact, I think the lady made sure that our plate was piled really high. It tasted wonderful, though it's always quite difficult to eat spag bol tidily, and I couldn't help dribbling a bit down my T-shirt. My hand was bright orange too, because I fed Alfie a little portion under the table.

When our plate was empty we felt very full.

'Yum!' I said, rubbing my tummy.

'Yes, double yum,' said Mum. 'I don't think I could manage any pudding even if we could afford it.'

Just as she said this, the lady came in carrying a great big cake with sparklers on top.

'Oh my goodness!' said Mum. 'A birthday cake! She must have guessed when I said we were celebrating! Oh, Jess! I'm having a birthday cake after all!'

'And you can have your birthday wish, Mum!'

'I haven't got anything left to wish for,' said Mum. 'Still, I suppose I can think of something if I try hard!'

But the lady was taking the cake over to the big table. All the people there started singing, *'Happy birthday to you! Happy birthday to you!'*

'Oh, for goodness' sake!' Mum said – or words to that effect. 'It's someone else's birthday cake!' She peered over at the table.

'Happy birthday, dear Peter! Happy birthday to you!'

'Peter!' Mum exclaimed.

A slim good-looking guy with fair hair was standing up, smiling bashfully.

'It can't be!' said Mum.

He made an attempt to blow out all the candles when they stopped sparkling. He only managed a quarter of them.

'It *is*!' said Mum, and she stood up and dashed over to the big table.

'Mum! Mum, what are you doing?' I asked, trying to grab hold of her.

She ran right up to the fair-haired man. 'Peter Ingham!' she declared. 'You were always hopeless at blowing out candles. Let me!' She took a deep breath

and blew hard – and every single candle went out.

'Tracy Beaker!' he said. He looked as if he was going to throw his arms round Mum, but then he thought better of it and just flapped them awkwardly in the air. 'I was just thinking about you too! I saw this fantastic vintage pink Cadillac parked on the seafront. Remember you always used to go on about your mum coming to drive you away in a Cadillac?'

'It's mine!' said Mum. 'But what are you *doing* here, Peter?'

'A while ago I came here on a nostalgic trip – remember our camping holiday? And then I got a job just up the coast and I live down here now, Tracy,' he said.

'Is this the Tracy you always go on about – the one from the children's home?' said the woman sitting next to him. She looked very pretty in her silky blue dress.

'Yep, that's me,' said Mum. 'Are you Peter's partner?'

The whole table laughed.

'He's my boss – or he will be next term. He's going to be our new head,' she said.

'You're a *headmaster*, Peter?' Mum asked incredulously.

'Yes, I know – it's mad, isn't it?' he said. 'These are my friends from the school. We're all teachers, so maybe you won't like us! What do *you* do now, Tracy? I always thought you'd be a writer – you were so good at making up stories when you were a kid!'

'I've done a bit of writing, yes,' said Mum. 'But now I'm considering moving into the area as an antique dealer. And this is my daughter, Jess.' She beckoned me over.

'Oh, good heavens, she's the spitting image of you! Hi, Jess! Are you as fierce as your mum, eh? She used to scare me silly at times,' Peter said, grinning.

'Yes, she's good at that,' I said.

'Come on, Pete! Stop chatting up your old girlfriend and cut your cake!' someone shouted, and the others joined in.

Peter went pink. 'Shh, you rowdy lot.' He picked up a knife. 'Cut it with me, Tracy. We have a tradition to keep up! We share our birthday cake.'

So they cut it together, and then Mum closed her eyes, and I knew she was making a wish at last. I don't know what she wished for. She won't tell me. But I hope it comes true.

HAVE YOU READ THEM ALL?

LAUGH OUT LOUD
THE STORY OF TRACY BEAKER
I DARE YOU, TRACY BEAKER
STARRING TRACY BEAKER
THE WORST THING ABOUT MY SISTER
DOUBLE ACT
FOUR CHILDREN AND IT
THE BED AND BREAKFAST STAR

HISTORICAL HEROES
HETTY FEATHER
HETTY FEATHER'S CHRISTMAS
SAPPHIRE BATTERSEA
EMERALD STAR
DIAMOND
LITTLE STARS
CLOVER MOON
ROSE RIVERS
WAVE ME GOODBYE
OPAL PLUMSTEAD
QUEENIE

LIFE LESSONS
THE BUTTERFLY CLUB
THE SUITCASE KID
KATY
BAD GIRLS
LITTLE DARLINGS
CLEAN BREAK
RENT A BRIDESMAID
CANDYFLOSS
THE LOTTIE PROJECT

THE LONGEST WHALE SONG
COOKIE
JACKY DAYDREAM
PAWS & WHISKERS

FAMILY DRAMAS
THE ILLUSTRATED MUM
MY SISTER JODIE
DIAMOND GIRLS
DUSTBIN BABY
VICKY ANGEL
SECRETS
MIDNIGHT
LOLA ROSE
LILY ALONE
MY SECRET DIARY

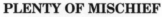

PLENTY OF MISCHIEF
SLEEPOVERS
THE WORRY WEBSITE
BEST FRIENDS
GLUBBSLYME
THE CAT MUMMY
LIZZIE ZIPMOUTH
THE MUM-MINDER
CLIFFHANGER
BURIED ALIVE!

FOR OLDER READERS
GIRLS IN LOVE
GIRLS UNDER PRESSURE
GIRLS OUT LATE
GIRLS IN TEARS
KISS
LOVE LESSONS

CHECK OUT JACQUELINE WILSON'S BRILLIANT WEBSITE!

Did you know there's a whole Jacqueline Wilson town to explore? There's lots of fun stuff, including games, amazing competitions and exclusive news. You can generate a special username, customize your online bedroom, test your knowledge of Jacqueline's books with exciting quizzes and upload book reviews! And if you like writing, make sure you visit the special storytelling area!

Plus, you can find out about the latest news from Jacqueline in her monthly diary, chat to other fans on the message boards and find out whether she's doing an event near you!

Join in today at
www.jacquelinewilson.co.uk